WILD SCOTTISH FORTUNE

THE ENCHANTED HIGHLANDS
BOOK SIX

TRICIA O'MALLEY

LOVEWRITE PUBLISHING

For Alan, whose love will always be home to me.

GLOSSARY OF SCOTTISH WORDS/SLANG

- Away and shite – go away, you are talking nonsense
- Bit o' banter – Scots love to tease each other; banter is highly cherished
- Bladdered – drunk
- Bloody – a word used to add emphasis; expletive
- Bonnie – pretty
- Brekkie – breakfast
- Braw – beautiful, good
- Burn – river, small stream
- Clarty – dirty
- Crabbit – cranky, moody
- Dodgy – shady, questionable
- Drookit – extremely wet; drenched
- Eejit – idiot
- Extension – addition to a house
- Get the messages – running errands, going to the shops/market

- Give it laldy/laldie – do something with vigor or enthusiasm
- Goes down a treat – tastes good; successful
- Hen – woman, female
- "It's a dreich day" – cold; damp; miserable
- Lorry – work truck
- Mad wi' it – drunk
- Och – used to express many emotions, typically surprise, regret, or disbelief
- On you go then – be on your way; get on with it
- Scran – food
- Scunner – nuisance, pain in the neck
- Shoogly – unsteady; wobbly
- Spitting chips – angry, furious
- Tatties – potatoes
- Tetchy – crabby, cranky, moody
- Tea – in Scotland, having tea is often used to refer to the dinnertime meal
- Wee – small, little
- Wheesht (haud your wheesht) – be quiet, hush, shut up

You are confined only by the walls you build yourself.
– Andrew Murphy

CHAPTER ONE

Orla

"Surely you just need to jam it in there."

"When does jamming something in ever help the problem?"

"Depends, is your date in a huff with you or not?"

I rolled my eyes at the two men currently bent over a lock on a stall door in an old outbuilding outside MacAlpine Castle. Munroe Curaigh of Common Gin was opening a new branch of his famous distillery here, and I'd bid for the project, knowing it would give my crew steady work for months if we'd got it.

And we'd landed it.

We were already two months into the project, and I'd been able to hire in more help, as well as take on a few other local projects like the rebuilding of Ramsay Kilts, which had recently suffered a tragedy.

Such a shame, that fire. I still couldn't believe his brother had started it. *Who does that?*

I was excited to work on the kilt shop, largely because the space wasn't exceptionally large, which meant Ramsay and Willow required explicit attention to detail. I always enjoyed the challenge of crafting out useful small storage or interesting details in unique spaces.

The distillery, on the other hand, was a much larger project where form needed to meet function. The building itself held considerable history, which Munroe hoped to preserve, and we were working with a team to blend the old with the new in a seamless design that should offer a light and airy workspace for his crew.

"I'd suggest a gentle touch," I said, interrupting the two men, coming to the intricate latch at the stall door. "As most women prefer that over getting jammed." Both men straightened as I slid my hand softly over the locking mechanism and turned it lightly, unhinging it so the door opened smoothly.

"Ah." Munroe cleared his throat sheepishly.

"Your technique is noted," the other man said, a twinkle in his gray-green eyes.

"Your future dates can thank me," I said, and Munroe winced.

"Apologies for our crudeness."

"I'm well used to it, lads," I said, continuing through to the tack room that we were converting into a front office.

"Orla, this is Finlay Thompson. Our Chief Operations Officer. He's just arrived in town to have a look over everything and will be moving here once things are up and running."

I glanced over at Finlay, my eyes taking in his crisp gray trousers with a muted tartan print, well-shined shoes, and gold watch peeking out from beneath his collared shirt.

Posh bastard.

"Are you here to clean then?" Finlay asked, smiling at me, and Munroe cursed under his breath.

"Aye, that's me. The cleaner. What would you recommend needs cleaning in here, sir?" I tipped my head at him, pretending to give a wee curtsy, and his eyes narrowed.

"Well, I imagine everything, no? Och, it's quite dusty in here. Will need a good brush down." Finlay surveyed the room that was smack dab in the middle of a literal construction site, covered in sawdust, and had the gall to suggest it needed a good dusting. Clearly the man didn't know his head from his arse, and I opened my mouth to tell him just that when Munroe intervened.

I knew Finlay's type.

Hell, I'd dated his type.

They walked into everywhere they went, assuming they knew what was what, and acted like a cock of the walk. He had the air of confidence about him, a man used to getting his way, and I didn't doubt that most things in life worked out exactly the way he wanted.

It didn't hurt that he looked like he'd just stepped out of a glossy magazine.

The man was seriously good-looking.

But in the way of a man that might roll back his cuffs and go a few rounds, if the need called for it.

I shouldn't find it appealing, and it was probably my incredibly long dry spell that made me find him attractive.

It certainly wasn't the nonsense he was spewing from his mouth.

"Finlay. This is Orla Clarke. Owner of Clarke Construction and our head builder and project manager. Basically your partner for the next six months as we finish the buildout."

"You're Clarke Construction?" Finlay didn't even bother to conceal his surprise.

It was a reaction I was used to. I was a female in a male-dominated industry. I'd been on more job sites than I could count at this point, and still most people mistook me for a delivery girl dropping off food to the site or something of that nature. Maybe I could have chosen an easier industry to break into, but my first love was construction work, and I'd fought hard to end up where I was.

Which meant I'd developed a fairly thick skin through the years.

"Aye," I said, accepting his hand when he held it out. "At your service."

"My apologies," Finlay said, holding my hand a moment longer than necessary, his lips curving up in what must be a practiced sultry smile. "I shouldn't have made assumptions."

"Everything good here, boss?"

All three of us turned at the word "boss" but it was my head joiner, Derrick, who was extremely protective of me as if I was his own daughter. He'd likely overheard the conversation since sound carried easily on an open job site.

"Aye, all good, Derrick. Thanks for checking in."

"When you're ready, I'd like to review the install on the

cabinets by the storage room. I think we can integrate sliding shelves depending on the weight of the contents."

"I'll be right there." I gave Derrick a quick nod and then turned back to the two men, hands on my hips.

"Are there any more doors you need me to open for you, gentlemen?" I gave Finlay a tight smile and he winked at me, appreciating my thinly veiled insult.

"No, Orla, go on ahead. We'll catch up with you shortly." Munroe squeezed my shoulder in thanks. I liked him. He was a fair man who was besotted with his fiancée, and his employees loved him. Low staff turnover at a business always spoke highly of a good boss to me, and I'd found my dealings with him to be smooth and easygoing.

Finlay, though? I'd wait to decide what I thought about the man.

"Nice to meet you, Orla. I look forward to working with you."

I withheld comment, giving him a curt nod and a wide berth as I left the room.

The *Finlays* of the world and I did not mix well, but I knew how to get on with them when it came to work. For now, I'd bite my tongue and crack on with my job, knowing I'd have one more challenge to deal with now that Finlay was on the project.

I glanced back to see him watching me as I walked away, a considering look in his eye.

Och, the man was going to be a problem. I could sense it already.

CHAPTER TWO

"None of the workers will go in there."

"Seriously?" I scratched my jaw, casting my gaze across the land behind the construction site to where a worn stone outbuilding stood, shrouded in trees, and looking for all the world like a witch's cottage from a childhood fairy tale. MacAlpine Castle loomed in the distance, a stately presence towering over our building operation, and I could almost imagine a highlander appearing between the trees, sword in hand.

The more I looked at the cottage, the more I got an impression that it wanted to be left alone, and the very idea that an inanimate object could project a feeling like that piqued my interest. *Was it Munroe's comment that the workers avoided this building that made me feel that way?* Scotland was full of abandoned outbuildings and ruins. It wasn't all that unusual to stumble across one, so what made this one so different?

"Aye. A superstitious lot, they are. Claim it's haunted. Once one of them refused to go in, the rest followed suit."

"Bloody hell." I sighed. Turning, I scanned the busy site behind me. Orla seemed to run a tight ship. I'd only been on-site for two days now, but I hadn't come across a worker that wasn't busy with one task or another once. I'd worked on enough of Munroe's buildouts, from retail stores to distilleries, to learn that this wasn't always the case with job sites. I had to hand it to the pint-sized powerhouse. She seemed to run things efficiently and her crew respected her.

She was also breathtaking.

Auburn hair tucked into plaits, wide sky-blue eyes, and a mouth made for kissing was a stark juxtaposition against the canvas overalls that seemed to be Orla's daily uniform. Her overalls were navy-blue today, and loose enough that identifying any particular aspect of her shape was largely impossible. I wondered if that was a deliberate choice, helping to keep unwanted advances at bay, or if she just enjoyed the comfort.

I'd steered a wide berth from her after I'd neatly insulted her by insinuating she was the cleaner, embarrassment still making it difficult for me to fully bridge that gap I'd created by my assumption. I would have to address it soon, as Munroe wanted me working closely with her. He needed to oversee the launch of his newest flavor of gin and wouldn't be as widely available on-site.

"Your thought was to use it for a tasting room?"

"Aye, just a wee spot for a sample of gin flights, and maybe the merch shop could go in there as well. That way people could have a separate destination after the tour is finished, so we can utilize the space in the distillery for the actual operations."

"What does Orla say about it?"

"I asked her to focus on other areas for now. But I'd like to get an idea if this is an option or if I'd have to hire another crew in to deal with it."

"Right then. I'll crack on and have a look. When are you off?"

"Heading out now. I'll be through to Edinburgh for the next few days, so I'm sorry I won't be here to introduce you around. Lia's invited you for dinner anytime, she's asked me to tell you. Or if you pop down to the pub, there's good scran on there as well."

"Aye, right. That's you on then. I'll fend for myself well enough."

"Don't forget. We've got this charity gala coming up soon."

"Och, don't remind me. Mum's on me about bringing a date."

My uptight mother, who had thrown herself into every charity under the sun when my father had passed on, was co-chairing a gala in Edinburgh focused on aiding the reduction of child hunger in Scotland.

"Do you have one? Lia's making annoyed noises about having to find a dress." Munroe grinned. I liked his fiancée, a highly talented chef at Grasshopper, a rustic elevated comfort food restaurant located inside MacAlpine Castle. She was down-to-earth, beautiful, and clearly most comfortable in the kitchen. Outside of it, she was a jeans and leather jacket kind of woman, but I imagined she would be stunning in a ballgown as well.

"Remind me again when I have the time to date?" I raised an eyebrow at Munroe, and he grinned.

"You're the only one forcing yourself to work this hard, Finlay. Not that I don't appreciate it. But you're no use to anyone if you burn yourself out."

"Work doesn't burn me out. It lights me up."

Which was only partially true, but Munroe didn't really need to know the ins and outs of all that. We were friends, but it was a friendship based on our business dealings, and I'd never opened up to him about what drove me to work as hard as I did.

It was nobody's business but my own, after all.

"Can't say I'm complaining. I'm lucky to have you on my team. Why don't you ask Orla?"

"Ask her what?"

"To be your date to the gala? You could just go as business partners. But she might get a kick out of it and you'd both be representing Common Gin."

"I doubt a gala falls within her duties as project manager."

"Fair enough. Just a thought. All right, that's me off then." Munroe squeezed my shoulder before turning.

"Oh, speaking of ... if you're heading through the site, can you send Orla out to meet me at the outbuilding if she's not too busy? I'll just pop through and see if I can get an idea what's got the lads spooked."

"Not all lads," Munroe gently reminded me, and I laughed.

"Damn it, I've already stuck my foot in it once." Orla's

team was made up of both men and women, and I needed to adjust my language quickly, so I didn't insult someone else. I didn't like making mistakes like that, not ones that tarnished my image, so I not only made a mental note to do better, but I also keyed a quick reminder into my phone to put it as a calendar alert. "It's habit. I've just worked on so many job sites that were mainly men."

"I like that she's challenging stereotypes. Her work backs it up."

"I don't doubt it. From what I can see, she's highly talented."

"Her crew love her as well. That's always a good sign. Right, I'm off. I'll send her your way."

"Safe drive." I was already turning back to the cottage, wondering what had the crew so nervous. I took my time wandering in the direction of the outbuilding, scanning the site for any inconsistencies or areas of concern.

The stone building was beneath a canopy of trees, with leaves and old branches collected in piles on the slate roof and moss clambering up the sides. As usual for Scotland, it was a cloudy day, but the light around the cottage seemed to darken the closer I got. Was it a trick of my mind or just the fact that the canopy of trees was thicker here? A ripple of unease shifted through me as I stopped in front of the worn wood door with an ornate knob. Bending, I squinted at the scratches embedded in the wood around the handle. What had been trying to get inside here?

The hairs on the back of my neck rose, and I jumped when a crow cawed loudly over me. Looking up, I squinted at three crows sitting in a row on a branch above the cottage.

"Well, isn't that perfect?" Like I needed anything else to spook me out. Shaking my head, because I was clearly just winding myself up, I turned the knob and stepped carefully inside the building, my eyes immediately going to the ceiling to see if the space was structurally sound.

Right, okay. Yeah, this place was creepy.

Yet, also intriguing. The door opened directly into a main room, but I could see that the building itself stretched much farther back as part of the wall across from me had crumbled. If that was a supporting wall, it was best that I not explore much farther into the room, because I wasn't the least bit interested in having the roof cave in on my head. Murky light filtered through dirty windows, and a musty breeze wafted through the broken panes. The floor was dirt, whatever wood that had once covered it long gone now, and a few broken chairs were piled in the corner by a massive stone fireplace.

Were those bones in the fireplace?

Intrigued, I stepped gingerly forward, my eyes narrowed on the pile in the fireplace grate.

The door slammed behind me.

Whirling, I held my hands up as the temperature of the room dropped to frigid, ice crystals forming on the windowpanes, and my breath came out in visible puffs in front of my face. Icicles dripped from the ceiling, a virtual ice cave forming around me, and I dug my nails into my palms just to feel the pain.

This isn't real.

Whatever was happening was a figment of my imagination—too much work and too little sleep, that was all.

Keeping calm, I eased myself toward the door, reaching out for the handle.

A shriek, more demonic than human, reverberated off the walls of the room, and I froze as an icicle shot directly at my head. I recovered my wits seconds before it hit my face, ducking and pivoting to avoid the blow. When it shattered against the wall at my side, the fragments piercing my cheeks with their icy cold, I'd decided I'd had enough.

Maybe it wasn't real. But it sure as hell *felt* real and I needed out. Now.

Grabbing the knob, panic rose as I struggled to open the door, something blocking me from moving. Another icicle shattered near my head, and I ducked, throwing my arms up to protect myself as they pummeled against my back.

"Stop!" I shouted, grabbing the knob, pulling as hard as I could, but the door was wedged securely shut. "Help!"

Another shriek sounded, fear lodged in the very marrow of my bones, and I realized I could very well die here. What the hell was wrong with this door? No matter how hard I tugged, turned, or pushed, it was lodged tightly shut. Ice crusted over the hinges, and I tried to chip it away with my hands, scratching at the door, but to no avail.

"Please, help," I begged.

Turning, certain that I was about to meet my maker, I gasped as a woman in a green dress, hooves poking out from the bottom, flitted through the window. Tossing a rock at the door behind me, she gave me a lingering look, as though she was sizing up my very soul, before the ice cave disintegrated around me. The shriek came again, lessened in its power now, and the floating woman nodded to the door behind me, urging me to go.

I didn't need to be told twice. Turning, I grabbed the knob, wrenching the door open before tumbling outside, gasping for air.

"Whoa there, lad. What's wrong?"

Orla sprung from where she crouched on the ground, cuddling two dogs, and I bent at the waist and gasped for air. The panic that had grasped me now thickened around my neck, making it difficult for me to take a full breath, and I sincerely thought I might pass out as I struggled for air. Sweat dripped down my back as Orla took my arms in her hands.

Her work shoes had hearts on them.

I hadn't noticed before that her worn leather steel-toe boots had tiny hearts etched into the leather, but it was all I could focus on as I struggled to breathe, staring down at the ground. *What the hell just happened?*

And what was I supposed to say?

That the cottage was haunted?

She'd laugh in my face.

One of the dogs, a corgi-type mix, a fat tartan bow at her neck, waddled forward into my line of sight and bumped her head against my leg, looking up at me with her tongue lolling out.

"Here then, just breathe, lad. In and out. Nice and slow." Orla basically cooed at me, rubbing her hands up and down my arms, her warmth and nearness soothing me. My legs shook, and she must have noticed because she insisted on easing me to the ground. "Sit here. Just sit."

"My trousers." *Of all things to be worried about now.*

But I had this innate need to take care of my things. I worked hard for everything I had, and I didn't like when my clothes got dirty.

"I'm sure you can afford another pair." Orla sat with me on the damp ground, at ease in her overalls, and kept quiet. Her shoulder touched mine, companionable, but not overbearing, and I reached out to run my hand across the dog that was currently trying to clamber into my lap.

"Is she yours?" I asked, needing to distract myself from the icy panic that was still lodged in my core.

"Lady Lola is the woman of the castle. The one growling over there is Sir Buster. He puts on a tough show, but he'll get jealous of you giving attention to Lola soon enough and make his way over to fuss at us."

I glanced to the chihuahua in a tartan collar who was currently pretending he wasn't the least bit interested in either of us, occasionally shooting us a glare and raising his lip in a growl.

"Is that right?" I increased my attention to Lady Lola, whose chunky bum wiggled in delight at my scratches, and sure enough Sir Buster approached.

"See? He's pretending he doesn't care, but he wants in, you ken?"

Once close, Orla scooped up the trembling chihuahua, and we sat in silence, a dog each, until my heart stopped thundering in my chest. I appreciated that we could sit like this, in quiet, while I tried to gather my thoughts. Many other people would have been yammering at me to tell them what happened, but Orla seemed to innately understand what I needed in that moment. Which was to claw myself back from the edge of a full-fledged panic attack and get my footing under myself again.

Lady Lola flopped her body onto my thighs, and I sighed, automatically brushing the dog hair from the wool.

"Don't like dogs?" Orla's tone suggested I must also like murdering babies then, and I slid a glance her way.

"Don't like dog hair," I corrected.

"Allergies?"

"Not particularly. Just ... messy." I didn't have it in me to explain that even though I bought expensive things, I didn't buy a lot of them, and took care of what I had.

"Messy can be worth it for the joy they bring." Orla made kissy noises at Sir Buster, who now looked like he worshipped the woman, and I couldn't say I blamed him. When she pursed those pretty lips of hers and blew kisses, I wanted to lean over and have a taste. "I've always wanted a dog."

"Why don't you get one?" How were we having such a normal conversation after I was almost murdered by flying ice knives?

"I'm worried I wouldn't be home enough for a puppy." Orla shrugged. "Want to tell me what happened in there?"

"Not particularly." What was I supposed to say? That I'd had a hallucination brought on by too much caffeine and too many nights of little sleep?

"Right then." Orla stood, depositing Sir Buster on the ground, and dusted off the seat of her overalls. "I'll just check it out myself."

Panic returned, and I jumped up, catching her before she opened the door. Wrapping my arms around her short body, I pulled her back tightly against my chest, imprisoning her.

"Don't go in there," I begged.

"Finlay." Orla's tone held a note of warning, and I immediately realized how inappropriate I was being. Her body was imprisoned against mine, and I was struck with our size differences. I could sense the strength in her, and how she'd instantly gone on alert when my arms had come around her. It wasn't unlikely that she'd been harassed more than once on the job, and here I was trapping her against my body.

"Please don't go in there," I amended, easing slowly back, but keeping one hand on her arm. "I don't think it's safe."

Orla turned, giving me an assessing look.

"So it's true then."

"What's true?"

"What my team told me about this building."

"What did they tell you?" Was I just going to parrot questions back at her to delay telling her what I'd seen? Absolutely. I was so far outside my comfort zone in this moment that I needed to somehow restore order to my world. If that meant a verbal rally with Orla, so be it.

"Why don't you tell me what happened first?"

"Tell me what your workers said."

"Are you always this difficult?" Orla demanded, hands at her hips.

"I'm just trying to get a clear answer."

"So am I." Orla's expression grew frustrated.

"Just tell me then."

"*You* tell me first." Orla threw up her hands, turning to

16

look at the cottage again. Her brow furrowed, and her face took on an expression as though she was very far away for a moment, her eyes seeing something that I couldn't.

"Not much to say."

"That's it? You came barreling out of here like the devil himself was chasing you and that's all you can say?" Orla arched a brow at me.

"Yes?" I asked.

"Och, not gonna fly, lad. Give it up."

"I don't want to talk about it. I'm fine," I promised. It was true enough. I was already embarrassed about how she'd seen me, in a sheer panic, on top of the fact that I'd insulted her the other day. Last thing I needed to do was make her think I was delusional too.

"Och, is that the way of it then?" Orla's temper peaked. "You look like you've been chased by a banshee, not a drop of color in your face and hands so cold they're like ice. Yet you say it's fine. Right, then. That's just grand, isn't it? Nothing to see here? Is that right?"

"I'm sorry I was rude to you the other day." I neatly changed the subject, walking backward away from the cottage, hoping to draw her with me. Orla's eyes narrowed, seeming to understand what I was doing, and after one lingering glance back at the front door, she fell in step beside me, the dogs racing in front of us back toward the castle.

"Don't bother yourself. I'm used to it," Orla said, hands in her pockets as we wandered back to the job site.

"Still. Doesn't mean I should have assumed your role on-site. I'm sorry for it and I'll work on being better."

"Well, now. That's refreshing." Orla's grin was like the

sun splitting the clouds. "Didn't take you for one to humble yourself."

"I have my moments."

"Aye, I see that. Or maybe whatever happened in that cottage scared you enough to be apologizing."

"No, I wanted to apologize before then."

"Will you tell me what happened?"

"Tell me what the workers say."

"They say the place is haunted." Someone called Orla's name, drawing her attention away, and she stood before me, torn between our conversation and the job.

"It might well be." There, that was all I was going to say about it. The last thing I needed to do was relive the harrowing experience that still made my gut churn.

"If that's the case, I'll invite you to stay away from it, Mr. Thompson. I'll sort it out soon enough."

"Wait, what? That's not your job—" I made to grab her arm as she turned to walk away but then stopped, reminding myself that I'd already touched her without her permission once today.

"It's my site. Which means it's my problem. Good day, Mr. Thompson." With that, Orla returned to her workers, and I was left wondering when I'd gone from Finlay to Mr. Thompson to her. Turning, I glanced back at the cold and foreboding cottage, and now I had a new thing to worry about.

How was I going to keep Orla Clarke away from that cottage?

CHAPTER THREE

Orla

The day flew by with one problem after another, keeping me away from investigating the outbuilding on my own. I had to hand it to Finlay though. Despite looking like he'd had his arse handed to him in a fight, he shouldered on through the challenges of the day, never showing that he'd been given the fright of his life. Or at least that was how it had seemed to me. The man's face had been devoid of color, and sweat had dripped from his brow. I knew a panic response when I saw one, and I was just grateful I'd been there with the dogs to help calm him down.

Stretching my arms over my head, I rotated my chin, trying to work out the kinks in my neck. My crew had left the site for the day, but I had just wanted to finish sanding a strip of the floor in the side room that we planned to convert to storage. I was hoping the wood would be strong enough to not have to replace, but I needed to sand it and test it for weakness before we could start a buildout in that room.

"Sore neck?"

I jumped, my hand dropping to the back of my neck as I turned to find Finlay at the door.

"Goes with the territory." I shrugged, studying his face for signs of wariness about what had transpired earlier that day. Finding nothing, his façade firmly back in place, I took a breath and tried not to be annoyed about being interrupted. "You're here late."

"I could say the same for you." A corner of his mouth quirked up when I rolled my eyes.

"Do you always do that?"

"Define that."

"Just like ... I don't know. What's the word in tennis? Parry? Lob back and forth? I say one thing and you toss it back at me?"

A flash of amusement heightened Finlay's good looks and my annoyance deepened that I was even remotely aware of how this man looked. I shouldn't care. He was my client's manager, technically a boss of sorts to me, and exceptionally not my type. Remembering how he'd flicked the dog hair off his trousers, I tried to imagine this man hunkered down in the middle of dirt and sawdust.

Nope. Couldn't see it.

Even now, surrounded by the mess of a construction zone, Finlay looked like he'd just walked out of a boardroom. A gold watch flashed at his wrist, his trousers showed no wrinkles, and only the tiniest of smudges at the cuff of his shirt indicated any sort of struggle in the cottage earlier today. And there had been. I'd heard him banging to get out.

Which reminded me. I needed to detour past that cottage on the way out today. I needed Finlay to wrap this conversation up so I could be on my way.

"Parry can be used in tennis. It can also be used in sword fighting. Or boxing even. Lobbing is when you toss something lightly to another person."

"So both would work here."

"Lob would only apply if you lobbed something back at me, which would then turn it into a parry."

"Mr. Thompson, may I be frank?"

"Oh, please do." Finlay's grin deepened, even though I sensed he was annoyed at me calling him Mr. Thompson.

"I'm finding this conversation a wee bit tedious, and I'd like to finish up my work so I can crack on with my evening plans. Is there anything you're needing?"

"What are your plans?"

"Is divulging my evening plans required as part of my job description?" I raised an accusatory brow at him.

"Now who is parrying?"

"See earlier note about my annoyance." I put my hand on the handle of the sander, indicating I was about to drown his words out.

Finlay simply crossed his arms and rocked back on his feet, clearly amused by me.

"My plans are much the same as they are most nights. To crochet and listen to murder podcasts. Any other questions?"

"More than before, certainly."

"Technically I'm off the clock, so you'll have to ask them another time." Bending over, I flicked the sander on, the loud noise drowning out any follow-up questions. I didn't look up as I moved the machine over the floor, concentrating on the rhythmic motion, watching as the grain of the old wood exposed itself to me. By the time I switched the machine off, having sanded far more than I had planned to avoid having to converse further with Finlay, the ache in my neck had intensified.

I added a neck massage to my evening plans.

I'd recently splurged on one of those personal massagers that wrap around your neck and shoulders and plugged directly into the power point. I had to say, next to a very different type of massager that I had tucked in my bedside drawer, it was my new favorite toy at home.

The evening air was damp, bringing with it the scent of musty earth after a soft rain, and I lingered for a moment as the last of the light held on. I always loved this shift of winter giving over to late spring, when the daylight hours became much longer, and we could say goodbye to blustery winter weather. MacAlpine Castle stood, proud as she ever was, the waters of Loch Mirren a mirror at her back.

What would it be like to live in a castle?

I honestly couldn't wrap my head around having so much space to myself. Well, not by myself, since loads of people needed to live in a castle to keep it running, at least in olden days, but still—calling such an impressive structure your home had to be kind of mind-blowing. I'd grown up basically on the streets, in a wee town outside Edinburgh. My mother's half-sister had barely been able to provide for her own children, let alone the added burden of myself after addiction had claimed my mother's life. Four of us children had shared a bedroom, and I was outside more often than not, which is why I always loved the shift of winter giving up the last of its hold and settling over to the gentler days of spring.

Not that spring in Scotland was all that warm, but when you spent a lot of time in the elements, even the smallest shift in temperature was deeply noticeable. By the time I'd turned sixteen I was largely on my own, barely passing by to check in with my frazzled aunt, and I wasn't sure which one of us had been more relieved when I'd finally stopped going around to the house. By then, I'd found a crew of others just like me, but it had been Jacob, sweet silly Jacob, who had saved my life.

His grandfather had owned a workshop. It was where Jacob had disappeared to when the bruises from his father were too large to hide. There, his grandfather had first taught him, and then me, how to build.

I'd forever be grateful for the gentle teachings of Grandpa Lou. He never once made me feel unwelcome for being a girl or not part of his family, and it was there I'd learned a very important lesson.

Nobody was going to save me but myself.

Having a skill such as being able to build with your own two hands? Well, it had opened a world of possibilities for me.

"A man has a fortune in his hands, Orla. You just need the right tools." Grandpa Lou had lectured me over and over, in one form or another. *"As long as you can build something for yourself, Orla, you'll have all the fortune you ever need."*

The old man had been right.

I now had what to most might not seem like much, but to me it was a veritable fortune. A solid work lorry, a successful business, and my very own one-room cottage that seemed as opulent as MacAlpine Castle, at least to me. Someday, when I had time, I planned to add a sunroom to the back of the cottage. A place where I could have a few plants and crochet in peace at the end of a long day.

Detouring toward the outbuilding, I picked my way along the uneven ground, the light growing dim around me. Perhaps I should save this for tomorrow. But if I could at least get a sense of what was haunting this cottage, I could do some research tonight.

Maybe I could free it.

Maybe not.

I was still learning about all this ghost stuff, since it had only been a year or two since I'd started seeing more of them.

Yes, more.

There was one that had been with me for a long time.

I used to think of her as my imaginary friend. Until I'd grown too old to believe in imaginary friends and realized that all of those late-night conversations I was having were either with a walking, talking delusion, or I, indeed, had a ghost who visited me regularly.

It took a while to accept the ghost aspect over the delusions, to be honest.

"Orla!"

I jumped, pulled from my thoughts, as Sophie, the new owner of MacAlpine Castle, called to me from across the garden. The dogs were with her, and at her shout, they turned and raced toward me. Joy immediately flooded me at their approach. Meeting them halfway, I crouched to pet Lola while Sir Buster did his act where he pretended to want nothing to do with me.

Such bluster.

I understood it, though. The tough guy act. I'd had to put it on enough in my own life, hadn't I?

"Hiya, Sophie. How are you getting on then?"

"Great, thanks. I was hoping to catch you." Sophie, a fresh-faced American, with strawberry-blonde hair, a friendly manner, and welcoming smile always put me at ease. I liked her. She said what was on her mind, and I appreciated not having to navigate things left unsaid, unlike with Finlay.

"Were you headed to that building?" Sophie inclined her head to the outbuilding behind me. "I didn't realize you'd started work on that yet."

"Was just planning to have a wee look." I tossed a look over my shoulder at the cottage, a flicker of movement catching my eye through the dirty window.

"By yourself? Even though it's haunted?"

At that, I turned and gave Sophie a surprised look.

"You've heard that as well then?"

"Of course. Your crew talks." Sophie gave me a considering look. "Want me to come with?"

"You *want* to go in a haunted building?"

"I live in a haunted building." Sophie shrugged.

At that, I caught sight of a highland coo sneaking up behind her, and my eyes widened until the light caught him just right and I realized it wasn't a real coo. Well, it was, but he was a ghost.

Och, this was a first.

I opened my mouth to say something, but then, not wanting to appear unbalanced to the owner of the castle, I snapped my lips shut. The coo crept closer, like a wee cat sneaking up on a mouse, and my mind whirled. What was he trying to do? Was he going to pounce on her?

Sophie caught my look and let out a long-suffering sigh. "He's behind me, isn't he?"

"Um, I'm not sure what you're referring to." I didn't like to lie, but I wasn't entirely sure how Sophie would respond to me seeing ghosts, so I protected myself first. Always.

"Clyde, I swear to God, don't make me hang up warning signs about you and ruin your fun. You've already scared me twice today." Sophie turned, hands on hips, a scolding note in her voice.

Laughter bubbled inside me as the coo's shoulders dropped, his eyes going wide and beseeching.

"Don't give me that look. You know we have a *one scare a day* rule. You've already violated it."

Clyde sniffed, hanging his head.

"Aww," I said, feeling sorry for the big guy, and then pressed my lips together when Sophie shot me a look.

"So you see him?"

"I, um, yes. The big ghost highland coo?"

"Yes, this is Clyde. He's friendly, except when he scares people within an inch of having a heart attack." Sophie sighed, turning back to me, her face resigned. "He made Lia pee her pants."

"He did *not*. This sweet guy?" Clyde perked up at my words, sidling over to me, and I grinned at him. "You're very handsome."

The coo preened, clearly pleased with my praise.

"Ghosts don't bother you then?" Sophie gave me a considering look, and once again I felt like I was dancing along the edge of something unknown. I wasn't sure how much of myself to divulge, but then remembered that Willow from the kilt shop was good friends with Sophie.

Shite. I'd made the mistake of revealing to them that I could sense ghosts. It wasn't typical for me, but I'd had a really stressful day and hadn't slept when I'd met with them to go over their project. With my guard down, I'd let it slip that I could sense ghosts. Which also meant that Willow had likely relayed this to Sophie.

It wasn't a huge secret, I supposed, as some of my crew knew that I had a sense of whether a building was haunted or not. They respected me for it, being able to sense energy, and we hadn't much talked past the basics of it all. They didn't care, so long as they could work in peace, and I did my best to make sure whatever project we took on was safe for them.

In all elements, I supposed.

"I wouldn't say I'm super chuffed about them. Though Clyde seems sweet," I amended. I had a soft spot for all animals.

Animals were a lot easier to understand than humans.

"But you see them, don't you?"

"Aye." No point in lying about it. Not when a huge ghost coo was currently sniffing at Sir Buster's bum, causing the dog to growl.

"I wonder why that is. Not everyone has the skill."

"Is it a skill?" That was the first time I'd considered the

ability to be a skill. Largely since I didn't have much say in it.

"You tell me. Some would say it is a great ability to have. Communicating with the dead? People pay a lot of money for that."

"It's not like that. I don't summon them to me." Instantly I realized that I was revealing far more than I had intended.

"Ah." Sophie turned. "The light's fading. I'd rather we looked at the building another time. Why don't I walk you to your car and you can tell me more about it?"

"Not much to tell." I fell in step beside Sophie. "I don't choose the interactions. It's not like I'm a medium. I just can go into a building and see if it is haunted. It's largely attached to structures. I've yet to see a ghost wandering the forest or whatever."

"So you're a house witch."

"What?" I stopped in my tracks, my eyebrows furrowing on my forehead.

"A house witch. I mean, that's what popped into my head when you said that. But maybe there's another term."

"What does a house witch do?"

"I don't honestly know. But I'd say they can probably see ghosts in houses and get rid of them. Have you removed any unwanted spirits from a house before?"

"I have." I dug my boot into the gravel by the car as a trickle of anxiety worked through me at the word witch.

Historically, people weren't kind to those who considered themselves witches. I didn't want the label—not if it meant more disapproving eyes on me, and the very thought of it made my stomach turn. I would hate to lose everything I had worked for because of this.

"Doing it with a spell? Or a ritual? Something to clear them out?"

I gave a curt nod, wary now.

"Sounds like a house witch to me."

I winced.

"And you can build houses. That's even cooler, right?"

I gave a tentative shrug. I wasn't sure where she was going with this, but I hoped wherever she landed wouldn't put me out of a job.

To my surprise, Sophie beamed at me.

"Orla, I think you're just the woman we've been looking for."

CHAPTER FOUR

ORLA

I didn't get to my crochet and true crime podcast after all.

Sophie had drawn me with her, promising just a quick chat.

Inside, Hilda and Archie, the castle caretakers, had joined us, insisting I stay for dinner while Sophie had basically blown my mind with a fanciful tale of Kelpies and magick, enchanted waters, and an ancient magickal Order that I, it seemed, was a part of.

The Order of Caledonia, to be precise.

Apparently it was a magickal Order that protected the Clach na Fìrinn, the Stone of Truth, basically one of the holy grails that many, many, many people had searched for the world over. This stone was so powerful that anyone who possessed it would hold all knowledge of humankind, which, I could understand, was a very dangerous tool. The kicker? It was basically sentient, understanding the need for its own protection, and the Order of Caledonia had sprung up to ensure the Stone never fell into the wrong hands. When the last of the Order had died over a year ago, the safeguard had fallen into place—the Kelpies—and now they haunted Loren Brae, driving away anyone who moved too close to the island where the Stone was buried. Until the Order was restored, the Kelpies would continue to threaten the town, and even I'd seen how much the village had deteriorated over the past year.

It wasn't like I was immune to hearing the Kelpies scream at night either.

By mutual agreement, nobody much spoke of what we'd all heard on the icy winter winds that barreled over Loch Mirren, but whispers had reached my ears.

Now, having confirmation that the Kelpies were real and that the people at MacAlpine Castle were quietly fighting to restore the Order, was both a revelation and an affirmation in the same breath.

I'd felt it, hadn't I?

I'd be lying if I said I hadn't.

I supposed, part and parcel with seeing ghosts, was the ability to sense enchantments and, well, when I'd moved to Loren Brae several years ago, drawn here by budding work opportunities and the need for a quieter way of life, I'd sensed an otherworldliness to the village. Maybe that's what had pulled me here all along.

The Order of Caledonia.

Me. A supposed member of an ancient magickal Order.

31

Once my disbelief had been suspended, a trickle of excitement had buoyed me on my way home.

I'd never been a part of something before.

Not really.

No family to speak of. A few scattered friends on the streets, drawn together more by what we didn't have than what we did. Grandpa Lou's workshop had become a haven to me, but even then, I'd understood that it wasn't really mine to keep.

When we'd lost Jacob, I'd run—*and kept running*—until I'd landed in Loren Brae, finally ready to set down roots and try to build something for myself. My crew was now the closest thing I had to family, and even then, I knew they went home to their own lives, while I returned to a quiet cottage. On my own.

The way I liked it.

If you were alone, nobody could hurt you by leaving.

But now, *now*, Sophie wasn't just asking that I believe her wild tale about the Order of Caledonia. She was asking me to join. To pledge. To accept my role to protect Loren Brae, to step into the magick that was granted with the role, and to be a part of something so much more.

My inner child jumped at the chance.

Adult me had severe misgivings.

So far, the Order consisted of women. Several of whom I already knew. Groups of women made me nervous. Fabulous foreign beings with their makeup and fancy purses and innate femininity, none of which I grasped or understood. Frankly, groups of women *terrified* me. I had no idea how to navigate the nuances of sisterhood, let alone listening to conversations of little concern to me. How could I care about the latest fashions when every pound I earned went toward ensuring the security of my future?

Granted, I knew I was being unfair to women in general. I'd met several, particularly since coming to Loren Brae, who didn't seem to give a hoot about fashion, instead preferring to discuss their favorite hobbies like gardening or hiking, something that I could at least carry on a basic conversation about. Even Willow, an actual fashion designer, who basically sparkled her way through life, had never made me feel uncomfortable. Instead, once she and Ramsay had hired me to oversee their rebuild after the fire, she'd made an extra effort to get to know me.

It appeared I still had a lot of my own shite to unpack if I wanted to change how I viewed sisterhoods.

And that was what this was, truly, at its core. Hilda had even told me that the Order was at its strongest when filled by women.

You're a house witch.

The words floated through my brain as I pulled my lorry to a stop in the spot next to my wee cottage, a long breath escaping me as it did every time I returned to my home.

It had taken me years to save enough to purchase this wee place and I'd gotten it at a steal because of the amount of work it had, well, *still*, needed. After I'd closed on the property, I'd bought myself a bottle of wine, made a small charcuterie board, and had sat on the bare floor. I'd lit a candle, looked around the space that nobody else could call their own but me, and had cried like a baby.

I'd given myself six precious weeks off work, my first real holiday, and I'd sanded, cleaned, built, and worked myself into exhaustion. The result was a livable space that shone with love. Unlocking the door, I stepped into the cottage, tension easing from my shoulders the minute I closed and locked the door behind me—*always locked, mind you*—and stood in my space.

Mine.

I'd never take this for granted.

On the far end of the room, a woodburning stove doubled as one of the main heating elements in winter. A deep-set love seat in soft earthy tones sat along the wall under the front window, pulled close to enjoy the warmth of the fire, and a soft tufted rug in muted greens had been placed across the hardwood floors. Directly across from the sofa, a kitchen cooktop and range of cabinets were tucked under the window that looked out to the back garden. I'd opted for roughhewn shelves above the counter, allowing the softness of the stone walls to show and keeping a lightness to the room that you wouldn't get with heavy cabinetry. A few of my pretty dishes were stacked neatly on the shelves, including my favorite mug.

It was a mug with a drawing of Batman and Robin on it that read *"Yer ma wee pal."*

Jacob had given it to me the week before he'd gotten in a fight outside the pub. He'd fallen badly, his head not standing a chance against the steps. Pronounced brain dead shortly thereafter, I'd lost the only real friend I'd ever had.

Grandpa Lou had followed six months later, and I'd promised myself to work hard in his honor. *I'd never felt so alone as I did in that moment.* Since that awful time, I'd buried myself in my job and hadn't looked up until now, on a random Tuesday, when an American woman pulled me aside and invited me to join a magickal Order.

It was an opportunity to be a part of something more.

To help the people of Loren Brae.

Where some people might jump at the chance to be a hero, I had to admit, at least to myself, that the very thought scared me.

Being a part of something more, a family, a group of friends, an Order—well, that meant I was responsible to them. For their feelings. For my actions. My words. Everything I did or didn't do would affect others. And while that may come naturally to many, to me it was a terrifying burden.

The only people I currently wanted to be responsible to were my crew. My team. I'd handpicked them, giving some a chance when many others hadn't, and their loyalty was something I didn't take for granted.

I stored my boots neatly by the door and automatically crossed to the fire to throw a few small logs on. Though spring was at our doorstep, the nights were still cold. Luckily, I didn't need to think about scrounging up food tonight. Hilda not only fed me a delightful dinner of chunky vegetable stew, but also sent me home with extras. I sensed she had an innate need to nurture, and I was never sure how to act around those types. Mothering was such a foreign concept to me that I often felt out of my element around women that tried to do that for me.

Once the fire was lit, I crossed to my sleeping area, separated from the room by a see-through bookshelf that I'd built myself. Modeled after a popular style from IKEA, I'd scraped together enough spare wood to create a beautiful design, with open-wood boxes stacked on top of each other, and had filled the shelves with second-hand shop finds and some of my favorite books. I'd flirted with the idea of building an actual wall between the bed and the rest of the room, but this open book-shelf design had allowed for a separation of space without having to frame it off completely. The result allowed for the flickering light and warmth from the fire to filter through to my bed, and the space was cohesive and airy.

On one shelf sat a bowl with a goldfish in it, who perked up when I walked closer.

"Sorry I'm a wee bit late tonight, Goldie."

Goldie, as in Goldie Hawn, was a goldfish that I'd bought on a whim because my very soul ached for a companion of some kind. I desperately wanted a dog but had resigned myself to spending time with them as a volunteer at the shelter instead, and so a goldfish had been the compromise I'd made with myself. I'd known next to nothing about fish, but I'd been surprised how much I'd grown attached to Goldie. She, or he, I wasn't entirely sure, always perked up when I came home, swimming in excited circles around the bowl, and would follow me as I walked around the room.

Now I grinned down at her as I tapped some flakes of fish food into the bowl, happy to be important to at least one thing in this world.

Which was a silly and morose thought to have, I told myself, as I stripped and tucked myself into the shower in the narrow bathroom attached to the corner of the cottage. I was important to my crew, wasn't I? They relied on me to pick projects that would give them solid work. They relied on *me* and *my* decisions.

Which was a direct contradiction to the nerves that kicked up when thinking about joining the Order. My need for belonging warred with my fear of never belonging anywhere at all.

By the time I showered and had crawled into bed, I hadn't landed on which direction I wanted to go with Sophie's invitation to join the Order. I was just picking up my crochet project when movement caught my eye.

He's handsome.

A woman in a green dress settled at the foot of my bed. I knew, if I bent forward and looked at where her dress ended, I would see goat-like hooves sticking out from the bottom of her dress.

The Green Lady.

A glaistig.

Stories abounded about her, in hundreds of variations across Scotland, and I wouldn't be the least surprised if there were more than one of these "Green Ladies" perpetuating these myths. But, from all accounts, she'd attached herself to me. She was the first ghost I'd ever seen, but certainly not the last, and the only one that had traveled with me as I'd moved across Scotland.

"Who is handsome?"

You know who. The one who got stuck in the cottage.

"Finlay Thompson. He's my new boss. Of sorts. What happened in the cottage?" I settled back against my pillows, comfortable with the Green Lady, as she'd been having these bedside "chats" with me for years. At first, it had been terrifying. Now I took comfort in her presence. She'd shown, time and again, that for some reason she felt protective over me.

The first time I'd seen her, she'd saved me from a mugging by scaring the shite out of the man who'd grabbed my arm as I walked the streets, not having a place to go home to that night. I'd been just as scared as my attacker, but when she'd ranged herself in front of me, protecting me while she terrorized him, I'd come to realize she was looking out for me. We hadn't spoken, not that first night, but I'd thanked her before running away.

Through the years, she'd grown more confident with visiting me and we'd developed a friendship of sorts, an affinity, you could say. She wandered the world, lost and alone, and I supposed I could identify with that feeling. Two lost souls we were, finding companionship with each other, and I had come to have an odd sort of affection for this woman who never told me about herself no matter how much I prodded.

Bad energy there. A woman unfairly tried and executed.

"So, like a poltergeist?"

The Green Lady just shrugged a shoulder. I'd learned that she didn't know the explanations that humans had come up with for ghostly or mythological apparitions. I'd been dying to ask about her goat legs for years, but any gentle nudges in that direction had resulted in her disappearance.

"And she went after Finlay, didn't she? He was terrified."

She made the building an ice cave and attacked him with icicles. The door was locked when I found him, but I let him out.

"So that was why he fell out of the door. He'd been locked inside. That's strong magick for a ghost, isn't it?"

Blood magick. She was very hurt.

"Och. That doesn't sound great. Any suggestions to help her?"

Take your time with it. You won't free her from there easily. You need to join the Order.

At that, I straightened.

"You know about the Order of Caledonia?"

Of course.

"Sophie thinks I'm a house witch. I don't know how I feel about that."

Witch is a powerful word. A blessing for some. A curse for others. You're lucky that you get a choice in which way that path unfolds for you these days.

"And if I join this Order? She says I'll get magick."

You already have magick. Joining the Order just makes you stronger.

"I do?" This was news to me. Seeing ghosts had never felt very magickal to me, but maybe I needed to expand my definition.

"What if I fail them?"

And what if you don't?

With that, the Green Lady disappeared from the foot of my bed, leaving me to contemplate whether I was ready to join something that would anchor me to Loren Brae forever. A part of me warmed to the thought, the feeling of coming home making me almost giddy with excitement, but like anything in my life, I needed to proceed with caution.

Goldie zipped tight circles in her bowl, mirroring my thoughts, and I drifted off to sleep.

CHAPTER FIVE

FINLAY

I hadn't told anyone about my encounter in the outbuilding.

I was new to Loren Brae, new on the construction site, and was still feeling things out. I often found it best to get the lay of the land first, because if I needed to implement change, it was better I did so with an understanding of the dynamics of what I was stepping into rather than coming in like a wrecking ball. Nuance mattered, particularly on buildouts, because many who worked on our construction sites also lived in the towns we built in. Small towns were their own puzzles to be solved, and I approached each project with a careful curiosity, knowing that we weren't just providing jobs for the construction workers, but also that the business we were growing would benefit the community.

I never wanted to give anyone a reason to dislike me, or the Common Gin brand. Reputation mattered, and Munroe knew that I cared just as deeply about his company as he did. He was a great boss, and he took care of his employees. I was proud of the work we did, the jobs we provided, and the community we had created. We even had a line of craft mocktails in the works for those who didn't drink alcohol.

The music of a busy construction site greeted my ears when I arrived the next morning, handsaws whirring, hammers slapping against wood, a morning radio show recapping the match from the night before. The air was still brisk, sharp enough that I cradled my hands around my thermos of coffee, and I took a moment to examine the building from the outside.

I could just see it. The finished project. Granted, I'd seen the mock-ups, which were stunning in their own right, but I loved nothing more than watching something that was once in disrepair come to life. I imagined this must be how gardeners felt, coaxing a seed to bloom, and being on a buildout was my favorite aspect of my job. Spreadsheets, finances, and profit and loss ledgers were a touch less appealing, but I thrived equally on-site as I did behind my computer. The nice thing about Munroe was that he didn't force me to solely take meetings and be on the phone at all times, as he knew as well as I did that I needed to get out of the office to remain a cheerful human being. Because of that, he'd structured his operations team to share their duties, and we were in constant contact as we shifted our roles to accommodate for what the company needed. It worked well, this balance of responsibilities that Munroe had created, and it pleased me that I'd been picked to be on-site for the Loren Brae project.

I'd needed a break from Edinburgh for a while.

As much as I loved my mother, she'd become overbearing to the point of neurotic since my father had passed away. After his death, a heart attack taking him in his lover's bed, we'd discovered just what kind of man my father had really been. I'd sensed hints of it through the years, but the unraveling of his lies had undone my mother and now she focused all her attention on me, desperate to control my very existence, because her own foundation had shattered.

Yes, some time in Loren Brae would suit us both. Even now, my phone pinged, and I glanced down to see a reminder from my mother about securing a date for the upcoming gala. It was the one engagement that I couldn't get out of, as not only was she a co-chair, but Common Gin had heavily sponsored the event. I didn't see the need for a date, but I might just take one to shut my mother up.

Orla strode around the side of the building, in green canvas overalls today, her hair plaited down her back. She carried a heavy stack of timber at her shoulder, and I jumped forward, wanting to help.

"Here, let me get that for you."

Orla turned, somehow managing to look at me without swinging the wood around and knocking my head off, showing she was well used to being on a construction site. I mean, of course she was. She owned her own construction business. Her eyes took a lazy meander over my outfit, stopping at my shoes, and she sniffed. I glanced down.

What was wrong with my shoes? They were steel-toed boots, proper foot attire for a construction zone, and I'd purchased them recently after my old ones had taken the brunt of a tar spill.

"I'm just fine, thanks. Is there something you needed, Mr. Thompson?" Orla waited patiently, as though the weight of the timber on her shoulder wasn't a bother, and I felt awkward for stopping her and making her hold the bundle longer.

"Is there anything that you need help with today?" I moved over and held the door for her, propping it open, and then followed her to where she put the wood down next to a stack of boards. She took off her gloves and tucked them in a pocket before turning to me.

"What do you know about building?" Orla arched an eyebrow at me.

"I know that's a hammer." I pointed to a tool tucked at her belt. Orla looked down, her lips pursed in disdain, and I suppressed a grin. It was easy to poke at her a bit, knowing she'd give the banter back, and I hoped to build a better relationship with her after we'd gotten off on the wrong foot.

Sunlight speared through the window, catching her eyes, and she blinked at me, her dark lashes fanning against her cheeks, and I had this sudden urge to pick her up and carry her away, to protect her from what harm life could bring her. It was so unusual for me to think such a thing that it took me a moment to realize she was speaking to me.

"Och, I'd say it's best you stick to your fancy office, and I'll stick to my job, no?" Orla held out a hand to indicate her sawdust-filled "office."

"This *is* my office for the next six months," I said automatically, trying to shove away the protective feelings that had whirled up inside me, unbidden, for this tiny powerhouse.

By all accounts, Orla did not need protecting. And certainly not from the likes of me. If I'd been any less confident in who I was as a person, my ego would be taking a hit by the indication that I was less manly for not working in the trades. Luckily, I knew who I was and what I brought to the table. I wasn't someone who needed to prove my *manliness* to anyone.

"I suppose that's true enough," Orla admitted. "Is there anything you want to go over with me?"

"Actually, there is." I gestured with my cup of coffee to the hallway. "I wanted to discuss the storage room, as we'll need to separate the botanicals. Has that been drawn into the plans?"

"I believe so, but it depends on the quantity and method of storing them."

My eyes caught on a wee badge on her collar, and I leaned a touch closer to see.

"Is that a goldfish?"

A faint wash of pink swept across Orla's cheeks, and instantly I was charmed. I'd yet to see her unsteady, even when I was in the middle of a meltdown yesterday, so this response intrigued me.

"Aye," Orla said, shifting and glancing away.

"Does it mean anything special? Or is that the logo for your company?"

"What in the world would a goldfish have to do with a construction company?" Orla's gaze whipped back to mine, and she regarded me as though I was daft.

"People have chosen stranger mascots, I'm sure."

"Name one."

"Freddo," I said, and Orla's mouth dropped open.

"What's wrong with Freddo then?"

"I mean, he's a frog. What does a frog have to do with chocolate?"

"The bars are in the shape of a frog." Orla crossed her arms over her chest, narrowing her eyes at me.

"Aye, that's true enough. But why? Why would anyone want to eat a chocolate frog? If I see a wee frog in the wild, it's not like I point at it and think that I want a chocolate version of it. They're not particularly cute or appetizing looking, are they?"

Orla's mouth opened and closed as she considered my words.

"Some people eat real frogs. Not the chocolate ones. So they probably think a chocolate frog would be lovely."

"Aye, that's true enough, though not particularly to my taste, I'll admit. Still, if I was launching a chocolate company, I'm not sure a frog would be my first choice of mascot."

"Maybe you're just bad at choosing mascots then. Because Freddo is iconic, isn't he? Seems they knew the way of it."

I laughed. "You're likely right. Then your goldfish is Clarke Construction's mascot?"

"Och, no." Annoyance swept over Orla's pretty face, seeing how she'd been nudged into explaining herself more. Pulling details out of this woman was difficult, but I supposed I was much the same. I could understand wanting to keep a wall up. It's why I spent a lot of time asking questions of other people. Not only did it allow me to gather information, but people always enjoyed talking about themselves. Except Orla, it seemed. "I have a wee goldfish at home, all right?"

"What's his name?"

"*Her* name is Goldie Hawn."

"A fashionable name for a wee fish."

"She's a diva."

"Blows bubbles when she doesn't get her way?"

Orla's lips quirked, and I considered it a win. While I hadn't made her outright laugh yet, I now understood this was a challenge I'd undertake.

The clouds moved, and sunlight shifted again, highlighting her gorgeous blue eyes. She blinked, her dark lashes feathering across her cheeks, and the moment drew out ... and I realized I was outright staring at her.

"Sometimes she even gives me the fin."

I chuckled, imagining a fish flipping Orla off.

You should ask Orla to the gala.

Munroe's words drifted back to me and while I'd first rejected the notion, now it didn't seem so out there. She was working with Munroe's company, wasn't she? Orla might enjoy a fancy night out with posh food at a charity gala.

"Orla, there's a charity ball soon that my mum is on me to bring a date. Fancy going with me?"

Orla's mouth dropped open and she narrowed her eyes at me, instantly making me realize I must have overstepped.

"You need a date because of your mum?"

"She's relentless." Mentally, I kicked myself. Not quite the way a woman wanted to be asked out. Embarrassment rushed through me. Usually, I handled these situations much better, but there was something about Orla that put me off my game.

"Um," Orla said, and I knew she was about to say no.

"I'll pay you," I rushed out.

Pay her? You idiot. Seriously, had I just offered to pay her to be my date?

"Pay me?" Orla squeaked. The pink on her cheeks heightened.

"Yes, of course. Common Gin is a major sponsor as well. So, it would certainly fall within a business scope. No reason not to be reimbursed for your time."

"Let me get this straight. You want to pay me to be your fake date to a gala so your mum will leave you alone? But also to represent the company?"

Och, I'd bungled this.

"Aye?" Even I didn't sound convinced, but I was already knee-deep in this, so I might as well keep going. "Just think, you'll get to dress up and eat tiny food passed around by snooty waiters."

"I don't have a dress." Instantly, Orla's face changed. *She was now the one who was embarrassed.* Lovely, just lovely. Not only had I insulted the woman by offering to pay her for a date, but I'd made her uncomfortable about not having a dress.

"Neither does Lia," I said, throwing Munroe's wife neatly under the bus. "She was grumbling all about it. Munroe's assured me that there is a dress budget."

Liar, liar.

Orla's eyes shifted over my shoulder, and she shook her head lightly, as though arguing with someone behind me. I turned, but the space was empty and when I looked back her expression was smoothed.

"To be clear ... you'll buy me a dress, pay for my time, and I get free dinner?"

"I can't promise that the dinner will be fabulous, but yes to the other things."

"How much?" Orla demanded, her eyes taking on a calculating look.

"Two hundred and fifty pounds." I named what I thought would be a nice price for a date but not insulting.

"Make it five hundred and I'm in. The animal shelter is saving for supplies for its extension."

She was going to use the money for an animal shelter? I felt even worse.

"What animal shelter?"

"The local shelter. I volunteer there a lot because I can't have a dog. They need more space and I've offered to build the extension for them, but they still have to acquire the supplies even if I can get it for them at cost, you ken?"

Great, now I felt like a right shite about what I'd just fumbled my way into. I'd just wanted her as my date because I enjoyed bantering back and forth with her, and she intrigued me. Yet somehow, I'd managed to make her think I needed to please my mum and that I paid for companionship. Could I be any more awkward?

"Why can't you have a dog?"

"I told you yesterday while you were trying not to cry outside the outbuilding."

Right, okay, I guess things *could* get more awkward.

"I was not crying," I insisted. Had I been crying? I couldn't quite remember.

Orla's expression softened.

"One of these days, you'll need to tell me what happened in there."

"I ate something bad for lunch. Fish. It was a bit off."

Wow, I was just full of mistruths today, wasn't I? It wasn't like me to fumble out so many excuses and now I needed to retreat. Or do something to make up for it.

"Uh-huh," Orla said, clearly not believing me.

"Listen, since it is for charity and I happen to like dogs, irrespective of their messy fur, I'll donate one thousand pounds to your shelter. In turn, I'd love for you to be my date to the gala, and I'll see about Munroe arranging a dress shopping date for you and Lia. Does that suit? You've met Lia, right?"

"Aye, she's great. A thousand pounds, eh? That would be just enough to get the shelter what they need. I can't possibly say no to that. Sure, Mr. Thompson. I'll be your date."

I pinched my nose and sighed.

"Can you please call me Finlay?"

"Is it a requirement of my fake date?" Orla arched a brow at me.

"Yes," I said, not caring if it was or not.

"Fine, *Finlay*. The dogs will thank you."

With that, Orla turned and pulled out her tape measure and carpenter's pencil, dismissing me.

"I'll send you the details regarding the dress and all that." Munroe had given the both of us each other's numbers in case of any issues that would arise on-site, but I'd yet to message Orla with any questions. Apparently, now

I had to arrange a personal shopper. Retreat was my only option at this point.

"Great, thanks." Orla was already marking the wood and making notes in a wee notebook, and I stepped out, feeling as awkward as a teenager who'd spoken to his crush for the first time.

How the hell was I going to find a personal shopper?

Annoyed, I went back outside and took out my phone.

"Hi, Willow? Yes, I need your help."

CHAPTER SIX

ORLA

A gala.

By the time I'd finished my work, early, because apparently I needed to partake in a magickal ritual, I'd managed to work my head around the idea of going to an actual gala. Well, sort of. I needed to find Lia and ask a million questions about protocol. I didn't know about proper manners when it came to fancy table settings or if I needed to do certain dance steps. Would I have to curtsy to someone? I didn't even know if I could curtsy. It was those details that were worrisome to me, not the idea of spending time with Finlay.

It was fun to ruffle his feathers.

I couldn't help but poke at him, just to see his smooth exterior crumble. He was the type of man that exuded confidence, his charisma filling a room, and it made me feel better to see a few cracks in the carefully erected façade he wore.

Barking pulled me from my thoughts, and I crouched as Lady Lola rounded the corner with Sir Buster at her side. Repeating the routine where Sir Buster pretended he didn't want my affection, I rubbed Lady Lola down until she was writhing in ecstasy before scooping up an annoyed Sir Buster and continuing to the entrance of the castle. There, I found Archie pulling a weed by the doorstep. The older man was wearing dark jeans, a gray jumper, and had a knit cap pulled over his white hair. Bushy eyebrows lifted when he saw me.

"That's a good lad then," Archie said, nodding toward Sir Buster in my arms.

"He puts on a good act, but I know he wants cuddles."

"He's all bark."

"I can understand that." There were definitely similarities between Sir Buster's diminutive size and his bluster, an act that I'd put on more than once in my life. Archie's bushy eyebrows drew low over his forehead, and he gave me an assessing look.

He wasn't a talkative man, but I suspected he didn't miss much. The quiet ones usually didn't.

"Are you ready for the ritual this afternoon?"

I shrugged, lifting my hands lightly in the air. I'd worn my newest overalls to work today, a black pair that I'd added some flair to with bright pink stitching at the leg cuffs, and my goldfish badge at my collar. How did one get ready for a ritual? The word alone made me think I was about to start spitting blood before my head rotated in a circle on my shoulders.

"I have no idea how to answer that."

Archie crossed his arms over his chest, a glimmer of a smile on his face.

"It's not so bad, lass. An ancient ritual of words and magick, but nothing all that scary. More ... *powerful* ... is the word I'd use."

"Are you a part of the Order as well?"

"I'm a caretaker." Archie gestured out to the expansive gardens that rolled away from the castle to the line of trees dotted along the base of the hills. "Not just of this land, but of those who are sent to protect it, to protect us, and to protect the Clach na Fìrinn. My job, more than anything, is to facilitate and guide, ensuring that the Order of Caledonia is strong enough to withstand threats."

"From the Kelpies?"

"From humans, lass." Archie shook his head, turning to look out where the afternoon light glimmered on the waters of Loch Mirren. "Humans will commit unimaginable horrors in the pursuit of fortune. Power. Knowledge, even."

The man was speaking my language. I'd seen enough on the streets to know the baser side of humans and didn't doubt that the greater threat to Loren Brae had nothing to do with magickal beings at all.

"I don't doubt it," I said, following his gaze out to the loch. "Yet the Kelpies seem to be the most imminent threat. Will they actually hurt someone?"

"They've killed. They'll do so again. Our goal is to complete the Order, which sends them to rest, and then the combined powers of the Order of Caledonia will protect the Stone."

"For how long?"

At that, Archie pursed his lips.

"As long as the Order of Caledonia is intact, the wards strong, the protection will hold."

"But what does that mean? For me, specifically? Does that mean I have to live in Loren Brae for my whole life?" The very thought made me feel itchy, which was silly, because hadn't I just put down roots when I bought my wee cottage? Still, commitment to anything made me a touch uncomfortable, like water dripping down your wrists under the sleeves of your jumper, and I fidgeted under Archie's assessing gaze.

"No, it doesn't. But it will require that you ensure the wards remain strong, so you'll need to travel back, ideally, yearly, to meet with the others to strengthen the protections."

"Brilliant. A yearly commitment then."

"Something like that, yes. Is that a problem? I was under the impression you're living here."

"I am now. But what if I want to move to Sri Lanka?"

"Do you want to move to Sri Lanka?" Archie tilted his head, a smile hovering on his lips.

"I don't know. I might. I hear they have elephants there."

"That they do. You could certainly visit and test it out."

"That's a lot of money to travel back and forth every year to protect a stone," I pointed out.

"Responsibility comes with restrictions." Archie pinned me with a look. "As you well know, heading up a company and all."

"Aye. It's just ..." I shrugged, searching for the words to articulate what my misgivings were. "How do I know I want to take this on when it means I'm essentially committing my whole life to this group? What happens if I want to leave?"

"Leave town or leave the Order? Nae bother if you want to leave town, lass. Many of our Order have lived around the world. I don't rightly know if anyone has tried to leave the Order before. I believe most have considered it a high honor to protect one of the strongest magickal items in the world."

He wasn't wrong. It was an incredible honor. Wee Orla, plucked from the streets, destined to protect the Stone of Truth. It read like a fairy tale. The only problem was that I'd stopped believing in fairy tales a long time ago. Because of Grandpa Lou. He'd been the only one to be straight with me.

I'd been waiting around for a Prince Charming, when in fact, I was the only one who could rescue myself. His words, and his tutelage, had changed the trajectory of my life, and now I stood before a fork in the path that would once more change the course of my future.

I turned, crossing my arms over my chest as I looked out over the loch. A low beat of energy hummed, coursing through me, as the blood of those who came before me rose in my veins and I imagined their power seeping into me.

What had the Green Lady said to me?

You already have magick. Joining the Order just makes you stronger.

It scared me, this joining of things, and yet, maybe I'd been connected to this all along. Destiny was fickle like that, wasn't it? A thousand choices leading to where I stood now, and yet, here I was.

Right where I was needed.

Nobody had ever really needed me before. If anything, I'd been a burden. Aside from at work, of course, but there I was fully in control. Maybe if I viewed this as an opportunity, a chance to connect more deeply, to help others, then I could accept this role.

The Green Lady appeared, walking gracefully across the garden, Clyde winking into sight at her side. She stroked his ears, Clyde tossed his head, delighted at her touch, and the two strolled closer to where Archie and I stood.

It was a stark reminder that I'd never been normal, never would be normal, so why break my pattern now? Joining the Order of Caledonia would set me apart for the rest of my life, and at the same time, it might give me the grounding that I'd been looking for all along.

"You're right." I turned back to Archie. "It is an honor. One which I'll gladly accept, even though I don't fully understand my role."

"What questions do you have?" Archie, I was beginning to realize, could be patient—at least when he chose to be.

"Sophie mentioned I had to pass three challenges. What does that mean?"

"The Stone doesn't accept just anyone joining the Order, you see, lass. There are many factors at play—your bloodline, your potential for magick, your character. Once we've determined you're a likely candidate to join, passing three challenges is a way for the Stone to test your mettle so to speak."

"To see if I'm worthy." How about that? Much like any other time in my life, I'd have to prove I was worthwhile.

"Aye. Pure of heart. Strong of character, you ken?"

Archie leveled a look at me. "It's a safeguard, though how the challenges present are different for each person."

"Will I have to fight a dragon?"

Archie's eyes twinkled. "Unlikely, no. So far, the challenges have been of character, heart, mental strength. That kind of challenge. Physical strength doesn't much matter if morals are impure."

Lovely. Now I would be tested if I had good character? Surely I'd screwed up enough in my life for the Stone to fail me, or whatever, in these tests.

"I think I'd prefer to fight the dragon."

Archie laughed, clapping a hand on my shoulder.

"You'll do just fine, lass. The challenges are usually tied to how your magick manifests, and I'm told you've already started showing your strengths. I suspect you'll be of great use to many lonely souls caught on this realm."

He knew.

It threw me, how in a matter of weeks, more people knew about my ability to see ghosts than in my whole life. It was a secret I'd fiercely guarded, and the casualness with which people threw around my gift was unsettling to say the least.

"You think that is how my power will manifest? With ghosts?" I looked up at him.

"You won't be the first to have her magick start showing before the ritual. It makes sense. But I may be wrong."

The Green Lady moved into sight behind him, and she gave me a single nod, a pleased look on her face. Her dress flowed around her, and it was the happiest I'd seen her in a long while. She tossed a pebble in my direction, as she had a curious habit of doing, and the dogs startled, barking at the unexpected intrusion. Archie turned, tilting his head as he looked at the garden.

"Something's there, isn't it?"

"Aye," I whispered. He felt it, even if he couldn't see her.

"Dangerous?"

"Not to us, no."

"Want to tell me more?"

To my surprise, I found that I did, but Sophie opened the door and popped her head out.

"There you two are. Hilda's making noises about dinner being late. Shall we crack on with the ritual then?"

For some reason, her words took my nerves away. If Hilda was worried about dinner being late, then surely the ritual couldn't be all that awful. My mind made up, I smiled at Sophie.

"Aye, lass. Let's crack on."

The days were getting longer now as we edged toward summer. The late afternoon light cast a soft glow as Sophie, Archie, and Hilda fell into step alongside me as we wandered across the back garden toward the easternmost part of the land. Archie seemed to be heading things up, while Hilda carried a bundle of sage, and Sophie chattered like we were all friends going on a wee picnic together. For some reason, her casual acceptance of ancient rituals and the ease in which she prodded me for information about the gala—news travels fast in small towns—lessened some of the tension that banded my gut.

The trees were thicker on this side of the property and we strolled alongside a wee burn, the gentle lapping of water a soothing backdrop to our walk, and Sophie pointed up at three crows that flew alongside us.

"Those are my crows."

"Your crows?"

"Yup, I've been training them. Did you know they're incredibly smart? Now they bring me gifts and whatnot because I'm feeding them regularly. It's quite fun to see what they'll bring next."

"That's so cool." I'd never given much thought to a bird as a pet of sorts, but now I squinted up at them, as they circled above us, and realized it might be fun. Could I be a bird person? Maybe. It was hard to tell with these things. I'd never thought I could be a fish person, but here I was, mother to one sassy goldfish.

"That's us ready then." Archie crouched and brushed some dried grass from a small plaque in the ground. I leaned over to see a Celtic insignia on it, and two horse heads intertwined beneath. "We start at the easternmost spot, and we'll repeat this ritual at the four cardinal direction points. The goal is to announce your arrival. You must indicate your intent to join the Order—as with magick everything revolves around intention—and your willingness to step into your power. It's all spoken word, so just follow along with what I say. There is no blood magick or sacrificing virgins, I promise."

Despite my nerves, I grinned. They were doing their best to make this easy for me, and I appreciated it, though I didn't quite like the unknown that came with all of this Order of Caledonia stuff. Movement caught my eye, and I glanced over Archie's shoulder to see that my Green Lady had joined us, and she gave me a gentle smile, nodding toward the plaque.

It was a stark reminder that I'd spent my entire life living with the unknown—from where I would sleep each night to where my next meal would come from at times— and it hadn't broken me. There was no reason that I wouldn't be strong enough to deal with the gift of power.

Hilda lit her bundle of sage, the smoke drifting into the air, holding a slightly sweet scent.

"I've added dried orange to the bundle—it's high energy, joyful, and good for communicating with your angels."

Angels? I glanced to the Green Lady who smiled once more at me, giving me a small shake of her head to indicate she wasn't an angel. I didn't doubt that, even though she'd protected me on more than one occasion. I supposed guardians could arrive in many forms, angels or not.

Trust them.

The Green Lady's words whispered through my head, and I took a deep breath, releasing my inhibitions. A pebble bounced lightly near the plaque, and Archie glanced over his shoulder, but she'd already winked out of sight.

"Huh," Archie said, rubbing the back of his neck.

"Must have been the crows," I said, pointing to where they circled above us. I wasn't ready to share the Green Lady with anyone. She'd been my own little secret for years, and while I suspected this group would be the ones to accept me having a friendship with a ghost, I'd bide my time on any such revelation for a while longer yet.

"I, Orla Clarke, announce my arrival as the newest member of the Order of Caledonia." Archie waited while I quickly repeated what he said, while Hilda wafted the sage around us. Sophie stood respectfully back, and I clutched my hands together at my waist, staring down at the plaque rooted to the earth in a way that I'd never been able to do.

Maybe this would be my time to finally do so.

"I accept the responsibility of protecting the Clach na Fìrinn. I vow to help restore the Order of Caledonia to its fullness, and understand the responsibility placed upon my shoulders. It is with these words I establish the Order of Caledonia as the first line of protection for the Clach na Fìrinn and alert the Kelpies to my arrival. I accept the power bestowed upon me."

I repeated the words Archie murmured, and I swear I felt a surge of energy ripple through me, as though the energy of those who came before me was reaching up and twining around my soul.

"Have you chosen a weapon?" Archie asked.

It had been part of the task given to me, even though I was told the weapon was more metaphorical than real. Even though I felt a bit silly, I'd landed on the one thing that had given me the only good fortune I'd had in my life. Tugging at the tool belt I still wore, I held up a small claw hammer, one that Grandpa Lou had given me, and Archie smiled. "Excellent choice."

"Thanks, it's meaningful to me."

"Orla has chosen her weapon and accepts her role. We'll now move to the next spot."

We repeated the ritual three more times, and as Sophie had said, it didn't end up being a huge deal.

And at the same time, it was everything.

I was now a part of something bigger, a protector of

one of the holy grails, and a member of a sisterhood of magickal women.

This could be the beginning of something incredible. Me, Orla Clarke, plucked from a simple life to that of a powerful woman.

I wasn't sure who this new Orla was yet, but I hoped I liked her.

CHAPTER SEVEN

ORLA

"I hope Willow knows I'll be wearing my boots under this dress."

I grinned as Lia grumbled her way to Willow's makeshift fitting room, where she'd taken up shop in the castle while Ramsay Kilts was being rebuilt. Apparently, Munroe and Finlay had enlisted her help to create gala-worthy dresses for Lia and me, and neither of us were all too pleased about it. Well, it wasn't that having a custom-made gown by Willow was a horrible thing—the pretty American was delightful to work with—but it was just the thought of hanging up my overalls and slipping into a fancy dress that made me feel like I had an itch I couldn't scratch between my shoulders. At least Lia was equally as unamused about the gown and gala affair as I was, so I had some comradery as we followed the narrow hallway that led from Lia's kitchen to the fitting room.

A flicker of something—almost a shifting of energy—alerted me.

"Clyde incoming."

"Thank you." Lia whirled, grabbing my arm, her eyebrows reaching her hairline. "*Finally*, some advance notice."

Clyde popped out of the wall ready to surprise us, only to find Lia standing with her arms crossed and a scolding look. His face fell.

"Clyde. What did I tell you about surprising me after ... *the* incident?" Lia demanded. The ghost coo's shoulders drooped.

"Is this incident where you peed your pants?" I asked, and Lia sighed.

"I see that story has already made the rounds."

"Who doesn't love a good peeing the pants story?"

"Seriously, I consider myself a fairly, like, street smart person, you know?" Lia continued past Clyde, air booping him on the nose, and he grinned up at her, his tongue lolling out. "Raised in Boston. Used to dealing with some rough neighborhoods and whatnot. I don't scare easily. Imagine my surprise when Clyde came along. Muggers, I can handle. A ghost coo? Yeah, it took a bit to adjust. I've warned him not to jump out at me again, but I think he must be excited that you're a newcomer. How did you know he was coming before he showed himself? What's up with that?"

I also pretended to scratch Clyde's head as we passed

him, my hand moving through the coldness in the air by his ears. I didn't know how to explain that I could sense ghosts before I could ever see them, let alone *feel* them like I could with Clyde. It wasn't as real as actually scratching the ears of a Highland coo, but it wasn't as though my hand passed through nothing at all. It fell somewhere in between, as though I pressed against something semi-permeable, but I don't know how else to explain it. As for knowing when he was about to appear, all I could say was that my senses went on alert.

And not in the way they did when Finlay was around.

That man made me take notice, no doubt about it.

He'd made himself somewhat scarce after he'd bumbled his way through asking me to the gala, which I still wasn't certain if he'd meant for it to be a date or not, and I hadn't seen much of him over the past couple of days. He was on-site though, as I split my time between the distillery and Ramsay Kilts, and my crew reported that they enjoyed working with him. Which was good, because if I'd heard that he was being difficult, then I'd have to run interference, something I never enjoyed.

My phone buzzed in my pocket, and I pulled it out to check another incoming inquiry from my website. Just last night I'd realized that I needed to put up a notice by my contact form that my crew was scheduled out for quite a while because business was really picking up. I didn't have the time to deal with answering potential new clients. Yet I couldn't just *not* respond. That was just bad business. Clarke Construction was important to me, built on my name and my word, so even though my precious sleep hours suffered, I would often work late into the night to make sure payroll was met, invoices were paid, and messages to current and new clients were answered. It was beginning to take its toll, but at the moment, I just didn't have a viable solution to avoid it.

"Here we are," Lia said, stopping in front of a wooden door that was propped open. "You ready for this?"

"How are you supposed to ready yourself for a custom fitting?" Lia laughed, but I was being serious. This was so out of my wheelhouse that I truly had no idea what to expect.

"I'm going to have to deal with it soon enough when I start with wedding dresses." Lia was marrying Munroe at an undisclosed date sometime supposedly in the next year. They'd postponed the wedding due to her mother receiving treatment for cancer, and from what I was told, everything was going smoothly. They anticipated being able to pick a date soon.

"Ladies! Welcome to my lair." Willow popped up by the door, wearing leather wide-leg trousers, a sparkly tank top, and had her hair piled in a messy bun on her head. Every time I saw her, she sparkled or shone in some way, and I appreciated her complete disregard for the Scottish weather to express herself.

"When you say it like that ..." Lia pretended to shudder.

"Knock it off or I'll put you in something with ruffles. Sooooo many ruffles."

Lia gasped.

"You wouldn't."

"I'm just evil enough to do it."

"And here I thought we were friends."

"Then you'll pretend to enjoy every second of this because from the looks of it, you're scaring Orla."

"I'm fine," I promised, my voice sounding far meeker than I'd intended. I cleared my throat. "Seriously, this is lovely. Thank you for doing this for us."

"Ah, there's the Scottish hospitality. Ever polite even though she's secretly dying inside. Come in, come in." Willow grinned and squeezed my shoulder as I walked inside the room.

"Aren't you cold in just a tank top?" Lia wondered.

"I don't like to wear anything too bulky when I'm taking measurements. Then once I get to work, I won't notice much else until I get my design down."

I clenched my jaw, hanging back a bit, as Lia turned a circle, hands on her hips.

"They did a good job with this room."

"Isn't it great? I mean, I'm excited for Orla's design for the new shop, but this isn't a bad substitute for now, is it?"

The walls of the room were the lovely thick stone mirrored through much of the castle, and the ceiling arched over Palladian windows that overlooked the walled garden below. I caught a glimpse of Archie stalking down the garden, a rake in hand, the dogs at his feet.

In the center of the room stood a small, elevated platform, with a line of standing mirrors across from it. Across the room, alongside the far wall, were several long tables pushed together to create a massive worktop for Willow. Rolls of fabric, several sewing machines, and various boxes crowded the space, and Bob Marley's music drifted lightly in the background.

"Reggae?" I asked, raising an eyebrow at Willow.

"My mood changes. Today's a reggae day because I needed the sunshine as it's been misty and cold much of the day. I was promised spring, but I don't think we're quite there yet."

I laughed. This was the warmest spring we'd had for a while.

"Don't you dare laugh at me, Orla. I was promised spring!" Willow glowered at me, lightly stomping her foot as she crossed her arms over her chest.

"You'll get it, I'm sure. For about two days. Enjoy the sun when it arrives." It was true enough, I supposed. I was so used to the mercurial changes of Scottish weather that I didn't much think about rain or sun anymore, as you'd likely get patches of it several times in a day, particularly as winter shifted to summer. Layers were the key to surviving the seasons in Scotland.

"That's it. Ruffles for the both of you."

I grimaced, and Willow laughed, clapping her hands together like she was the Wicked Witch of the West.

"Come to me, my pretties ..."

"Cut it out or I'm out of here," Lia said, pulling her jumper over her head and dropping it across the back of a green velvet chair.

Did we have to get naked? Is that what was happening here? I'd never undressed in front of a group of women before and instantly became awkward and unsure of myself. I couldn't just ... stand naked on a podium ... could I? In front of people? And all those mirrors?

My horror must have shown on my face because Willow dropped the act.

"Orla, have you ever been to a fitting before?" Willow asked, cluing in to my actual discomfort versus Lia's pretend annoyance.

"No." I shook my head. "I really don't know what I'm supposed to do."

"Ah, okay. Let me walk you through it." Willow came close and touched my arm, the contact making me jerk slightly. It was barely noticeable, I was sure of it, but it wasn't unusual for me. I wasn't used to people casually touching me, so I always responded oddly, I supposed, when it happened. "Are you wearing a T-shirt under your sweater? Erm, your ... jumper?"

"Aye."

"That'll be fine then. I just need you to take your sweater off and then I can get close enough measurements. I'll have you stand on the podium in front of me, and I'll take your measurements here." Willow tapped at my shoulder. "May I touch your side?"

"Yes." She must have sensed my nerves, because she asked, and I realized that was likely what made her a good designer.

"I'll take measurements around the bust." Willow tapped lightly by my ribs, waist, and hips. "And through here. Then I'll measure the length of your leg, or what we call the inseam. That way I can tell how long to make the skirt."

"Do you need our shoes to go with it?" Lia asked. "So you know the length?"

Willow turned, grinning at Lia.

"I'm assuming you'll be in those boots or similar?"

"You betcha." Lia nodded, her face set in a stubborn expression.

"Same for you, Orla?"

"Um, I don't really have any fancy shoes." Embarrassment rushed through me. What kind of woman was I that I didn't even own a pair of heels? Most women my age likely had several pairs and probably wore them on date nights. My previous "dates" had largely consisted of pizza takeout or a night at a local pub, none of which had called for a fancy dress or heels.

I was *so* out of my element.

"Not a problem at all. The dresses will be long enough to cover your shoes, or if you want, I'm happy to go shoe shopping with you."

"Shoe shopping?" I must have said it in the same tone as someone who had just sniffed rotten fish, and Willow gasped, holding a hand to her chest.

"Don't tell me you hate shoe shopping."

"What's there to shop for?" I looked down at my work boots, admiring the little hearts etched in the leather. I had two pairs of work boots, one my "clean" pair, and one for dirtier jobs. Next to those, I had a solid pair of wellies, and a pair of trainers if I ever felt like going for a walk. What else did I need?

Willow closed her eyes and pretended to count to ten.

"Before I kidnap you and force you into the car to teach you the joys of shoe shopping, I'll ask first. Do you want a nice pair of shoes to match your gown?"

Worry filled me. Would it be a huge faux pas if I didn't wear the correct shoes at a gala? I mean, this was a fancy event with a custom-made gown. I didn't want to embarrass myself.

"I'll do whatever you think is best. I don't want to look stupid," I said.

"But why should she buy a pair of heels she'll never wear again?" Lia pointed out, coming to my defense.

"I'm not saying she has to. But I bet we could find a happy medium. One that isn't work boots, for either of you. Here … let me show you." Willow crossed the room and opened her laptop, typing away before turning the screen. "What about these?"

Lia and I stepped closer, bending to see what looked like satin ballet flats.

We both hissed in response, and Willow rolled her eyes before turning the computer back to herself.

"Fine, too far. Right, what about … this?"

"Oh, that's not bad. Can we pull that off?" Lia asked. On the screen were a pair of silver sparkly Converse low-tops, looking very cute, but serviceable as well.

"I don't see why not. If you're dancing and twirl and your skirt comes up, people will just catch a glimpse of sparkles. Or if you cross your leg and your shoe shows. Again, sparkles. It will look more thoughtful than work boots, but you'll both be comfortable."

"I'm not opposed to this. Orla?"

"Um." I realized that I, too, was not opposed to this idea. I didn't want to feel awkward at the gala, like I was some interloper, and I trusted Willow to lead us in the right direction. If sparkly Converse were the answer, then I was happy to compromise there. "Och, surprisingly, no, I'm not opposed. They look comfortable. Those are brilliant, Willow."

"They are. I have two pairs. You'll love them. Once we decide on your dress colors, I'll order a matching pair in your sizes."

I opened my mouth to ask how much they would cost, but Willow cut me off.

"Billed to the men, of course. You're representing Common Gin, and I'm told the owner has deep pockets."

"Oh, he does. In fact, charge double for making us go through this torture," Lia insisted.

I laughed, pulling my jumper over my head and stepping onto the platform that Willow had indicated. She approached, a pencil behind her ear and tape measure in hand, and I held my arms out when indicated. All told, it was relatively painless, even though I felt a bit awkward when she wrapped the tape measure over my bust. I knew she was only doing her job, and she wanted to make sure the dress didn't fall off me.

"There, that wasn't so bad, was it?" Willow nodded for me to step down, all while jotting notes in her book.

"Nope, you're right, pretty painless."

"I'm the one who should be moaning, having to make two dresses on such short notice," Willow grumbled, pointing for Lia to climb onto the platform.

"That's why I said charge him extra. Three times for making us go," Lia complained as she climbed up.

"Speaking of ... what's up with you and Finlay?" Willow asked, glancing at me, and I jumped, surprised at her question.

"What do you mean?"

"Well, he asked you as his date, didn't he?" Lia looked at me in the mirror.

"I mean, not really. He's paying me."

"What?" Both women stopped what they were doing and turned to me in shock.

"Um ... he's paying me?" I repeated, realizing, now, that it made me sound like an escort.

"I need immediate details," Willow demanded.

"How on earth did that happen?" Lia asked.

I wasn't used to women, hell, *anyone*, questioning me about my life or really showing much interest at all. I couldn't tell if they were angry with me for agreeing to be paid to go to this gala or if they were angry at Finlay. I wasn't good at reading social cues most times, particularly in groups of women, and my stomach churned. I wished I hadn't said anything at all.

"It's nothing, really. It's a donation to my favorite animal rescue is all." There, that made it sound less escort-y, didn't it?

"Orla, why don't you tell us what happened?"

"Um, it's not a big deal. It was just a suggested donation to the animal rescue. It's not like he's paying me to, you know ..." Great, if they hadn't been thinking that before, they likely were now.

"You know what I think we need?" Lia asked.

"What's that?" Willow turned back to Lia, wrapping the tape measure around her hips.

"A drink. Let's go to the pub after this. I know Shona wants to meet Orla now that she's a part of the Order, and we'll have ourselves a nice glass of wine and can discuss everything. How does that sound?"

Terrifying.

Not that I was going to admit that to these women who were not only trying very hard to be my friend but were also a part of the same magickal Order that I'd just joined. I'd known that getting along with the other women would be part of the deal when it came to joining the Order. It might be nice, I told myself, to have some people to talk to about all this magick stuff.

A cat wandered into the room, brushing against Willow's legs, and she looked down at him.

"Hi, sweet baby," Willow cooed. "Calvin says I'm stressing you out."

"The cat ..." I looked down as he approached me, rubbing against my leg, and I instantly crouched, helpless to resist the advances of any animal. I loved when people's pets came to me for a cuddle. It felt like I was the chosen one, every time, and it was my favorite part of any site visit.

"Yes, he's my familiar. He communicates with me through imagery. He's very sweet, but not as fancy as Lia's familiar."

"I would hardly call Brice fancy." Lia laughed.

"Brice? Familiar?" What were they even talking about? At my confusion, Lia sobered.

"We're all witchy women of some sort in the Order of Caledonia. Which means we get a familiar. Someone to help us on our quest, so to speak. Calvin is Willow's. Mine is a touch more unconventional, though I would argue that Shona's is as well. Since I'm a kitchen witch, I get a house broonie."

"Och, go on." I laughed, realizing they were just having me on. Broonies were definitely not real. I'd grown up with tales of the little house elves and knew that stories of them were often used to keep children in line.

"Brice? Can you pop in to meet Orla? Calvin's here," Lia called.

A blur of motion, a shimmer of energy, and all of a sudden, I was staring down at a wrinkled wee man, in faded overalls, who seemed to be having one big love fest with Calvin, who instantly jumped into his arms.

"Holy shite," I breathed.

CHAPTER EIGHT

ORLA

A drink was one hundred percent called for after meeting a broonie in real life for the first time. Brice turned out to be quite shy, seemingly very sweet, and well-besotted with Calvin. The two frolicked together like long-lost best friends, and the result was decidedly endearing. Not that I wanted a broonie, because I wasn't sure I could really deal with another magickal being popping into my life regularly, but Lia assured me he stayed in her kitchen and was generally quite helpful when he wasn't up to mischief.

The Tipsy Thistle was the main pub in town, and really, from what I could gather, the hub for which all gossip, news, and important events was disseminated. They served a good meal, prices were affordable, and the owner, Graham, was not hard to look at.

Not hard at all.

He'd spotted us upon our arrival, nodding to a table by the fire, and we'd settled in, Sophie, Agnes, and Shona joining us shortly after our arrival. The pub was half-filled, some men tucked at the bar to watch a match turned low on the telly, and Celtic music lilted lightly in the background. The fire took away most of the chill, as the fog had descended on our walk to the pub, and I was grateful for its warmth. A quick bite, a drink, and I'd be home soon enough to feed Goldie, who seemed ever patient with her varying dinner times.

If a fish could be considered patient, that is.

"Well, now, to what do I owe this pleasure?" Graham stopped at our table, crossing muscular, tattooed arms over his chest, his grin widening as his eyes landed on me. I hadn't much chatted with him in the past, having only come in for a meal with my crew, and now I was surprised at the heat that stirred inside me as he focused his attention in my direction. Damn it, but the man was seriously good-looking. "An entire table full of the prettiest ladies this side of Loch Mirren. Surely my luck is changing, and the gods have decided to smile upon me once again."

"Och, wheesht, Graham. It's a ladies' night, can't you see?" Agnes, a slim woman with a springy crop of curls and a mile-wide smile, glared at him.

"I see well enough, don't I, darling? And what kind of man would I be if I didn't express my appreciation for the beauty bestowed upon me on this dreich night?"

"I know it's his thing and all, but it's very effective." Sophie fanned a hand in front of her face. "Go on, Graham. Flattery will get you everywhere."

"And likely a fist planted in my face by Lachlan." Graham chuckled.

"Well-deserved at that," Agnes said.

"Och, darling, I can't still be in the bad books with you now, can I?" Graham focused his attention on Agnes, and I noticed something shift in his expression. Longing flashed behind his eyes before it was quickly shuttered, and I wondered what the story was there. Was Agnes out of her mind? Surely Graham would be fun to date, no?

"That you are, and you well know it." Agnes sniffed and studied the menu, though even I knew the contents of the menu having been here a few times already. Agnes ran a bookstore in town, and I suspected she could recite the menu by memory.

"What did you do now?" Sophie asked Graham.

"He had two American lasses through here the other night. Helped them both home, didn't he then?" Agnes arched an eyebrow at him.

"They weren't sure how to get there, what with the foggy night and all," Graham said.

"Loren Brae's not so small that Google maps doesn't work here."

"It's important to be hospitable," Graham insisted.

"Two of them?" Shona, a quiet woman with long blonde hair and luminous blue eyes, shook her head. "Fair play to you, lad."

"You're on his side then?" Agnes leaned over to Shona.

"I am on no sides here. Though I am failing to see the issue that Graham, a seemingly unattached man, went home with a woman."

"Women," Sophie corrected, sweetly, and Agnes bristled.

"Of course he can do what he wants. If he wants to be a loose man."

"I thought you were a progressive woman, Agnes," Lia said. "Are you slut-shaming Graham?"

"Och, it's *not* slut-shaming." Agnes slapped her menu down. "I'm just suggesting, as an owner of a business in town, that he act with some decorum."

"Surely helping my clientele to not get lost in the dark is a gentlemanly service?" Graham beamed at Agnes, and I stifled a laugh. Whatever was going on here, it was amusing to watch.

"Oh, it is. It is," Agnes conceded with a sigh. Looking around the room, her eyes lighted on two handsome young men, Americans by the flags on their backpacks, and she smiled. "It's foggy tonight again. Will you be helping those lads home as well?"

"If they need it," Graham said, not missing a beat.

"Or maybe I should." Agnes tapped a finger against her lips, a considering look on her face.

"I'm sure I can direct them." Amusement had left Graham's face. Agnes stood, easing past me, and crossed the room to stop at the lads' table, while Graham fumed at ours.

"Do you drink wine, Orla?" Sophie asked.

"I do." Every once in a while. I wasn't a big drinker, in general, as I didn't typically like feeling out of control.

"Two bottles of Cabernet for the table, please, Graham."

"Right away." Graham left, his face a mask, and my

eyebrows rose as Agnes threw her head back and laughed, dropping a casual hand on the shoulder of one of the lads.

"Is it just me or could you cut the tension with a knife between those two?" I asked, wincing as soon as the words were out. Here I was, not wanting to talk about Finlay paying me for a date, and now I was sticking my nose in someone else's business. This was not like me, as I'd learned to not ask a lot of questions growing up.

Don't ask questions you won't like the answers to.

I'd learned that little lesson very quickly.

Not that it necessarily applied here, as I had no interest in Graham or stepping on any toes in that direction. But it felt intrusive for me to ask about a relationship between two people I didn't know very well.

"With my sword," Sophie assured me. Nudging Shona, she nodded toward me. "Orla met Brice today. What do you think she'll think of Gnorman?"

"Gnorman?" I asked and Shona's sunny face lit up.

"He's my garden gnome." Shona pitched her voice lower, leaning in. "In fact, I have two of them. As in real-life gnomes. It comes with being a garden witch."

Heat flushed through me, and I sat back, my world recalibrating around the knowledge that not only did magickal beings apparently frolic left and right all through Loren Brae, but that for the first time maybe I wasn't alone in my oddity.

It's not easy being an orphan.

It's even harder being one who sees ghosts.

Agnes returned to the table, a smug expression on her face, and I just looked at these women, so varied in their appearances. Shona wore a simple blue jumper and had dirt under her nails, Sophie was in a UCLA sweatshirt, Willow was in her sparkles, Lia was in a leather jacket, and Agnes had on a pretty red blouse. And there was me. In canvas pants and a cream, ancient woolen jumper that kept me warm against the damp. A mismatched group we were, if I'd ever seen one, yet somehow those very differences soothed me. It was as though anything would go here, and they'd still accept you into their fold. I certainly hoped so, as a quiet yearning for acceptance filled me.

"Lovely lads. Traveling through," Agnes said as she dropped into her seat. Graham returned with two bottles, opening both with a flourish, studiously ignoring Agnes as he poured.

"Food tonight, ladies?"

We put our orders in—mac and cheese with a side salad and chips for me—and settled back with our wine.

"So, Orla sees ghosts. I think that's going to be the power that manifests for her. She's a house witch," Sophie said without preamble, and I jerked, spilling wine on my jumper.

"Damn it," I said, switching out the wine glass for water and dabbing at the jumper with a damp napkin. It wasn't the jumper I was much fussed about, it was the fact that she'd just exposed me, casually, to an entire group of women that I didn't know that well. One being my client, as well.

"Welcome to the Order," Shona said. "It's an adjustment, isn't it? Being part of something bigger?"

"I ..." I wasn't sure how to answer that. I still felt like the kid standing outside the playground, watching the other kids play together. "I honestly don't know what to think."

"Neither did I." Lia held up her wine in commiseration. "Not until I found my spell book and saw my grandmother's name in it. Then the connection came through for me and I felt I was where I belonged. Hey, I wonder if your family will be in there too. I can look. What was your grandmother's surname?"

I froze, unsure how to respond, not wanting to spill my dirty past all over these lovely smiling women. What was I supposed to say? That I didn't know my own grandparents' names? How my mother ditched me at an early age before succumbing to her drug addiction and her half-sister barely raised me? There were no family albums to pore over, fun stories of the past, or memories of those who came before me.

"I don't have family." It came out fast, the words whipping across the table, and I saw the expression I hated the most on people's faces. Sympathy. It fell like a wave, crashing across the women, and my stomach churned. *Now comes the pity party.* This was my least favorite part, next to the inevitable questions, and my shoulders hunched.

"That's just fine then, isn't it? You've got one now." Agnes squeezed my arm, nodding to the women around the table.

"Yup, that's part of it," Lia agreed. "Annoying as these bitches can be at times. They're *my* bitches."

"Has ladies' night taken a dominatrix-y turn?" Graham appeared with a basket of bread. "If so, I fully support this direction you all are taking."

"If we do, men won't be invited to watch," Sophie promised him.

"That's certainly a loss." Graham disappeared and the knot of tension inside me loosened slightly.

"I lost my mom when I was young," Willow said, reaching for a piece of bread. "I think my favorite thing about the Order is not only do you get to be magickal, but you also get to be magickal along with other cool women. Plus, I mean, how freaking cool is it to know there's so much, like, weird and amazing things that exist out there? It's kind of blown my head off to know all these things, like, just *exist*, you know?"

"Listen, I thought I was well on the way to losing my marbles when gnomes started talking to me," Shona assured me.

"Or eyes peered at me from the dark corner of my kitchen pantry," Lia chimed in.

"Or cats started projecting images into my head." Willow tapped a finger on her forehead.

"What is your power?" I asked Willow, realizing I didn't know what she could do.

"I can see the future," Willow said, and my mouth dropped open.

"No way," I breathed.

"Yup, though I can't really control it. It's not on demand, but it more comes to me in flashes."

"I have voice command, which helps with keeping the Kelpies back." Sophie tapped a finger at her chest. "Shona is a garden witch, so she grows magickal herbs. Lia is a kitchen witch, so she has food-based spells. Willow sees the future, and you, my friend, apparently sense ghosts. Which in my opinion, makes you a house witch."

"Ghosts aren't just tied to houses," I pointed out, taking a healthy gulp of my wine after speaking. It rattled me to talk about these things so openly.

"Yeah, but you build houses. And you sense ghosts. And I think you mentioned you can help them ... move on?" Willow tucked a strand of hair behind her ear, and I flushed, unused to such undivided attention upon me. No, that wasn't it. I was used to my crew focusing on my instructions and guidance. This was ... kind and ... personal. It warmed my curious and lonely soul.

"I don't know what I do. Not sure if there's a name for it or not. Some I help move on. One has stayed with me for ..." I snapped my mouth shut, glancing at the almost finished glass of wine. I *never* spoke about the Green Lady.

"Ohhhhh, you've got a ghost familiar already? That's so cool," Lia said.

"Want to tell us about it?" Agnes asked, and the table quieted, waiting.

Did I? I was so used to hiding her that my instinct was to shut this conversation down. But she'd told me to trust the Order, hadn't she? So far, she'd been the one constant in my life that had protected me.

"I don't know what to say," I admitted, folding and refolding the napkin in my lap. "She just showed up one day. I was in the middle of getting jumped and I—"

"Excuse me, what? Getting jumped? Orla, that's *awful*," Sophie said, her eyes huge. And to her it likely was. Life played out a little differently when you had to fend for yourself though.

"Right, anyway, so, she just appeared. Scared the crap out of him and me to be honest. But she stayed with me after that."

"What does she look like? Does she have a name?" Agnes asked, her bright eyes curious.

"She's never given me a name. I've asked, repeatedly. She wears a green dress and ..." I paused. How was I supposed to explain she didn't have human feet?

"The Green Lady!" Agnes exclaimed and my mouth dropped open.

"You know her?"

"Aye, or *of* her. She's quite famous around Scotland, though some will say there's more than one of them. Cloven hooves, right?"

"Talking about me, darling?" Graham stopped with a tray of food and winked at Agnes.

"Only if those are horns I see peeking out of your thinning hair."

Graham audibly gasped, his eyes widening.

"You didn't just say that."

"Aye, I did."

"Damn it, Agnes, are you really that mad? It's not like you to be downright mean."

"Och, I'm just tetchy today, Graham. Ignore me. I promise your hair isn't thinning." Agnes waved her words away.

"There she is. I was hoping you'd be back." Before Agnes could stop him, he dropped a kiss on her cheek, and she swatted him away. Not before she disguised a grin, though.

"So, a half-woman, half ... goat? Haunts you?" Sophie brought us back on topic.

"Yes, but she's very nice. She's not great with details, and she doesn't like a lot of direct questions, but she, I don't know, guides me? Helps me?" I dug into my mac and cheese, my stomach grumbling after an active day of work.

"The Green Lady, also known as a glaistig, has a ton of different stories about her. It's not unlikely that there are many 'Green Ladies' so to speak." Agnes made air quotes with her fingers. "Some stories speak of her being threatening and leading travelers astray. Some speak of her as the Goddess of the Hunt and people would make offerings to her. Others say she is benevolent and looks after weary travelers. A few stories suggest she is even fae."

"Fae?" I'd never considered that. She'd always struck me as exactly what she was—a ghost.

"Some, aye. That she was once mortal and cursed, hence the goat's legs. It wouldn't be uncommon to see such myths associated with the Fae. They have many curses and trickery in their stories."

"She won't tell me. I've asked."

"So you *can* communicate with her?"

"I can. She does speak to me. But she's very picky on what she wants to talk about. It's not ... I don't know." I shrugged. It wasn't like we hung out for hours on end. She'd pop through and say something to guide me and then disappear.

"It wouldn't be unusual if she positioned herself as a protector of sorts in your life, which is what it sounds like, right?" Agnes stabbed a piece of lettuce with her fork. "She often helps lost travelers find their way."

And if that didn't describe me to a T.

A lost traveler in life, that is. But I was finally finding my way, wasn't I? For the first time ever, things were falling into place for me, and my hard work was paying off. I was beginning to be cautiously optimistic that I'd actually clawed my way out of an uncertain past and was finally building a foundation for myself—a future that I could rely upon. And maybe some new friends to help make life less ... lonely.

CHAPTER NINE

ORLA

"Did you hear there are otters up by the Auld Mill?" Derrick, my head joiner, asked me as we measured for custom cabinetry to store the botanicals as Finlay had requested. Well, the cabinetry was more for the tools and smaller storage containers, as the botanicals themselves would be held in larger opaque containers to protect the ingredients. I was told they were stored before a maceration process that would extract the flavor to be added to the gin. Examples given to me were dried citrus peels, juniper berries, and grains of paradise. It sounded interesting, but my job wasn't to figure out how to make the gin. I just needed to create the space for Munroe to succeed. Which meant I was more interested in—*did this room need to be regulated for humidity?* What type of electrical wiring needed to be run through here to heat or cool the space?

Would I need an extractor fan to pull any moisture from the room? The precision required here wasn't about the process of gin-making so much as keeping the ingredients in tip-top condition so Common Gin could create the best product possible.

Humidity and temperature control were everything—not too warm, not too cold, not too dry, and not too moist.

The botanicals needed a stable environment.

Much like myself, I realized, as I studied the small window in the storage room and wondered if it would be a failure point for humidity control. I might need to create custom shutters for the window or perhaps seal it up entirely, just to make sure the space was safe.

"Yes, someone mentioned something about protected land," I said, tuning back into the conversation. Derrick was well used to long pauses in a conversation with me while we worked, otherwise nothing would ever get done, and I made a mental note to talk to Finlay about the small window.

"They want to make a visitor center of sorts. For the otters." Derrick grunted as he got down on his knees and pried at a corner of the floor, testing the wood.

"That'll be grand, won't it?" Any talk of animal rescues piqued my interest, and while I didn't know much about otters, the pictures of them I'd seen holding hands—wait, paws—were pretty cute.

"Running into some problems though." Derrick grunted again, shifting on his knees, and dropped his reading glasses onto his nose. He was in his early sixties, not likely to retire anytime soon, and I was lucky to have him on my crew. Not only was he protective of me, having two daughters of his own, but he was a master joiner, and his craftsmanship showed it. I'd found him when I moved to the area, and he'd been happy to head up my team, as he'd just been leaving a partnership with a dissolving commercial construction group. Clarke Construction had kept him rooted in the area, and his wife was equally as happy to not have to move elsewhere for work.

"Is that so? Such a shame." I knew as well as anyone the holdups that came with renovations, from delays on materials to unreliable tradesmen.

"Haunted, I'm told." Derrick didn't look at me, but he paused, waiting for my reaction.

We never spoke of it, yet he knew, in some capacity, of my ability to see ghosts. During the second project he'd worked with me on, an extension on a house, the crew had been spooked by a supposed apparition of the ghost of a little girl. I'd stayed late that night, speaking to her, and had helped her to move on—clearing the energy in the house so we could proceed. What I hadn't known was Derrick had come back for his wallet he'd left in his toolbox and had seen me talking to an empty room.

The next morning, he'd mentioned he'd returned to the house, and I'd frozen, unsure of what to do. Derrick had patted me on the shoulder. *Things are calmer in here now.*

That was it. He'd never mentioned it directly, and we'd moved on, the crew happy to work in a space not fraught with unseen tension. I'd worried, for weeks, that Derrick would gossip with the crew or share my secret, but he'd never once said a word.

Again, protective.

He was a good man and I understood what he was telling me now.

"Is that right?"

"Seems so. Loren Brae has a lot of such activity. But it's holding up the project."

"Is the visitor center a good thing? Maybe it's better for the otters if nobody is there." I had to consider the possibilities from both sides before I went and did something about it. Because I knew, in his own direct way, that Derrick was asking me to act.

"The organization has raised enough money to buy the land around it, which will give the otters more protection from any future development, but they'll need ongoing funds for the maintenance and whatnot. Plus they want to educate people. Turn it into a nature center of sorts. Even have a Zen Garden, I'm told, for people to relax and have a spot of tea."

"It's a beautiful building," I admitted. "What organization is this?"

"An Irish couple, actually. Brogan and Kira. They have a center over in Grace's Cove on the West Coast of Ireland. Now that they've seen success with their first nature center, they're expanding their reach across Ireland, and now Scotland, looking for otter habitats that can be protected."

"Isn't that something?" The paths people took in life always interested me. Particularly when so few opportunities had been offered to me. Rescuing otters hadn't been high on the list of profitable ways to keep a roof over my head. But it cheered me to know that people like that existed in the world and did something to help.

"They do good work, I'm told." Derrick sat back on his heels and glanced at me.

"Och, sure, I'll give it a look." This was the closest I'd ever gotten to acknowledging what Derrick had seen that day. Derrick gave a sharp nod.

"The wife has a particular liking for the otters."

Ah, that made more sense now. Derrick had a deeply entrenched sweet spot for his wife, and I admired his quiet devotion to her. I wanted that someday, for myself.

At least I thought that I did.

"I also like otters," a voice interrupted us, and I turned to see Finlay standing in the doorway.

"Just gotta grab my toolbox," Derrick said, standing and exiting the room, giving Finlay a quick nod as he passed.

"Are you bidding to work on the Auld Mill project?" Finlay stepped farther into the room, and my attention narrowed to a pinhole, all focus on him and his deeply handsome face. It was like he'd sucked the air from the room, and all I could hear was my heart thundering in my ears as he drew closer.

We hadn't spoken much since he'd asked, er, *paid* for me to go to the gala. This was the first time we'd been alone since, and nerves kicked low in my gut as I tried to steady my breathing. There was just something about Finlay that put me on my back foot, whether I was ready to fight or flee, I wasn't entirely sure, but his presence certainly threw me off kilter.

"Nae chance." I shook my head. "I've got more on my slate than I can handle at the moment."

"Then why are you going to take a look?"

So he'd heard more than I'd thought he'd had.

I shrugged, looking away and focusing on the window across the room.

"It's for a good cause. In case they want a second opinion, I can offer it."

"Maybe it's best if you stay away from there."

"Excuse me?" I whipped my head around, glaring at Finlay. The man had paid for one date. *One*. He certainly didn't get to tell me what to do.

"I just think, given the rumor that it's haunted, that it's best if you stayed away from the building."

I raised an eyebrow at him and put my hands on my hips.

"Surely you aren't presuming to come in here and tell me what I can and can't do with my time? Particularly when it would be after hours and off the clock. Or are you thinking you're the boss of me in all aspects of my life now?" I left the rest unspoken—the part where he'd paid me for a date—and Finlay stepped closer. He stopped just short of invading my space, yet his presence had invaded it since the moment he'd walked into the room. His nearness was palpable, and when his gaze drifted over me, goosebumps shivered down my skin as though his hands followed where his eyes went. I wondered what he saw when he looked at me.

Not that I should care, but now that I was going to a gala with him, I kind of, actually, really did care.

Did he think I was pretty?

Annoyed at myself, and my response to him, I waited, my hand resting at the hammer slung in my tool belt. It comforted me, though I likely looked like I was holding onto a holster.

A wolfish look slipped across Finlay's face, and heat bloomed low inside me.

"Of course, I'm not the boss of you ... in some aspects of your life, that is ..." Finlay let the words linger, and my mouth went dry at what was left unspoken.

But I could be, in other areas, if you let me.

I knew what he was leaving unsaid, my *body* knew it as well, based on the desire that rippled through me, but my mind refused to accept that a man like Finlay would be interested in a woman like me. Even though he strapped on his fancy work boots and showed up at the site every day, we were still worlds apart, him and me.

"Mr. Thompson." I enjoyed the annoyance that flashed in his eyes and turned to the window, neatly changing the subject. "I need to ask you about this window. I'm told this room needs to be tightly regulated when it comes to humidity and temperature. As it stands, this window is drafty at best, which, naturally, we'd refit and seal with a new one. However, my question is, would it be best to seal it completely? I'm told the botanicals are stored in opaque containers to help keep desired freshness, and I'm just wondering if this could be a potential failure point for your storage?"

Finlay moved toward the window, and I shivered as he passed me, his arm lightly brushing mine. A spark jumped between us, energy ricocheting up my body, and I had to force myself to ignore this response I was having to him.

It wasn't like I hadn't been with a man before.

But something about Finlay just captured my attention

in a way that I wasn't remotely comfortable with. He made me feel almost skittish, like a newborn foal finding its legs, and I couldn't say that I was a fan of this disconcerting feeling. Finding stability and centering myself was an equilibrium that I'd fought for, and my goal was to maintain that for as long as I could. A stable foundation, one that I'd built myself, was integral to me finding peace. Finlay, with his fancy galas and dominating manner, was not a part of the future I'd built for myself.

Finlay tapped a finger on the window, and then ran his hand along the seams, his lips pressed together as he studied the glass. I'd noticed he did that, gave any questions serious thought, and I appreciated that he genuinely listened to the crew when they came to him.

"While I hate to lose the light, as I love the character of this building, it might be best to seal it up."

"I could build shutters, on the interior, that you could open while you were working in here. Double-glazed window, a new sill, and you'd have this sealed nicely. I could foam pad the backside of the shutters, almost like you would for soundproofing, and that would help. If you really wanted to keep the window, or at least the aesthetic in here."

"I just wonder if that's being excessive for a small window, when it is likely easier to seal it up."

"Could be. But I agree, it is nice to have in here. Do people spend a lot of time in this space?"

"They will, yes. We're constantly adding new stock, monitoring, sorting, and rotating old stock. Everything is dated and inspected regularly to ensure the freshness of ingredients."

"Your employees could open the shutters while they worked and then close them up when they left. If they wanted the natural light."

Finlay squinted up at the ceiling.

"We'll do warm light in here. Not fluorescents. I hate working under florescent lights."

"Aye, they're a touch annoying, aren't they?"

"Horrible. I used to work in an office that only had that type of lighting. I swear I went home with a headache almost every day."

"I can imagine. It serves its purposes, but not for in here." I wanted to ask him about his job, the one he hated, and if he was happier now. But I didn't, not really knowing how to strike up a casual conversation with him, because what if I asked about something that was a bad memory in his life? It was one of the reasons I hated being asked questions about my own past. Difficult life experiences didn't always make for fun conversations, I'd learned, and I was now an expert at diverting to other topics.

"What the ..." Finlay's body tensed, and I felt the magick before I even turned.

A unicorn stood outside the small window.

Let me repeat that.

A unicorn stood outside the window. A glorious pearlescent horn jutted from her head, white mane flowed in the wind, and her coat shimmered as though she'd been dipped in opalescent paint. She snorted, tossing her head, and dipped her horn toward the window where Finlay and I now crowded together, our shoulders touching. I held my breath, my thoughts scrambling, as I witnessed the most beautiful being I'd ever seen before. It was as though her opal eyes held untold galaxies of knowledge, and a warm balm of love and acceptance washed through me, tears springing to my eyes.

"We have to see her!" Finlay grabbed my hand and tugged, dragging me from the room and out through the front door, racing around the side of the building together. But by the time we reached where she'd stood, the unicorn was gone.

A glimmer of a moment now lost.

I felt bereft, as though something beautiful, a piece of my soul, had been taken from me. And in the same instance, as though an incredible gift had been bestowed upon us.

"I've never ... I've seen some strange things in my life, but that was incredible. Och, lass, did you see her?" Finlay whirled and I jerked as he lifted me into his arms, twirling us both in excitement. My body froze, my typical reaction to uninvited touch, but Finlay was too ecstatic to notice.

Once I recovered from the initial shock of his arms around my waist, I realized that I didn't *quite* mind having him touch me. He held me out of sheer excitement, and I couldn't blame him. The unicorn had been extraordinary.

A shared moment. That was all this was.

"I did." I laughed at him, little bubbles of giddiness rising in me like a shaken bottle of champagne. "Unbelievable."

"Incredible. Just incredible." Finlay twirled us once more, and I enjoyed this unfiltered look at him, when he wasn't in "boss" mode. His excitement was palpable, like a child's on Christmas morning, and I didn't want to poke a hole in his joy by insisting he put me down. It didn't matter, not really, since I knew he wasn't a threat to me. I wasn't sure how I knew that, but I just did. Years of fending for yourself gave you a pretty good radar on who was out to hurt you.

"A fecking unicorn. Of all things." Finlay's gaze dropped to my face, and our eyes held, something deepening between us. The air grew thick with tension, the kind that made me squirm and wish for a moment alone with the toy in my bedside table, and his gaze dropped to my mouth.

Now it was time for me to get down.

I tapped his arm lightly.

"Permission to disembark, sir," I said, keeping my tone light, but needing to remind him he was holding me off the ground. On my own worksite of all things.

"Och, right. I'm sorry. Shite, I really have made a habit of grabbing you, haven't I? I'm sorry for it, Orla. I'll try to do better."

"Thank you." I wasn't going to placate him or tell him that I didn't mind, even when I didn't really mind all that much. Which was a thought to be examined later, as usually I was a stickler for appropriate workplace interactions. It's why I had women who enjoyed working on my crew as well. They knew that I ran a tight ship, and the men who worked with us respected the rules, just as the women weren't allowed to harass the men. Construction sites were notorious for lewd talk, but my workers kept it respectful with each other. It was a point I prided myself on. "Brilliant. Absolutely brilliant."

"Incredible." Finlay's face was alight with joy, as he searched the trees that lined the back of the building.

"Absolutely incredible. I can't believe it. Surely that wasn't real."

"She seemed pretty real, dinnae she?" I pulled my eyes away from his handsome face and forced myself to steady my breathing. A unicorn and being held by Finlay? It was senses overload for this girl, that was for sure.

"I wonder what it means. If anything. Should we not be building here? Was it a warning? What if this is her habitat and we're ruining it?"

"Och, that's not the feeling I got," I said, tilting my head as I considered it. "It felt ... soothing. Like she approved, or something. And we're not building all that much, are we? We're using what's existing here, with a slight extension. It's not like we're developers taking down the forest or something."

"True, true," Finlay murmured, hands in his pockets. He shook his head. "Just absolutely incredible."

"Aye." We stood in silence for a moment longer, and then I shifted, knowing I was needed back inside. "Well, I should crack on."

"Right, of course."

It felt weird, to just walk away from him, after a moment like we'd just had, but I didn't know what else to do.

I fist-bumped his arm lightly.

"Well done," I said, and then turned abruptly and stalked away, silently berating myself. *Well done? What the hell did that even mean?* And *this* was why I didn't make much time for dating. I was catastrophically awkward, even at the most mundane of times, and apparently, more so, in epic moments.

I'd punched his arm. *Well done?*

"Well done" what, exactly? "Well done" on spotting a freaking unicorn?

Och, I was going to be kicking myself all day for that one.

"Orla, any decision on the window?" Derrick called to me from the stockroom, and I forced myself back into work mode, grateful for the diversion.

Well done, indeed.

CHAPTER TEN

ORLA

The Auld Mill property was beautiful, just as Derrick had mentioned, and I leaned against my lorry and studied the building for a moment, assessing the situation. Situated on the banks of Loch Mirren, the cream stone building jutted out from the land, a small waterwheel attached to the side of the building where a burn flowed to the loch. Green hills, alight with the first wash of spring, hovered over the mill, strong sentinels ever on watch. Loch Mirren itself lay flat, hardly a ripple in her glass-like surface, and I was drawn to her shores to look out toward the small island that held one of the most powerful items in the world.

Icy cold gripped me, like a frozen corpse scratching at my heart, and I gasped for breath, whirling to look at the building. A shadow shifted in the bottom window, evil oozing out, like an oily blackness slipping across the uneven ground toward my feet. I froze, caught in the hold of whatever darkness seeped toward me, and it was only because of this being's stealthy power that I missed the shrieking behind me.

It was too late.

I was just too late.

An icy wall smashed into me, water crashing over my head, the force of the power thundering over me and dragging me into the frigid waters of Loch Mirren. I had one moment to gasp for breath before I was tumbled under the waves and tossed about, like a sock in a washing machine, and held under.

I wasn't sure if it was the icy water or the fact that I couldn't swim, but for some reason, I didn't fight. Instead, acceptance filled me as I was tossed about in the water, drifting into darkness, my body going numb as my need for air began to tighten my lungs. Blinking my eyes open, I strained to see through salty murky water, trying to gauge which way was up. Kicking out, flailing, my head popped briefly onto the surface, and I gasped for air just as another wave careened over my head.

But not before a pirate loomed, riding the wave toward me, his hand outstretched.

Surely I was hallucinating from lack of air and sheer panic.

In fact, seeing a pirate ride a wave, his mustache billowing in the wind, forced a giggle out of my lips, and for the fun of it—I put my hand out to him.

I mean, of course there wasn't really a pirate about to rescue me from an attack. I was delusional, slipping into the murky depths of Loch Mirren, knowing I didn't have the strength or acumen to fight the evil being from the Auld Mill on my own. I didn't really know, nor did I have the air or the mental capacity to understand what was happening.

Life-changing events really *do* happen fast. People always talk about what they would do in an emergency, but the reality is, you have moments, if not seconds, to make decisions that will change an outcome. And I, sad to say, couldn't quite get my legs or body to work well enough to claw my way back up to the surface of Loch Mirren.

Swimming lessons hadn't exactly been in my budget growing up.

A hand closed over mine and I was ripped from the water, propelled forward across the surface, and deposited in a heap on the beach, gasping for air. I didn't look up, didn't care what I would see, and instead crawled across the beach, forcing my body to move, move, *run*, away from the edge of the loch. Tremors shook me as I scrambled, clawing my way up the side of the hill, until I landed in a heap next to my lorry, my back resting against the tire as my entire body shook with adrenaline.

Footsteps crunched closer, and I wiped the water from my eyes, raising my head.

"Well, now, honey. I can't say I much enjoy swimming either, but if I'm going to do it, it'll be in that pretty turquoise sea right outside my doorstep at home in the Keys, not in this dark and dingy water."

A woman stood before me with luminous brown skin and wise eyes, wearing a tartan caftan with sparkles and feathers at the hem. A silky black turban wrapped her head and at the center winked a jet-black stone. I hadn't even known that caftans could be made with tartan, let alone sparkles and feathers, and I gaped at the woman.

The pirate hovered over her shoulder.

A ghost.

He was a ghost pirate, and somehow, he'd managed to help me from the water.

"I love seeing you swim, my lovemountain," the pirate all but purred.

"You just like seeing me in my bikini, Rafe." A loud chuckle reverberated from the woman, the sound filling me with warmth, and I tried to gather my thoughts.

I still wasn't entirely sure that I wasn't dead.

Movement caught my eye, and I angled my head, peering behind the woman's caftan to see three husky men in kilts, with their shirts off, mind you, leaning against a car. Their muscular arms were crossed over their burly chests, and they waited, a mix between male strippers and beefed-up security guards, and I blinked at them.

Right, I *had* to be dead. Was *I* a ghost now?

"Am I ... dead?" I asked. Wiping water from my face, I tried to fight through chills that wracked my body. My teeth chattered together, and I didn't think that my teeth would still chatter if I was dead.

"Lads! A blanket for this woman." The lady in the tartan caftan snapped her fingers, and then snorted, leaning over to whisper to me. "*Lads*. Don't you love saying that? I do. Sounds so proper. And here I am taking myself on a tour of the Highlands. Never thought I'd be one for a man in a kilt, but I have to say, I can see the appeal."

I goggled up at the men who approached, all muscles

and bare skin, and one crouched to wrap a blanket around me.

My eyes widened.

Listen, I've lived in Scotland my whole life. It wasn't unheard of to catch a glimpse beneath a kilt on a windy day here or there. But when a man crouches in front of you, wearing a kilt, while you're sitting on the ground, let's just say … it was enough to bring the heat coursing back through my body.

"Th … th … thank you," I stuttered, accepting the blanket, and the woman grinned at me.

"What's your name, child? I think we need to have a chat about that nasty bugger that just tried to kill you."

So she'd seen it too. And didn't seem much bothered by the darkness. Interesting.

The woolen blanket helped ward off some of the chill, and I tucked it more tightly around me as I stood, glancing back out to the now placid waters of Loch Mirren.

"I'm Orla."

The woman threw her hands to her waist and grinned, looking me up and down.

"Isn't that just fine, then, honey? I'm Miss Elva. Look at that, Rafe. Elva and Orla. Sisters from another mister."

"She doesn't look anything like you, my lovemountain." Rafe, apparently the name of the pirate ghost, adjusted his hat and sneered as the half-naked men in kilts returned to the car. "Nice skirts, *lads*."

The men clearly couldn't hear him, or I'm sure they would have corrected the pirate, as some Scots would— with their fists.

"She can be my sister if I want her to be my sister,

Rafe." Miss Elva scolded the pirate, and his cheeks pinkened. "She's clearly messing with magick and can see ghosts. That makes her more my sister than most, doesn't it?"

"Of course, my beauty. You're right, she's obviously your sister."

Nobody had ever called me their sister before, and yet, the word warmed me in a way that I hadn't known it would. Granted, this woman towered over me both in height and size, not to mention the clear strength of magickal power that emanated from her, and I very much *did* want to be her sister. She felt safe to me. Pulling the blanket more tightly around my shoulders, I gave her a tentative smile.

"You know about magick?"

"Ooof, child. I *am* magick." Miss Elva threw her head back and laughed that rolling laugh again and waved a hand in the air. "Do you not see this fabulousness?"

"I'll admit, I've never seen a tartan caftan before."

"Do you like it?" Miss Elva preened for me. "I made it before the trip. I'm a fashion designer as well as a practitioner of magick."

"It's pretty fabulous." It was at that. I'd never be able to pull it off, but Miss Elva owned the look.

"Now, honey. Tell me what that was all about? If it wasn't for Rafe having a fit while we were driving by, I'm not sure we would have stopped in time."

"I saw you. Before I went under again. *You* ... saved me. A hero." I turned to the ghost who sniffed and pretended to look unaffected.

"Can't let a pretty lady drown, can I? Though you

don't hold a candle to my lovemountain, of course. Could use some more meat on your bones. Do they not feed you here? Oh, you must be poor. The poor were always so skinny in my time."

I raised my eyebrows. There was a lot to unpack, and I wasn't sure which of his comments to respond to.

"Rafe! Take the compliment and shut up. You can't be calling people out on their body size. Or their money. Ignore him." Miss Elva gave Rafe a sharp look.

"Well, I'm sorry if I'm just a bit annoyed having to ride around with *them* all day." Rafe fumed, raising a hand to the husky men by the car.

"You're just mad Rosita didn't come on the trip. Doesn't mean I can't have my fun."

"Nothing stops you from having your fun, lovemountain."

"Damn right, Rafe. Best way to live your life."

I blinked, staying quiet as they argued back and forth, certain this was one of the weirder days of my life. Clearing my throat, I interrupted a tirade from Rafe about the level of nakedness of their car companions.

"The Kelpies are a threat to Loren Brae, but we're working on subduing them. So long as you don't go in the water, you should be safe."

"Is that right? Huh. That's just fine then. But that wasn't a Kelpie that tried to kill you." Miss Elva raised an eyebrow at the water and shivered.

"It wasn't?" I mean, it had happened so fast, I couldn't really say.

"Similar. A water creature. Likely a nuckelavee."

"A what?" This was all new to me.

"Child, don't you know your myths? Nasty beast. Dark, dark energy. Creature of the sea, but often terrorizing those on land. Sometimes as a water horse as well. But not Kelpies. Kelpies were sometimes known to be helpful. A nuckelavee, ooooh, honey. Nasty, nasty beast. Mm-hmm."

"Fun to ride though," Rafe said, pretending to wave a fake lasso in the air.

"You didn't ride a nuckelavee, Rafe."

"I most certainly did!" Rafe exclaimed, fury thundering his face. "How do you think I got to her so fast?"

"Mm-hmm, wasn't what it looked like from the shore."

"You couldn't see. Tell her, Orla."

"Um, well, I was kind of drowning, so it was hard to see what was happening, but it did look like you were riding a wave toward me."

"See? She saw me riding something."

"You were surfing the wave. Not riding a nuckelavee. That beast would've sent you right back through the veil."

"This is nonsense! Nonsense! How dare you insult me?" Rafe whizzed off in a fit, winking out of sight, and I just looked at Miss Elva. I had no frame of reference for how to handle this situation.

"He's a bit temperamental. But then, most men are, aren't they? Fragile egos, most of them. Anywho, I'm thinking we need to pack this menace back to where he belongs, right, honey?" Miss Elva nodded toward the Auld Mill.

"You can feel it?"

"Child, I can feel *that* a thousand miles away. It is not good. Granted, you have all sorts of magick and beasties wandering about in Scotland, don't you? Some the likes

I've never seen back home in Tequila Key, that's for certain. It's tough keeping my guards up or I'd be stopping every two seconds to see to one matter or another. But I'm on vacation, aren't I? I can't be responsible for solving the world's problems."

I didn't doubt she could. She was equal parts terrifying and soothing, and I had no idea how to proceed. Not that she seemed to expect much as she just steamrolled right over me and kept talking.

"Let's get this one fixed though, shall we? It's a nasty spirit in there and he needs to head home. Lads." Miss Elva snapped her fingers again and tossed a look over her shoulder at her entourage. "My bag."

One of the half-naked men strolled forward and hooked a large satchel on Miss Elva's arm. I was beginning to see the appeal of having these men at her beck and call.

"Um, what exactly is your plan?" I was dripping wet, the wind had been knocked out of my sails, and if the dark spirit inside this building was what had taken me down, well, let's just say I wasn't entirely pleased about trying to confront it. I had to imagine we looked quite the sight— me, scrawny, pale, my long red hair dripping down my back, and Miss Elva, large, powerful, tartan caftan billowing behind her. An odd pairing, indeed.

"Is that kelp down there?" Miss Elva nodded toward the shoreline where lumps of kelp and other seaweed tangled among the rocks on the shoreline.

"Aye, looks to be."

"Can you gather some while I get prepared?"

"How much?"

"Not much. Just enough for a spell."

"As I've never done a spell before I'm not quite sure how much you'll be needing."

"Never done …" Miss Elva trailed off in surprise, looking me up and down. "I thought you were magickal."

"Um." Was I? Maybe after the ritual I was. It was hard to say really. I didn't really feel magickal.

"No problem. I got this. You're lucky Miss Elva came along when she did, let me tell you, child. Nasty beastie, hiding out like we can't see him lurking all gross and dirty in there. Just a handful of kelp should be enough."

Something shifted behind the windows of the Auld Mill and Miss Elva sneered.

"Yeah, we see you, beastie. You'd better watch yourself."

Lovely, just lovely. Miss Elva was threatening a sea demon.

This was more than a ghost, and way out of my element, and now somehow, I had to help banish it with magick when I'd never even done a spell before. Well, the Order of Caledonia ritual notwithstanding. Even so, I was out of my element to say the least, but that seemed to be keeping with the theme of my life lately. Taking a deep breath, I dug in my lorry for my tool belt, added my special hammer, and grabbed a canvas bag to collect kelp in. Clambering down to the shore, I took a deep breath. To say I was nervous after nearly drowning was an understatement. I could only hope the "nasty beastie" stayed in the Auld Mill, quietly growling at Miss Elva. *I didn't love the water the first time, and I am not keen to go in again.* I quickly gathered the kelp, the salty brine stinging my hands, the scent pungent in the damp air. I was also surprised that nobody

111

in town had seen the commotion. *Were they all hiding indoors today?*

"You don't think those men are sexy, do you?"

I screeched at the voice at my ear, jumping to see Rafe hovering over me.

"Bloody hell," I gasped, almost dropping the blanket around my shoulders.

"I agree. That's where those *lads* belong. Look at them ... trying to gain her affection. They might get her for a moment, but she's mine for a lifetime." Rafe stared after Miss Elva, adoration in his eyes.

"I mean, they are handsome. If you're one for those muscular types." I glanced away from Rafe's scrawny arms.

"You would say that. Looking like a drowned rat and all."

"Pardon me?" Not that I was going to fight a ghost, but the thought drifted briefly through my mind.

"Rafe, you leave her alone. We need to get moving or we'll never get dinner, and you know how I get when I'm hangry."

"Aye, Rafe, run along." Rafe zipped away and I tried to bury the annoyance at being called a drowned rat. I knew I was on the thin side, but I didn't need to be reminded about how unwomanly I looked next to a curvy goddess like Miss Elva. I was all muscle and sinew brought on by years of hard work and conserving my meals. Not exactly screaming sexy or womanly here, but that wasn't really the objective when I was busy hammering nails and building things all day, was it?

Stomping back up the shoreline, I stopped by Miss Elva, bag in hand.

"I think there's enough here."

"Too bad it's damp. We need to burn it. I'll just use a little extra magick. The tough part's going to be getting inside so we can properly do the spell. Let's go."

"Um, just go? Inside? With the nuckelavee?"

"Yup. It's going to try to scare us, but we're stronger than that, aren't we?"

Were we? Because it had come pretty damn close to killing me moments ago.

"I'm sorry, but how do you know how to do any of this?" I squinted at the stranger who had appeared from seemingly nowhere sparkling in a tartan caftan.

"Child. I'm Florida's strongest voodoo priestess. Voodoo isn't my only magick, it's just one of my favorites. If you run in the right circles, you'll likely have heard of Miss Elva, honey, I promise you that."

"And you're in Scotland why?"

"It's called a vacation. Ever taken one?"

"I haven't, no." The words were out before I could stop them, and I realized with startling clarity that I really had never taken a vacation before. It was a luxury I'd never been able to afford. An afternoon in the park or down by the water on a sunny day was the closest thing to a holiday that I'd ever taken.

"Is that right?" Miss Elva made a disapproving noise while she rooted around in her massive bag. "I highly suggest treating yourself. Though Scotland is a bit colder than I prefer."

"Warmest spring we've had in a while."

"So I've been told. And yet, I'm from Florida. Let me

tell you ... this weather would have our iguanas falling from the trees."

"Um." Did iguanas climb trees? Why would they fall in the cold? Before I could ask, Miss Elva brandished a bottle in her hand.

"Got it. Let's get started."

"What are we doing exactly?"

"First a protection spell for us. Then we'll enter the property, summon Mither, and have her deal with the nasty beastie. After that, we'll ward the place and I'll be on my way to get some food."

She made it sound so easy.

"Mither?"

"Mither o' the Sea. Mother of the ocean, basically, and the only one who can control this one in there." Miss Elva nodded toward the building.

"I don't know what I'm doing." Nerves hummed, causing my stomach to twist. "How am I meant to help? What if I screw it up?"

"Don't you worry. I'm used to working with people who mess up spells regularly. Just focus on the intent, draw on whatever power you can feel inside you, and align yourself with me. I'll lead the spell and we'll get rid of him quickly."

"You make it sound so easy."

"It can be, if you don't screw it up. No sudden movements. Don't step out of the circle. Stay focused. This one in there? Honey, he's going to put up quite a stink. He's having himself a good ol' time up here. He's not going to want to go back. Stay with me, stay focused, and we'll send him packing."

"Right. Och, I'm nervous."

"Just channel that right into what we want to accomplish."

Miss Elva marched forward, and a soft wailing took up from inside the building, like nails scratching on a chalkboard, and the hairs at the back of my neck rose. Hurrying after her, I clutched the bag of kelp and hoped I hadn't gotten myself in over my head. Miss Elva muttered to herself, rustling around in her handbag, before turning and handing me a small burlap bag about the size of my palm.

"Into your pocket it goes."

"What is this?"

"Your protection."

"Right."

I shoved it in the damp pocket of my overalls, wishing I was at home curled up on the bed watching Goldie spin circles in her bowl. A lump formed in my throat as I thought about who would feed her if I had died today. Poor fish, reliant only on me.

"Basil and bay, protective herbs of might, in this mojo bag, they merge with light. By the guidance of spirits, this spell I weave, protection granted to all who believe."

At Miss Elva's words, a gentle wash of energy coursed over me, and I swear I could see a soft tinge of light surround us. Miss Elva stepped forward and knocked sharply on the door three times.

I gasped as it blew open, slamming against the wall, and the howling increased.

"I'll just be by the car," Rafe called from over our shoulder. "Making sure your friends are safe."

"Damn fool pirate," Miss Elva said, sliding me a look.

"Too scared the demon will take him back through the veil with him."

"Would it be easy to do?"

"Oh, we've lost Rafe a time or two, I'll admit it. He's right to keep his distance. Come on then, stick close."

Miss Elva strode inside and I glued myself to her back, stopping short of holding on to her caftan like a child grabbing the hem of her mother's skirt. She stopped abruptly once inside and quickly sprinkled a circle of salt around us.

"Black salt, for protection," Miss Elva said.

Behind her, movement shifted, a dark shape shimmering into solidity for a moment, and my mouth dropped open.

It didn't have skin.

Thick veins, black with blood, corded yellow flesh, with arms that draped almost to the ground ending in claws. He was only solid for a moment, his strength waning as he faded into transparency, as though someone was sliding the button down on a photo editing program to make him more see-through.

"Bloody hell," I gasped.

"Stay with me, Orla. Intent is everything. Kelp?" Miss Elva ordered.

I dug in the bag and held out the damp kelp.

"Into the middle of the circle. We'll use our magick to start it on fire."

I dropped the kelp, making a loose pile between us, trying to ignore the wailing that was beginning to make my entire body shake again. Miss Elva shook a loose white powder on top of the kelp, and then using a blowtorch style lighter, she ignited it. The fire took, and a tendril of smoke drifted into the air.

The nuckelavee lost its mind.

Shrieking, it bounced around the mill, rattling against the walls, and threw loose rocks across the room.

"Gotta move fast now." Miss Elva grabbed my hands, forcing me to look up at her. "Remember. Intent is everything. Stay in the circle."

"Like I'm going to leave your side with this one running about," I muttered and Miss Elva grinned.

"In the name of Papa Legba, gatekeeper divine, let this sacred smoke cleanse and align. With this kelp, I banish all strife, warding off darkness, embracing the light. We call upon Mither o' the Sea, let this spell cleanse and set the Auld Mill free. No longer may the nuckelavee roam, sweet Mither, we beg of you, take his soul home."

A roaring sounded behind me, and I realized it was the waves thrashing against the building, the mill wheel creaking as it began to throttle and turn, the stream surging alongside us. I focused on imagining sending the demon home, trying to tap into that little ball of light I could feel deep in my core, which I likened to a battery. It must be my power source, my own little magickal battery pack, and I tapped into it the best that I could. The nuckelavee shrieked, one last long woeful cry, a sound I would never forget, before light flashed, and a window shattered. Glass flew across the room, narrowly missing us, and fell to the floor in pieces like an icicle exploding on the ground.

Silence fell.

I held my breath, my chest heaving with effort not to

run from the building and never return, and Miss Elva squeezed my hand.

"Don't move until I close the circle."

"I don't think I could if I tried."

Miss Elva quickly ran through a ritual of closing the circle, and then she squeezed my hand once more before stepping back.

"Your spirits here are strong. But the good are just as strong as the evil. Mither was surprisingly responsive. Which is good, seeing as how I'm starving. Rafe!" Miss Elva shouted, and Rafe appeared, hovering outside the doorway. "Let's go eat."

"Of course, my lovemountain. Anything for you, my beauty."

"Do you want to join us?" Miss Elva asked, and even though my inclination was to decline, I was fascinated with this wayward traveler who had saved my life.

"Aye, I do."

"Before we go ..." Miss Elva handed me another pouch. "Nail this above the door. Have them keep it there if possible."

"Nae bother." Pulling out my hammer and a nail from my tool belt, I secured the pouch by the door frame, happy to help keep this building free of darkness.

I stopped.

A vine of gold leaves was etched in a circle around the base of the wood handle that hadn't been there before. My eyes widened.

"Look at that. This is new."

"Mmm, child. It certainly pretties it up, doesn't it? I'd say the spirits are happy with your work."

"I didn't do anything."

"Of course you did. I wouldn't have been able to pull off that spell without your power. It's rooted here, which is why Mither appeared so quickly. Don't doubt your own magick."

With those mind-blowing words, Miss Elva strolled out of the building, her caftan billowing in the wind.

"Oh, child? Where should we go for dinner?"

"Um, I'd recommend The Tipsy Thistle. I can meet you there. I'd just like to put some dry clothes on." And feed Goldie.

She needed me. And even more surprising?

Perhaps Loren Brae needed me too.

CHAPTER ELEVEN

ORLA

Of course Finlay had to be at the pub when I arrived. Not only had I embarrassed myself earlier by awkwardly punching him on the shoulder after the unicorn sighting, but I was still rattled by the experience at the Auld Mill. Frankly, it had taken all my energy to force myself to change into a pair of faded trousers and a loose gray jumper. I redid my braids, chatting to Goldie the whole time, and had given her a few extra flakes for dinner before forcing myself back out the door. The adrenaline spikes from a wild day had left me feeling drained and I wanted nothing more than to drop onto my bed and sleep for ten hours.

But I was curious about Miss Elva, and Rafe *had* saved my life, so at the very least I could buy her dinner.

Two things I noticed immediately after registering Finlay's presence: The first? Agnes was looking positively joyful from where she sat at the bar. And the second? Graham looked decidedly grumpy, and I wondered what had set him off today. I followed his gaze to see Miss Elva holding court at a table by the fire, her entourage having donned T-shirts that fit like second skins in deference to the rules of being clothed at a pub.

They might as well have been naked for the thin cotton T-shirts showcased every last devastating inch of their muscular physiques and more than one woman was discreetly checking them out across the pub.

Much to Agnes's delight, I could see, as I stopped by her chair.

"Have you seen the eye candy?" Agnes hissed, gripping my arm. I jerked lightly, but didn't remove her hand, as her eyes were trained on the men across the room.

"Not only do I see them, but I also saw them with their shirts off earlier."

Agnes gasped, turning to me.

"You saw them naked?"

At that, both Finlay and Graham turned, zeroing in on me, and my cheeks flushed. Finlay had changed from work, wearing dark denim trousers and a blue chambray shirt, the cuffs rolled up to reveal his strong forearms. His gold watch winked at his wrist, and his eyes were alight with curiosity and something else that I couldn't quite put a name to.

Maybe I didn't want to put a name to it.

"Orla, honey! Yoo-hoooo!" Miss Elva called, waving from where she sat, as if the entire pub wasn't already watching her. The Tipsy Thistle was a hodgepodge place, as old buildings in the UK often were, with rooms added on here and there through the years. The room we were in now housed a large circular bar, various cozy seating nooks, and was peppered with random bits and bobs decorating the stone walls. Even so, it wasn't large enough that Miss Elva had to shout, but I was beginning to think that was her normal speaking volume. The woman seemed to live out loud.

One of her entourage stood, a strapping lad with dark hair and lively blue eyes, and crossed the now silent pub to stand by me. I looked up, and kept looking up, until I met his eyes.

"Four more pints, please. And whatever this beautiful lass wants." The lad grinned at me, and my insides did funny things as I remembered the lot of them with their shirts off. *Not to mention the full frontal thanks to their kilts and tendency to squat.*

"Um, a Coke is fine, Graham." Best not to drink around these men before I did something silly like ask if they could bench-press my body weight.

"That's fine, mate. I'll bring them over," Graham assured the man, and I bit back a grin, suspecting he wanted the beefcake to stay away from Agnes.

"Helllooooo," Agnes said, her smile widening at the man. "Welcome to Loren Brae."

"Thank you." The man's grin deepened. "We're certainly enjoying ourselves. You're welcome to join our table if you'd like."

"I—"

"I'll bring the drinks over, mate," Graham said, louder this time, and the man nodded, returning to where Miss Elva held court.

"That was rude," Agnes huffed.

It *had* been a bit rude, and deciding to ruffle Graham's feathers a bit, I leaned in.

"You'll have to come join us, Agnes. Miss Elva is a treat."

"Oh, I'd love nothing more."

"Why did you see them naked?" Finlay asked, leaning closer, and I straightened, surprised he'd ask me that question. He was technically my boss, and who I saw naked was really none of his business.

Not that I'd mind seeing *him* naked.

As soon as the thought hit my brain, my entire body heated, and I shut that idea down quickly. No, I most certainly did not remember his strong arms wrapped around my body, lifting me easily in the air, while twirling me like I was some heroine in a romance novel. Nope, I didn't recall every second of that moment in the slightest. Not at all.

"Are you asking that in a professional capacity then, Mr. Thompson?" I asked lightly, knowing I was baiting him.

Annoyance flashed, and Graham grumbled behind the bar. Agnes let out a soft coo of delight, clearly happy with the way things were going this evening.

"Mere curiosity, Ms. Clarke, since you announced it to the whole pub."

"Hardly the whole pub. Just a side comment to my friend Agnes. Were you eavesdropping on a private matter then?"

"Och, it's a private matter you had with them now?" Finlay's face turned stormy, and I hid my amusement. I wasn't one for games, never really knowing how to navigate flirtations, but I could see why Agnes enjoyed poking

Graham so much. Both Graham and Finlay were strong, handsome, smart men in their own right. Knowing you could affect them did feel a touch powerful, I had to admit. Not that I should even be thinking of flirtation. Finlay was a work relationship and needed to stay as such.

"Shall we take those drinks over for you, Graham?" Agnes asked sweetly and he glowered as he slapped a tray on the bar.

"I'm guessing that's a no," I hissed in Agnes's ear, and she chuckled.

"Let's go before their heads explode."

We crossed the room to where Miss Elva sat, reveling the men with a story about a Tiki bar in the Keys, and they pulled up two more chairs for us.

"Miss Elva, this is Agnes, a friend of mine."

"Ohh, child, aren't you a powerful one then?" Miss Elva slapped her knee and smiled up at Agnes who tilted her head in question as she sat.

"Am I?"

"If you don't know it yet, you'll find out soon enough." Miss Elva beamed at Graham as he approached with drinks, his face set in stone. "And look at this gorgeous one. Care to come on my travels with me, handsome? I'll make it worth your while." Miss Elva winked, and Graham almost dropped his tray of drinks. Setting them down hastily, he gave Miss Elva a quick nod.

"Appreciate the offer, but it looks like you have your hands full already."

"There's always room for more." Miss Elva pursed her lips.

Rafe appeared over Miss Elva's shoulders and hissed at Graham.

"Imbecile. Ungrateful beast."

My eyebrows winged up as I tried to pretend that I didn't see a pirate ghost throwing a hissy fit behind Miss Elva's back.

"You hear that, Graham? The more the merrier." Agnes slapped Graham on the back, and he turned a forced smile at her.

"Surely there is. Yet I'm busy running this pub, and what's that, Finlay? Another pint you say?" Graham hurried back behind the bar while Agnes's shoulders shook with laughter.

"That one has his eye on you." Miss Elva nodded to Agnes.

"Me and every other woman that crosses his path," Agnes said, rolling her eyes.

"Nah, honey. It's you. But you're not ready to see that, are you?" Miss Elva's gaze sharpened on Agnes, and I watched with interest, wondering how Agnes would respond.

"It's complicated," Agnes said after a beat of silence.

"Aren't they all, honey? It's why I never tie myself to one man. Aside from my sweet Rafe, that is." Rafe winked back into sight over her shoulder, an adoring light in his eyes.

"That's right, my lovemountain. I'll always be devoted to you even if you share your body with others."

"And why shouldn't I share? There's more than enough for me to go around. I can't help that I attract men wherever I go." Miss Elva boomed her rolling laugh and Agnes looked over at me, a question in her eyes.

"Um, there's a ghost here. A pirate to be exact," I whispered in her ear.

"Rafe?" Agnes guessed.

"That's the one."

"Interesting. A ghost lover. Very progressive."

"That's me, child, I'm open to it all." Miss Elva winked at one of the men across from her who reached out and trailed a hand down her arm.

"Can I be you when I grow up?" Agnes wondered out loud.

"Or at the very least, bottle your confidence?" I asked, and then took a hasty sip of my Coke. Usually I wasn't so bold in what I said to strangers, but exhaustion had dropped my guards.

"What's going on in this town? There's a lot of power here." Miss Elva leaned forward, bracelets jangling as she braced her elbows on the table.

"It's ..." Agnes glanced to the three men.

"Gentlemen, would you mind taking your dinner at another table? Looks like it's going to be us girlies for a bit."

"Anything you want." The men rose as one and we all, along with every other woman at the pub, watched them cross the room and take another table.

"Where did you find them? They're, like, perfectly matched," Agnes asked, turning back to the table.

"Aren't they just? Child, they just flock to me. I don't blame them either. They know a good thing when they see it." Miss Elva preened and I laughed. She was impossible in the best way, and I loved how confident she was with herself.

Graham arrived at our table, carrying a large tray of food, and my stomach grumbled.

"I ordered a bit of everything, does that suit?" Miss Elva looked at me.

"No problem at all. But I'd like to pay for it. You saved my life today."

"What happened?" Graham and Agnes asked in unison, and I bit my lip, annoyed with myself for saying anything. Small towns and all that.

"Just a small accident that I happened upon and was able to help our girl out of a bind. Hey, cutie, mind feeding my boys too? They eat a lot."

Graham looked down at the expanse of food on the table and then over to the table where the beefcakes had moved to.

"This is ... just for you three?"

"Do you think it's enough? I can always order more unless the kitchen closes soon?" Miss Elva fluttered her eyelashes and Graham quickly recovered.

"I reckon this is enough for you three. I'll get more on for the lads shortly."

"You're the best." Miss Elva beamed and then turned to us with a smile. "I love me some good girl time. I have the best friends in the world back in Tequila Key. Althea and Luna—both of whom are powerful too. Just like you ladies. Friendship is everything, particularly when you're dealing with nasty stuff like that beastie over at the mill."

Cutting a burger in half, I bit in, my stomach all but singing with happiness now that it knew food was coming.

"Orla, what happened?" Agnes whispered, shooting a glance over her shoulder to make sure Graham was gone.

"I went out to the Auld Mill to check why people said it was haunted. Apparently, a nuckelavee was keeping house in there."

Agnes sucked in a breath.

"Mm-hmm." Miss Elva nodded. "Nasty beastie."

"Tossed me right in the water. And, well, I can't swim, so that wasn't an ideal situation."

"Orla! How scary." Agnes wrapped an arm around my shoulder in a quick hug and I allowed it, realizing that it was nice to have someone actually care if I lived or died.

"Miss Elva got rid of it though."

"*We* got rid of it," Miss Elva corrected, biting into her haggis. She stopped, peering closer at her plate. "Do I want to know what I'm eating here?"

"Nope," Agnes and I said in unison.

"I'll take your word for it. Delicious, though."

"We've warded the Auld Mill. The building should be clear now. And get this—a gold vine showed up in my hammer."

"You passed a challenge," Agnes gasped, her hand at her throat.

"What's that now?" Miss Elva looked up from her food.

Agnes surprised me by answering her question. Normally, she would deftly swerve any queries from visitors about the Kelpies or other strange goings-on in Loren Brae.

"Orla's just accepted a role in the Order of Caledonia. It's an ancient Order of sorts, meant for protection of a particular thing that shall not be named. She has to prove herself before she's fully in."

"Ohhhh." Miss Elva fanned her face. "I do love an ancient Order. There's just something so sexy about rituals and traditions, isn't there? That explains the strong magick. I know what Orla's is. What's yours, girl?"

"Mine?" Agnes laughed and shook her head. "I don't have any. I'm a worker bee. A researcher. That's it."

"Mmm, if you say so." Miss Elva said it in a way that suggested she absolutely didn't believe Agnes but knew better than to ask questions of people who didn't feel like being asked.

"Orla, may I speak with you for a moment?" Finlay's voice at my back caused me to jump. I looked longingly down at my burger.

I suspected I knew what Finlay wanted to ask me—he was the type who wanted to run to the rescue of women, and I could just imagine Graham had relayed to him what I had said about the threat on my life earlier today.

Hunger won out.

"I'm sorry, but I'm starving. I can speak with you after dinner, if that suits?" Finlay's jaw clenched at my words, but he nodded once before turning on his heel and returning to the bar.

"And that one has his eye on *you*," Miss Elva declared, moving onto a sausage roll.

"What? Me? No, it's not like that. We work together."

"He paid one thousand pounds for a date with her," Agnes offered, and Miss Elva paused, looking up at me, her eyebrows raised to her turban.

"Is that right, child?"

"I mean, technically, but not in the way she's saying it."

"In what way does a man pay for a date then?" Miss

Elva leaned back in her chair, crossing her arms over her chest. *I wasn't going to be able to hide from this conversation.*

"He asked me, in a professional capacity, to be a date to a gala that his company, my client, is sponsoring. To make it worth my while, he's paying me so I can donate the money to the animal rescue."

"Seems to me you would have gone for free if it's your client."

"That's what I said." Agnes nodded at Miss Elva.

"I'm not a gala kind of girl. Plus, once he offered, I couldn't help but think of how that money would help the shelter."

"And he's paying for a custom-made dress for her," Agnes added.

"How do you know all this?" I turned to Agnes.

"Are you kidding me? We're Scottish. We love talking about how much everything costs. Did you honestly think he was going to pay one thousand pounds and order a custom-made gown and somehow manage to keep it quiet in this town?"

"Men don't do that unless they're interested," Miss Elva said.

"He's not. I promise you, it's not like that. He just made the whole thing awkward and ended up cornering himself. It was really just an accident."

"No Scotsman *accidentally* pays one thousand pounds for a date."

"No *man* does," Miss Elva corrected.

I really wished they weren't putting these thoughts in my head. Not that they hadn't already kind of been there, but so far, I'd been successful in silencing my inner monologue that questioned why Finlay wanted to take me with him to the gala. But now that other people were voicing the same thing I was questioning, heat bloomed on my face. How was I supposed to work around Finlay if I thought he fancied me?

Or if I might, just a teeny-tiny bit, actually fancy him?

Och, this was becoming complicated, and I didn't want complications. I wanted a simple, stable life.

"I have no idea what to say here," I admitted, looking up. "I just want an uncomplicated life."

"Well, now, child, why in the world would anyone want that?" Miss Elva threw her head back and laughed, slapping her knee. "Particularly when you have magick. Don't you know a complicated life is *so* much more fun?"

"Is it? It's hard to tell."

"You can still steal your moments of Zen in a complicated life. Trust me, Orla. Go to the gala. Wear the dress. Flirt with every man under the sun. Or woman, if that's your thing. Eat it up, enjoy it, and let Finlay fawn all over you. There's nothing finer than a man falling all over a woman. Trust me, I live my life by it."

As one, we all turned to look at the three gorgeous men in kilts who were waiting for Miss Elva to call upon them.

"I'd take her word for it, Orla. She seems to have it figured out."

"Don't I just, honey. Don't I just?"

CHAPTER TWELVE

FINLAY

I'd never gotten a chance to speak with Orla about her near-death experience, and I'd been up half the night worrying over it. She'd begged off our conversation, promising me she was fine but exhausted, and had left with Miss Elva and her entourage, dropping Orla off on their way out of town.

I'd be lying if I said it didn't bother me, just a bit, that she'd also seen those men in kilts naked. Perhaps more than a bit, even though Orla was right, it was absolutely none of my business who she chose to get naked with.

Images of stripping her out of her overalls and bending her backward over a work bench had filled my head, my body responding, and despite trying not to think of Orla's pint-sized body under my hands, I hadn't been strong enough to resist. When I had taken my pleasure, it had been with her name on my lips, and I'd woken up feeling a touch guilty this morning. She was an employee of sorts, after all, and I was certain Munroe would frown upon me trying to date her.

Hadn't he been the one to suggest I take her to the gala though?

In a professional capacity, I was certain, and yet I couldn't help but look forward to having an entire night to spend with her. Orla intrigued me. She was a contradictory mix of both wary and confident, seamlessly handling difficult projects and mediating employee relationships, yet standoffish and short when pulled into personal discussions. I wanted to peel back her layers, much like I'd peeled off her clothes in my dream, and discover who she was.

Which, again, was stupid. It wasn't like I had time for relationships. And Orla was most definitely a relationship type of woman.

The day my father had died was the day that I'd learned that everyone had secrets. In every action and word, my father had seemed perfect. The perfect husband, the perfect father, the perfect friend. *Everyone* had loved him.

He'd died in the arms of his lover, revealing a string of infidelities and ruining the carefully constructed image I'd had of him. The image he'd worked *so* hard to preserve. Add that with a dried-up bank account and debts owed, and I'd been forced to step forward to care for my mother in the way she was accustomed to so she didn't lose face in society.

In grieving him, not just the father he'd been, but the image I'd constructed of him, I'd become focused on creating security for both me and my mother, which was why I was so driven to succeed professionally. It also left very little room for relationships. Because of this, I'd always found it easier to stay unattached, to put the stakes up front, and to keep things casual with my lovers.

And Orla was anything but casual. She took her work seriously, treated most conversations with an intensity that I couldn't quite understand, and didn't strike me as a no-strings-attached kind of woman. Which meant, once again, that I needed to keep things professional with her. Friends at most.

Never lovers, no matter how much it now seemed I wished for her to unravel beneath my hands. Ever since we saw the unicorn together, I couldn't help recalling the feeling of her in my arms. She was relatively tiny, but strong. *She'd fit my body perfectly. I hadn't wanted to let go.*

Even now, my fingers clenched at the thought of touching her, and I realized that somewhere along the way, the quick-witted Orla had worked herself into my head.

Speaking of, I needed to stop by the shelter and pay what I had promised Orla as payment for her to attend the gala. It was the weekend, and I hoped they would be open, but I didn't want to delay too long in case they were waiting to buy the supplies for their extension.

After a quick shower and a bite of toast with my cup of tea, I left the wee rental cottage I was staying at and walked to the shelter, enjoying the soft spring morning. I always enjoyed spring, when the sunshine would burn off the crispy fog of morning, and the hint of new garden growth tinged the air. A cherry blossom tree hung her branches over the pavement, blush pink petals fluttering in the breeze, as though nature was throwing a party to welcome the arrival of summer. Loch Mirren was still, the morning light dancing across her surface, the trees that lined the shore mere smudges of paint on her reflection. It was quiet here, in a way that it rarely got in Edinburgh, and I glanced up as three crows swooped low over my head, following my path.

Could I get used to small town life?

Maybe. It certainly had its perks. A built-in friend group, beautiful natural landscapes, and a laid-back atmosphere. I hadn't even worn half the clothes I'd brought with me, finding there was very little need for suits and ties here. The meetings I had were done at the construction site, not in the boardroom, and I was enjoying being more hands-on, even if I had to work late a few nights a week to make sure the spreadsheets tallied up and the project stayed on budget.

I heard the barking before I even arrived at the shelter, and I smiled at the woman with kind eyes and a messy bun of gray hair behind the front desk.

"Good morning, it's a braw day, isn't it?"

"It is at that," I agreed, leaning an arm on the counter.

"Are you here to meet the pups then?"

"No, I'd just like to make a donation."

"Och, well, now. That's just grand, isn't it? We certainly appreciate every quid we can get. There's a box there." The lady nodded to a small donation box on the counter with a slit in the top.

"Uh, it's a touch more ... sizeable than that. Do you have a card reader? If not, can I get your bank details? I'll transfer it over."

"Brilliant. We absolutely could use it." The woman beamed at me like I'd just told her I'd managed to end world hunger and picked up a small portable card reader. "How much would you like to donate then?"

"One thousand pounds."

The card reader jostled in her hands, and she peered at me over the counter.

"Did I hear that correctly?"

"Yes, ma'am."

"Och, that's brilliant. Just brilliant. We'll be able to get our extension after all." A suspicious sheen glimmered in the woman's eyes, and I immediately felt awkward, never certain how to navigate a woman's tears.

"Yes, I hear it's needed. What are you planning then?"

"Let me give you a tour. I can show you where we're building out and you can meet some of the residents."

"Oh, I'm sure you're busy." Based on the cacophony of barking in the back room, her presence was desperately needed.

"Not too busy for our hero here."

I hesitated as I held my card up, looking around the small front room. If one thousand pounds could be life-changing for this shelter, maybe I should add more just in case they ran into any problems in the construction or needed more food for the dogs. If this donation was enough to bring tears, surely, they were in need of more? I thought of my well-padded savings account, just in case of a rainy day, and looked down at the threadbare sofa in the waiting room. Though I regularly gave to charities, it was usually from afar, not in the lobby of the organization that I was donating to. Now, seeing her excitement, I was helpless to not want to give more. Leaning forward, I dropped my voice, having heard other people in the back.

"Can you double that?"

"Excuse me?" The woman gaped at me.

"I'd like to double that if you promise to keep it a secret."

"I-I ... but of course. If you're certain?" The woman's mouth worked, her eyes alight with excitement.

"Yes, I'm certain. Will that be enough for your immediate needs or is there more?"

"Let me ... let me just check." The woman put the card reader down and walked over to a small desk. Opening a drawer, she pulled out a binder and flipped through the pages, walking back over to me. "If you're speaking specifically about the extension, this is the quoted budget for labor, materials, and how long it would take to get done. That doesn't include the ongoing food or vet care needed for the additional animals that will fill the space of course. But we do regular fundraisers and have volunteers, so I'm sure we'll make do."

I scanned the budget, seeing how Orla had donated all of her time for free, and guilt made my stomach clench. Here she was already working herself to the bone for us and she was still donating her free time to helping this shelter?

Yeah, I could do more. I also noted the budget was extremely lean, which meant Orla was likely also shouldering some of the costs of this build. Not only was she talented, but she was generous. She ... fit Loren Brae so well. *She's making a difference.*

Now it wasn't only guilt that sat beneath my breastbone, it was shame. *I could be doing more with my life than simply building a nest egg.* And this could be my first step.

"Here's what I'd like to do," I said, sliding the binder

back to her. "I'd like to cover this budget and then also set up a recurring monthly donation that will help with food for the dogs. Is that something you can arrange for?"

"I ... I, yes, I mean yes, of course we can. That's ... thank you, sir. Thank you," the woman gushed, jotting down the numbers I mentioned before patting her hands on her cheeks to dash her tears. "I need to get the paperwork set up for the recurring donation if you can just wait—"

"Finlay? What's going on?" Orla's voice behind had me turning. She'd come in from the back room, and her look sharpened at the tears on the older woman's face. "Barbara, what's wrong? What did you do, Fin?"

It was the first time she'd shortened my name, and the brush of familiarity made my insides warm.

"Och, Orla, he's a hero this one. I'm telling you, an absolute gem. He's paid off the extension, so he has."

"Ahem." I cleared my throat. Barbara had instantly violated my terms of not telling anyone about my donation. Her eyes widened and her face looked stricken.

"Och, I'm sorry. I promise I won't say a thing to anyone else. It's just ... she's the builder, the one who provided us with this budget. Surely, it's okay for her to know the budget's been met and we can proceed with construction?" Barbara pleaded with me, clearly upset that she'd broken her promise to me. Orla rounded the counter and looked down at the woman's notes before raising surprised eyes to me.

"This is much more than discussed. And a recurring donation?"

"It was needed." I shrugged a shoulder, uncomfortable now.

"Please don't be upset with me, I promise I won't say a word of it to anyone else. It's just Orla will be the one ordering the materials and ..." Barbara wrung her hands.

"I'm not upset," I promised her. "That's just fine that Orla knows. She's excellent at her job, you couldn't have hired better."

Both women beamed at me, twin rays of sunshine, and I shifted, feeling uneasy under their adoration.

"I need to get this paperwork set up," Barbara said.

"Why don't I show you around and you can see where we're going to build while Barbara finishes up?" Orla said, moving out from behind the counter.

"Sure, that'll be grand." I didn't want to be this close to Orla, not when I'd had such a deliciously naughty dream about her the night before. Here she was in faded denim and a worn jumper that did nothing for her shape. And yet all I could think about was running my hands beneath that loose jumper and feeling her skin heat under my touch.

Damn it. I needed to keep it professional.

Orla's hair was plaited back again, a few tendrils loose around her face, and she looked at ease here in a way that she didn't on-site. Maybe it was because she was off duty and this was a space she could relax in, but she walked more slowly and her face was relaxed, serene almost.

This is her happy place.

Another facet of Orla I hadn't yet uncovered.

"Are you ready for chaos? It's puppy playtime before we open for adoption. Helps get some of their energy out." Orla looked me up and down and sniffed.

"What's that look for?" I glanced down at my cuffed denims and polished boots.

"You might get a bit dirty. Dogs are messy." The way she said it was as if I couldn't handle a few stray pieces of dog hair on my clothes.

"That's just fine. These are comfy clothes."

"Of course they are." Orla rolled her eyes, and I shook my head at her, bemused.

"Why do you find that so hard to believe?"

"You're just a bit posh, Finlay. Nothing wrong with that, but I'd just say that *your* work clothes and mine are a touch different."

I glanced between her worn clothes and mine and shrugged.

"I'm only half the time on-site. The rest I'm in an office. I think it's called balance."

"It's okay to be posh, Fin."

There it was again, my name shortened at her lips, and I warmed to the familiarity.

"I'm not posh."

"Says the man with a gold watch on his wrist."

"What's wrong with my watch?" It had been a gift from my grandfather when I turned eighteen.

"Nothing at all." Orla smirked, pursing her lips together.

I wanted to kiss her.

The thought struck, sucking the air from my body, and I instinctively leaned forward, closing the distance between us, all thought leaving my mind so focused was I on her lips.

Orla pushed the door open at her back, breaking the moment, and pandemonium greeted us.

Loud barks erupted at our entrance, and furry bodies flew everywhere, racing around the room as we entered, and

Orla quickly shut the door behind us. A girl, looking to be in her late teens, monitored the dogs from the far end of the room, and a laugh escaped me at the absolute chaos that greeted us.

Dogs of all sizes, shapes, and ages ranged across the floor. A few of the smaller ones chased each other in circles around the room, while three older dogs lay against the wall, observing the chaos. One dog, which looked to be a lab mix of sorts, with dark brown fur and a few grays on his snout, nudged a puppy gently that tumbled into his face.

"Who's this guy?" I asked, deciding to start with the older dogs since the puppies were too chaotic to try and catch at the moment. Crouching next to the brown lab, I shifted so I could sit next to him and held my hand out gently, allowing him to sniff me first.

"This distinguished gentleman is named Harris, and I might just be in love."

"Kicking those hunky highlanders to the curb already?" I couldn't help but mention the strapping lads in the pub that, apparently, Orla had seen naked.

"They were never mine to keep." Orla sighed dramatically and threw the back of her palm against her head before kissing the top of Harris's head. "Harris is the only man for me."

"You're a lucky man, Harris." I wanted to ask more about the men from yesterday but knew it wasn't my place to do so. She had every right to a private life, didn't she?

A grin flashed across Orla's face before she buried her face in the dog's neck, stroking his ears slightly.

"He's just the best. Calm. Gentle. Loving. I hate that he's in here."

Her eyes were filled with adoration and the way the dog twisted to look up at her, swiping his tongue over her face, assured me this was a mutual adoration.

I jumped when a puppy tumbled into my lap, followed by two others, and they wrestled each other around my legs, clearly unconcerned for any of my body parts as they nipped and growled at each other. One puppy, a fuzzy white one with a black mark on his ear, grabbed the lace of my shoe in his mouth and tugged.

"Hey there. Tough wee lad, aren't you?" I booped his nose and he abandoned the lace for my finger, his sharp teeth sinking into my skin. "Och, that's a fierce bite, mister!"

"Are you okay?" Orla reached over Harris and grabbed my hand, bending her face low to my palm. I froze. Her hands were surprisingly soft for a builder, and warmth trailed across my palm as she examined the bite. Her warm breath heated my skin, and I shifted, feeling my body respond to her closeness.

"It's fine. Just a wee scratch." I needed to break contact before I embarrassed myself in front of her. Instead, I tussled with the puppies in front of me to distract myself from thoughts that were taking me down an entirely different route.

Her hair smelled like wood chips and lemon.

It was an unusual combination, but one that suited her perfectly, and I tried not to imagine her in the shower, lathering a lemony soap onto her supple body.

A sharp yip drew my attention to two puppies who had moved from playing into a more serious battle. Reaching over, I tugged them gently apart, taking the fiercely growling one into my palms and leveling him up to my face.

"Sir. You're going to need to tone it down." I admonished the puppy gently and Orla chuckled next to me as the puppy tried to paw my nose.

"Yes, lecturing him sternly will certainly get through to him."

"It certainly worked with me."

"Och, tough parents?"

I glanced at Orla as she made a strangled noise, like she was upset with herself for asking, and her eyes widened as she quickly looked away, shaking her head slightly as though she was berating herself. Was it because she didn't want to get to know me on a personal level? Or because she thought she'd crossed a line? Either way, I was even more intrigued about her now, so I decided to ignore her odd look and focused my gaze back on the puppy that was currently falling asleep in my arms.

"My father preferred things done his way. Rules were meant to be followed, and his word was law."

"And that knocked all the silliness out of you?"

"Something like that." I curled the now sleeping puppy into my side and looked out across the room as I thought about my childhood. Had I ever been a silly child? I didn't remember being so. As an only child, my parents' expectations had weighed heavily on my young shoulders, and I'd always been more prone to my studies than play. Maybe that was part of what had upset me so much about my father's lies. All those of me working hard and following the rules, never one to indulge in games, and my father had been playing games all along. With my mother's heart. With his family's livelihood. Apparently, he'd had a need for the adrenaline rush, and because of it, he'd come down harder on me. It was almost as if he'd been punishing himself through me, and it had made me a reserved child. I'd had to actively work against that inclination to become more personable in the business world, but it had taken years for me to do so.

So, no, I hadn't been much for silliness in my youth. I tried to make up for it now, when I had a moment to spare, but old habits die hard, and more often than not I used my downtime for work.

Rarely did I do something so frivolous as to spend a morning away with puppies in my lap.

Orla didn't ask more, even though I would have shared about my life if she had done so. Instead, we fell into companionable silence, her wrapped around sweet Harris, and me with a growing pile of puppies in my lap, as more wandered over and clambered onto my legs for a sleep.

"So much for these posh trousers escaping unscathed." I pretended to sigh heavily in disappointment.

Orla made a tsking noise.

"Such a shame, really. I hear dog hair doesn't come off."

"Nope, going to have to bin these clothes now."

Orla rolled her eyes, but then, in a surprise move, she punched my arm lightly.

Much like she had awkwardly the other day.

Her cheeks pinkened and she looked away.

Well, well. Wasn't that interesting? Maybe, just maybe, I wasn't the only one affected by being in each other's company.

Very interesting indeed.

CHAPTER THIRTEEN

ORLA

I tried to remember just how cute Finlay had looked with three puppies sleeping on his lap, while a team of hair and makeup people worked on me. It was the only redeeming quality I could think about him in this moment, as nerves twisted low in my stomach about attending the gala that evening. I should be at home on my day off, crocheting a blanket for Harris and listening to a podcast while Goldie blew some bubbles in her bowl.

Not at some swanky hotel in Edinburgh, in a fancy suite, stationed next to Lia, who was making similar noises of distress as I was.

"Why did we agree to this again?" Lia hissed, her eyes meeting mine in the mirror above the sink. They'd brought two chairs into the bathroom for us to sit on while they did our hair and makeup, if that told you anything about the size of the hotel suite we were in.

I could barely fit *myself* into my bathroom at home, let alone two chairs and a team of hair and makeup people. This had to be the fanciest bathroom I'd ever been in. I kind of wanted everyone to leave so I could pour myself a luxurious bath with loads of bubbles, and then open all the little jars by the sink to see what they held.

If Finlay and Munroe were going to spend this much money on hotel rooms, shouldn't I be using them to the fullest? Why even get a place this nice if we were just going to be out at a gala all night? It seemed like a waste of money to me, but who was I to tell other people how to spend their money?

To be honest, I hadn't even considered the need for a hotel room. But, of course, we'd need a spot to sleep. The gala was in Edinburgh, which was a fair drive from Loren Brae, and it wouldn't make sense to come home that night. I had checked the bus schedule to see the options to get home before Finlay had informed me that Munroe had reserved a block of rooms for us.

A shiver of excitement had danced through me before Finlay had immediately clarified that I would, naturally, have my own room.

Not a date, Orla. This was not a date.

I had to keep reminding myself of that fact because it was beginning to feel a little bit like a fairy tale. What with all the hair and makeup and a gorgeous dress that I was scared to touch, let alone wear. What if I spilled something on the dress? Willow would never forgive me.

"Did we agree to it? It feels a bit like we were steam-rolled," I said. Guilt immediately filled me. Finlay had gone above and beyond his agreement to pay for the extension at the shelter—something which I'd honestly wondered if he'd even do. One thousand pounds was an incredible amount to pay for a date, and I'd kind of expected him to not fulfill his side of it. When I'd seen him there, and gotten a look at the numbers that Barbara was writing down, my impression of Finlay had shifted.

He'd looked decidedly uncomfortable with our adoration, particularly when Barbara gushed all over him, tears in her eyes, pulling him into a long hug before he left. Honestly, I'd been certain the man would have eaten the adulation right up, enjoying the praise and being center of the limelight. Instead, he'd quietly accepted the praise, but Barbara later had sworn me to secrecy, telling me in no uncertain terms how upset she'd be if word got out about Finlay's gift to the shelter.

He'd asked her not to tell anyone.

Protecting me? Or himself? I couldn't quite be sure, but my feelings about Finlay were more mixed than ever. I'd reached out to the group of women in the Order, having asked them to keep the information about Finlay paying for the date quiet, and they'd all agreed. I hadn't thought about his side of things when I'd told my new friends about it, but now Finlay had me wondering about the person beneath the shiny layers.

This past week, I hadn't seen him much, as we'd received a large delivery of supplies that had been on backorder due to a holdup of container ships in the Suez Canal, and it had been all hands on deck to bring the project back onto a timeline that Munroe would be happy with. Finlay had been active on-site, meeting with me when I needed clarification on something, but we'd both bent our heads to work.

I had to say this for him—he didn't hide himself in a fancy office and bark orders. No matter how posh his exterior seemed. Instead, he was involved in every aspect of the buildout, speaking with my team and listening carefully when they gave ideas or suggestions on ways to circumnavigate various issues that always popped up on a build.

In the meantime, I'd also spent mornings checking the work of my secondary crew assigned to Ramsay Kilts and I was pleased to see the burned building coming back to life. It was such a sweet spot, nestled at the end of the lane, and I loved creating a mix of work and living space for Willow and Ramsay to thrive in. I also loved just how much the grumpy highlander doted on sunshiny Willow. Where Ramsay was gruff, and likely terrifying to some, he was basically a mashed potato with Willow, giving her anything she desired so long as she kept smiling.

It was seriously too adorable, though I'd never, ever, be caught dead calling Ramsay adorable out loud.

"You know why *I'm* going. Not sure why you decided to go." I looked over to where a stylist lightly pinned Lia's riot of curls back from her face.

"Because that's fiancé code. You kind of have to do these things once in a while to support your person." Lia scrunched her face up in the mirror and I smiled.

"Luckily it doesn't seem to happen too often."

"Thank God. Could you imagine? There's no way I'd

be able to run the restaurant and be a socialite. I love that we live far enough away from here that I don't have to be involved in events like this too often, but when I'm feeling the need for more stimulation than Loren Brae can offer, we can run over here for a show or something."

"Or a gala." I laughed at Lia's glare.

"I'm really hoping this won't be as painful as people seem to make galas out to be."

"Och, they're exhausting." This came from the woman currently curling my hair.

"I love them. I like to see what everyone's wearing," the woman doing Lia's hair chimed in.

"True enough. Sometimes they have a good guest, like a comedian or a band that's great fun. You'll enjoy yourself if you like to listen to all the gossip and see how fashionable everyone is."

Two things that I literally did not care for.

"Don't worry, Orla. I'll be by your side. We can escape for breaks when we need them." Lia reached over and squeezed my hand and I nodded, worry making me bite my lip.

"No lip biting, hon. I just lined them," the makeup artist gently chided me.

No lip biting. No cursing. No high-fives or fist bumps. Did I need to curtsy? Would I be shaking hands with people? What about if I screwed up which fork to pick up at dinner? I'd spent far too long the night before googling which fork was the proper one to use, but now as nerves kicked low in my stomach, all my careful research neatly fled my brain.

"Your hair is beautiful." I looked in the mirror where

the woman curled my long hair. For much of my life, keeping it long had been more out of budget constraints than vanity, but now that I could afford regular haircuts, I'd found that I liked my long hair. Even if I just plaited it back most days, it had become a part of me. I often tugged on my plait when I was thinking or wound it around my hand when I was nervous. As a child, I'd been teased for my ginger locks, but I'd grown to love my hair through the years. Not that I ever gave it much thought anymore, as who had time for mooning over hairstyles when I had a million things on my to-do list each morning?

"It really is, Orla. You should wear it down more often." Lia peered at me in the mirror.

"Safety hazard at work."

"I get it. I wear a bandana most days to cover mine," Lia agreed. "But this style really suits you. It's just so pretty. You look like a real princess."

I laughed. I was certainly anything but.

"I feel like I'm getting the princess treatment, that's for sure."

"Just wait until you have your dress on. As annoying as it is, Willow knocked it out of the park."

I do look like a princess.

It was the first thought I had when I looked in the mirror after Lia had helped zip me into the dress. I stared at my reflection, not knowing this woman, unaware that I could even look this way.

This woman? Well, *she* was beautiful. An ethereal flower, blooming at midnight, poised to catch a dew drop on her petals.

She was not *me*. There was no way this image connected to aching muscles, sawdust-covered hair, and slivers in my palms. It was the most disconnected I'd ever felt from myself, and I stepped forward, staring into the tall mirror.

Willow had gone simple, erring on the side of elegant and sleek, seeming to understand that too much pomp and circumstance would have sent me running for the hills. Emerald-green silk highlighted my ginger curls that cascaded over my shoulders and down the back where the dress dipped low. Cap sleeves, a sweetheart neckline, and a figure-skimming bias cut showcased my body, but the silk drifted across my skin and wasn't too restrictive. I turned, looking to my back, admiring how the skirt fell in a few soft flounces, tucked artfully into the material, and ended just at the floor. The dress was stunning, but it was also comfortable, and for that I was grateful. I loved wearing my overalls all day because they allowed me ease of movement, and there was nothing about this dress that made me feel uneasy or restricted.

Aside from the fact that I didn't know who I was in it.

Two thin plaits held my hair back from my temples, and the makeup artist had done something fancy to my eyes, making them look larger, and my skin looked luminous and glowing against my dress.

"Tinted lip balm." The makeup artist handed me a tube of lipstick. "You don't need a lot of color on your lips and if you're not used to wearing lipstick, this is a better option. Just touch up through the night."

"Thank you." I tucked it in the matching handbag that

Willow had made to go with the gown and took a deep breath, turning as Lia walked into the room.

"Oh, Lia. That's such a good dress for you."

"Isn't it? And she did put a damn ruffle on it, but I can't say I mind."

It was the tiniest of ruffles at the hem, a light touch of whimsy, and the blush pink highlighted Lia's dusky skin and made her look both elegant and extremely sexy.

"Munroe's going to swallow his tongue."

"I hope so. I feel kind of naked in this dress. But in a good way, you know?"

I shrugged not knowing how to answer that, just knowing that Lia literally glowed in the dress. She was going to make a beautiful bride when she did get married. Lia crossed the room and stood next to me in the mirror.

"We look damn good. These men are lucky to have us."

"Och, it's not like that. Finlay doesn't have me." My cheeks pinkened and I turned from my reflection, drawing a slow breath in to steady my nerves.

"Well, you know what I mean. To have us on their arms. And Munroe definitely will get to have me later if I can get him to keep his hands off me once he sees this dress. He's going to love it."

"If you disappear for a certain amount of time, I'll cover for you."

"Could you imagine?" Lia threw her head back and laughed. "Munroe's way too proper to steal away in the middle of a fancy function, but I'll know what he's thinking."

"You two are so cute together."

"Thank you. I'm lucky to have found him." Lia paused and then closed her mouth, shaking her head once.

"What?" I asked.

"Nothing. I just want you to enjoy yourself tonight. Don't put any ... rules on anything, you know? Just have fun. You look too gorgeous not to."

"It's the rules I'm worried about. What if I eat with the wrong fork?"

Lia gave me a look like I wasn't that bright, and my eyes widened.

"It wasn't the fork I was referring to."

A knock sounded at the door, interrupting our conversation, and we both turned.

"Come in," Lia called, and the makeup artist held the door open for Munroe and Finlay to walk into the lounge area of the suite.

Munroe's mouth dropped open and I beamed as he crossed to Lia, his heart in his eyes.

"This dress. I'm going to either kill Willow or pay her extra. You look like walking sin. In the best way."

"I told Orla I felt like I was naked in it." Lia winked up at him and Munroe reached out, his hands hovering inches over the silk.

"I'm scared to touch. For more than one reason." His expression turned wolfish, and Lia giggled, nudging him back with the tip of her finger.

"You don't get to mess me up yet. It took a team to put this together and I will not let you ruin their hard work."

"Are you certain? We can call this whole thing off and leave."

"Munroe! You're sponsoring this." Lia laughed,

squeezing his arm. Munroe wore a black suitcoat and his kilt, and the two made a striking pair.

A throat cleared and I turned to Finlay, realizing I hadn't even given him my attention yet, so caught up was I with watching Munroe fall in love with Lia all over again.

My breath caught.

Finlay looked incredible. He, too, wore a kilt in soft grey with red, black, and white threaded through it. A crisp white shirt and dark waistcoat made him even more polished, and my stomach twisted in knots at the thought of having a man like this on my arm tonight.

"Orla."

My name was a whisper at his lips, just a gasp of air before acceptance, a flash of ... something ... in his eyes. Quickly, he shuttered the look and cleared his throat.

"Orla. You look lovely. Willow's done a fantastic job and this color really suits you."

Not quite the hungry welcome from him as from Munroe, but I reminded myself that this was a professional engagement. What did I expect? For him to fall at my feet because he saw me in a dress and professed his love? The entire idea was idiotic. I wasn't even sure if I liked Finlay half the time, and yet now a part of me—a deeply buried part of me, mind you—might want him to see me at my best and be overcome.

Stupid, really. This wasn't a fairy tale, and I was no princess.

"Do you like it? I wasn't sure how I'd feel, but she's designed it so I can move easily." I twirled for him, showing the dress off, while Munroe did his best to fawn all over Lia without dragging her into the bedroom.

"The dress is beautiful, as are you." Finlay stepped closer and bent forward, and I leaned in automatically. He dropped his voice. "May I tell you a secret though?"

"Aye." My heart hammered in my chest.

"While this is beautiful and I certainly won't deny you'll be the belle of the ball"—Finlay swept his hand out to my dress—"never are you more beautiful than when you're in your element, building incredible things, with the creative light shining in your eyes. That, to me, is when you're luminous."

The breath left my body, and my eyes caught on his, the moment hanging between us.

Because it didn't matter how much makeup or hair or fancy dresses I put on. Finlay saw me for me, and he thought I was beautiful just as I was. I wasn't sure how that sat with me, because I'd been certain he'd prefer this polished version of me. The woman that I didn't recognize in the mirror. Instead, he'd complimented me but told me he thought I was prettier when I was at work. In my overalls.

How was I ever going to keep my defenses up against a man who saw me clearly and accepted me for who I was—just as I was? The very thought was terrifying, and I needed to shift back into business colleague mode before I did something stupid like close the gap between us and lay my lips across his.

Because damn it, I wanted to. I'd wanted to the day in the shelter, when he'd donated so much money to a good cause, insisting on anonymity. There'd been a moment then, too, when I'd wanted to lean forward and capture his mouth in a kiss. I'd tried to tuck it away all week, that yearning I had for him, and now it reared its head inside me and his words shattered me.

Finlay thought I, Orla Clarke, builder, was beautiful. Just as I was.

"Orla, I apologize. My fiancée distracted me. You look stunning," Munroe said, shifting my attention to him and breaking the moment between Finlay and me. I turned, a smile at my lips.

"I don't blame you. If Lia wasn't a taken woman, I was considering asking for her hand myself."

"Thank God she's wearing my ring tonight. I'm certain I'll be beating the men off her." Munroe grimaced, and then tried out a scowling look. "There ... does that look intimidating?"

We all grinned at the blond-haired man and his glasses.

"You're about as intimidating as a golden retriever puppy." Lia patted his cheek. "But I love you for it anyway."

"Excuse me, but puppies can be quite fierce." Finlay rushed to his friend's defense, holding up a finger. "I still have a bite from one from last week."

"Thank you, Finlay. You hear that, darling? I'm fierce." Munroe puffed his chest out and we all laughed. He checked his watch and then motioned for us to follow him. "Come on, come on. On we go. Let's get this over with."

At least I wasn't the only one nervous for the gala. I realized that maybe none of the people I was attending with tonight looked forward to a gala, but each had their own reasons for attending. Maybe this wouldn't be such a bad night after all.

Particularly when Finlay held his arm out for me to take.

Even if I wasn't a real princess, maybe I could just play one for a little while.

"Look," I said and poked my sparkle trainers with hearts etched on them out from beneath my dress.

Finlay peered down, a wide smile breaking out on his face.

"There she is."

CHAPTER FOURTEEN

ORLA

It was worse than I had expected.

The night had begun on a promising note, and I'd been positively cheerful when we'd entered the large ball-room, certain that I was well equipped for the night ahead. I'd done some research on what to expect at a gala and had spent some time memorizing which fork to use at dinner.

What I hadn't known was the charity the gala was for.

I could have kicked myself.

How could I have spent all this time preparing for a charity gala and yet never asked what the charity was for?

To help end child hunger in Scotland.

Of all things.

Photos in stark black and white were blown up and plastered around the ballroom of children just like I'd been. Hungry. Scared. Angry.

They need you. The signs proclaimed. Yet they had it all wrong. We didn't need rich people to pity us. We needed a better system in place to support those of us who were forgotten by our families, the government, and our schools. The government cast a wide net, trying to help where they could, but still many slipped through the cracks.

Like me.

"Mother."

I turned, swallowing my nerves and pressing my lips together as a woman in a dove-gray gown and pearls glided to Finlay's side. Clutching his arm, she tilted her cheek for a kiss all while her eyes flicked over me from head to toe.

I'd been assessed, quickly, and now the questions would begin. Street instincts told me I was up against a powerful force, and the way Finlay's entire stance and energy had changed when his mother had drawn close told me a lot about him. I tightened the shawl I'd been given with the dress around my shoulders, a chill dancing across my skin.

"Finlay. Don't you just look so very handsome? You take after your father you know." Finlay's mother beamed up at him, but I noticed the lines around Finlay's mouth tighten at the mention of his father.

"So you've told me. I'm sure he would have loved this event."

"He did love a good party, didn't he?" Finlay's mother sighed and patted a hand to her chest before finally addressing me. "We lost Finlay's father a few years back and still miss him dearly."

"I'm sorry for your loss," I said automatically, picking up on some sort of tension that bounced between the two. Was it grief? Or something else?

"Yes, well, we must carry on, mustn't we?"

"Mum, this is Orla Clarke. Orla, my mother, Sharon Thompson."

"Lovely to meet you, Mrs. Thompson." I nodded my head, even though a part of me wondered if I should curtsy. But she wasn't the queen, was she? There was no need to curtsy.

"And you as well, Ms. Clarke. And how did you two meet?" The way she asked it seemed to suggest the answer would determine if she liked me or not.

"Orla is a business colleague of mine, Mum."

"Is that right? You're a businesswoman, are you?" Sharon's eyes sharpened in a way that I didn't like, and I opened my mouth to lie, but I caught a glimpse of green over Sharon's shoulder.

The Green Lady. She was here, gliding through the ballroom, leaving a trail of people glancing around as a draft of cold air drifted past them. Most never saw her, but many could feel her presence. She stopped behind Sharon, lifting her chin and crossing her arms across her chest, meeting my eyes. A proud stance.

Don't hide yourself from anyone, Orla. You've worked hard for what you've accomplished.

"I am." I tore my eyes away from the Green Lady and smiled widely at Sharon. "I'm also a builder. I run my own construction firm, Clarke Construction, and we're working on the buildout for Common Gin's new distillery in Loren Brae."

Sharon recoiled, ever so slightly, but enough that I caught it. Something flickered behind her eyes, and I knew I'd been instantly judged and dismissed.

The Sharons of this world and I did not mix. It was the first thought I'd had of Finlay, aside from noting how gorgeous he was, and now I understood why I'd had it. Even if he wasn't anything like his mother, he still came from her, didn't he?

That wasn't fair, I reminded myself. We couldn't judge others on the sins of their parents. Otherwise I wouldn't have much to say for myself, would I?

"A builder. How ... charming." Sharon sniffed, lifting her chin and looking over my shoulder, a smile blooming. "I'm going to have to excuse myself here shortly. Duty calls and the Stuarts just came in."

"Of course, Mum. We know how busy you are." Finlay took a step back, turning and nodding at a well-dressed couple approaching.

"Orla ... I can't put my finger on it. You look *so* familiar. Did you replace our toilet in the downstairs bathroom?" Sharon said this a touch louder than one normally would as the couple came to a stop next to us. Interest bloomed on the woman's face as she looked me up and down.

"No, Mum. She wouldn't have replaced your toilet. She's not a plumber. Orla does complicated high-level remodels for top businesses in the industry," Finlay inserted, his arm coming lightly to my back. I allowed the touch, mainly because he was putting his mother in her place, and I smiled up at him, knowing it would annoy Sharon.

"Of course, I'm not sure where I've seen you before then." Sharon turned, dismissing me, and held her hands out to the couple. "Darlings! So delighted you could make it."

"Let's refresh your drink." Finlay tugged me away before we got swept into another conversation, even though my drink was still full.

"*She's* lovely." I took a sip of my champagne, scanning the opulent ballroom, while forcing myself to keep my composure. It didn't matter what anyone in this world thought of me. These weren't my people.

I was just the help.

It was true, too, even if they paid highly for my services. At the end of the day, I was still just a builder completing a project for them and they'd never think twice about me again. I wouldn't be rubbing shoulders with them at the club over the weekend or laughing with the wives while our husbands took a round of golf.

I barely had time to do my crochet projects and listen to my podcasts, both of which I dearly wished I could be doing at the moment.

"She's a difficult woman who has become even more so after my father died in the arms of his mistress."

"Oh." I pressed my lips together again, lip liner be damned, and touched Finlay's arm. His expression was stony. "That's a tough blow."

"It was. I ... I lost more than my dad that day. I hated that he hadn't been transparent with who he was as a person. It matters, you ken? And this image I'd had of him all along, well, it wasn't real. And it shattered my mum. She's much better at keeping up images. I guess transparency isn't as important to her as it is to me. And now with no money to speak of, well, I'm stuck keeping her in the life she was accustomed to."

"She doesn't work?"

"She won't work. I don't think she's ever tried."

"Must be nice." I blinked down at my glass, realizing I said that part out loud, and hastily put the glass on the bar. I would need to slow down on the alcohol if I was to get through this. I was a lightweight at best and I would need my wits about me to not shove my foot in my mouth repeatedly.

"For her, yes, I quite imagine it is." Finlay shot me a wicked grin, and I warmed. "For me it's annoying."

"Yet you take care of her."

Finlay sighed, tipping his glass to his lips, his eyes roaming around the room.

"She's still my mum and it was tough to see her hurting."

"That's fair." I squeezed his arm lightly before turning to the room. "Why don't you dazzle me with all the gossip and tell me who is who?"

"That, my beautiful lady, I can do." Finlay drew me to the side and we looked across the ballroom. Women wore everything from slinky, figure-hugging dresses, to gowns with wide skirts, discreet beaded fascinators tucked in their hair. They glided to and fro, greeting friends, colorful birds flitting around the room, an endless display of pomp and circumstance. The men, too, were equally as handsome, most wearing kilts, and the variety of patterns and colors made for a dashing group gathered in the ballroom.

"See over here? The man with the thinning hair and green tartan? Word is he'll only eat Monster Munch with tomato soup for dinner."

"Really? That is ... well, quite shocking." I pretended to be scandalized as Finlay drew me closer to a table near the front of the ballroom. A stage stood in front of it, with a podium and a large projection screen, and I assumed there would be a talk of sorts tonight.

"Orla! Should we sit?" Lia waved to me, standing by the table, and I realized then we'd been assigned seats.

"We'll all sit for a speech. Then dinner and then dancing," Finlay explained, as he wound me through the crowd, his hand a light touch at my back. I passed poster after poster of photographs of hungry children and my heart skipped a beat when I thought I saw one of Jacob. Pausing, I peered closer, but realized it wasn't him.

It might as well have been.

Every image looked exactly like I'd remembered it and it was a stark reminder that no matter how far you ran, the past still would slap you in the face when you least expected it.

"I'm starving," Lia hissed in my ear, grabbing my hand. "The food had better be good or I'm going to revolt."

"Might be fun to watch," I said, pulling my eyes away from a photo of a group of kids sitting on stairs outside a shelter. *I know those steps.*

"I wouldn't be above flipping a table or two," Lia assured me as we sat. "I get wildly hangry."

My eyes went to the poster again.

I remembered being "*hangry*" too. Hunger so raw it clawed your stomach until you felt yourself withering away as your energy sapped. Yeah, being hungry could make a body angry, that was for certain.

As soon as we sat at our table, surrounded by so much wealth and opulence, my stomach had churned. Couldn't they see how much they were spending on this gala? All of this could have been used to feed needy children, not stroke the egos of those who were out there rubbing elbows and making business deals. This felt ... distasteful in a way that I couldn't rightly explain. I fell silent as Sharon strode to the podium and launched into a speech about the needs of hungry children in Scotland.

The entire contents of which was wildly off base.

Had she ever even *spoken* with a needy child in Scotland? Or gone to a soup kitchen? Fury licked through me, and I took a shaky sip of my wine, unsure how to react. Huge photographs of sad children projected behind her as she spoke, each image lingering for a while before it melded into the next.

"If only the children would be able to access the resources we have for them, we could better set them up for success."

I narrowed my eyes at Finlay's mum. Was she insinuating it was the child's fault for not eating the food provided? Had she even tried some of the meals offered? Depending on the place, I could tell you from experience, the meals weren't great.

But none of that mattered when you were starving. Food was food.

Sharon paused as the next image flashed on the screen and she turned, gesturing to it.

I froze.

It was a photo of me, taken without my consent likely, my T-shirt showcasing my ribs and boney arms, my ginger hair unmistakable. I leaned against a wall outside the soup kitchen, freezing cold likely, waiting for my cousins to finish eating. There was no mistaking who was in the photo, even if my body had since filled out and I was much healthier now.

A roaring filled my ears, my entire body flushing with heat, as Sharon turned back toward the microphone, her eyes zeroing in on me.

Lia whirled, her face wreathed in sympathy.

"Tonight, we're lucky enough to have a success story here in our very audience ..." Sharon began.

I didn't wait to hear what she was going to say next.

I refused to be paraded around, particularly without my consent, as some success story of a charity I'd never even heard of. *No one had ever turned their head to care for me. To offer me a soft bed, warm food, or shelter against the elements.*

That, I had done for myself.

The hypocrisy in Finlay's mother's *empathy* was only fueling my disgust.

My pain.

Jumping up, I dodged Finlay's attempt to grab my arm and slipped to the side of the room, taking the first door I could find. Panic gripped me, sweat dripping down the back of my dress, and I hit the stairs at a dead run.

Thank God Willow had let us wear trainers or I would have fallen head over heels down the steps.

I heard my name, but didn't look back, couldn't think, couldn't breathe, and when the Green Lady appeared in front of me, taking my hand, I allowed her to lead me out.

Once again, saving me.

By the time I broke outside into the cool night air, dusk still lingering, I welcomed the cold. A light mist drifted, kissing my cheeks, and I gulped for air on the steps outside the hotel.

"Orla."

I couldn't turn, couldn't bring myself to look at the sympathy I knew I would see in Finlay's eyes.

"I'm fine, Finlay. I just needed some air."

What I needed was for him to leave. I didn't need to see the pitying look on his face that had been mirrored around the room that evening every time someone had looked at a photo of the children at the soup kitchens. Did anyone ever stop to think that maybe the children should be asked if they wanted their photos taken and put on display like that? Bile rose in my throat.

"I'd ask for my mother to apologize to you, but it will be hard for her to speak after I murder her."

My eyebrows winged up and I turned, certain that Finlay would have made an excuse for his mother's behavior. Instead it sounded like he was defending me. Confused, I tilted my head and searched his face.

Finlay glanced around at a few people who had stepped outside for a smoke and reached forward to touch my elbow lightly.

"Come with me?"

I nodded, understanding he was sheltering me from the curiosity I had likely created when I jumped up and ran from the ballroom. Finlay drew me around the side of the hotel, and to a set of steps that led to one of the many narrow closes that ran through Edinburgh's main streets. I loved Edinburgh for that reason, as each close was like a portal to another secret world and would often duck off the main street and follow a winding lane to a hidden part of the city. Now, I was grateful for the relatively quiet and safe space it provided. Finlay glanced up as several waiters propped a back door open, stealing a smoke, and he looked back at me.

"Hold on just a second." Finlay went over to the waiters and drew out his wallet. I turned away, watching the mist drift through a streetlight that had just winked on, and rubbed my hands over my arms.

My skin burned.

I'd never felt so exposed in my life, and I had been on the receiving end of many pitying looks before. Growing up in poverty, I had grown used to the looks that adults gave me.

I had just thought I'd finally left most of that behind me.

I really hoped that Finlay wasn't getting me food from the waiters. It would just add insult to injury, and I didn't think I had it in me to explain to him why it would hurt so badly if he did.

"Here, come with." Finlay was back and I steeled myself, turning to find him brandishing a fancy bottle of champagne and two glasses. The breath left me. I could accept that offering, at least.

Finlay climbed a few steps to the stone landing and put the champagne and glasses on the ground before slipping out of his coat and placing it on the ground before I could stop him.

"Finlay! Your coat."

"I don't care." Finlay's words were clipped, and I wanted to argue with him about the fine wool being on the damp and dirty ground, but I had enough street smarts to understand when a man was barely containing his rage. Though Fin was entirely controlled, the tension spilled off him and I eased myself up the steps, uncertain of how to proceed. "Sit. Please."

I sat.

Finlay joined me, his shoulder not quite touching mine, but the heat from his body still brushed my skin. The arch over our heads caught much of the misting rain, and I stared glumly out at the dark steps that dropped below me, winding away into another part of the city. I could go down those steps and keep going, never looking back, and leave it all behind. I'd done it before, hadn't I?

The pop of the champagne jolted me and then Finlay handed me a glass, which I accepted, watching the bubbles rise in the golden liquid. I had no idea what to say.

"Orla. I truly have no words. I can't make excuses or explain my mother's behavior. That was cruel in a way that I can't ever forgive, and you'll have to excuse me if I can't quite find the correct response right now."

"It's fine." I shrugged a shoulder and took a sip of the champagne. It tasted like starlight.

"It's anything but fine. She's grown tough over the past few years, since we lost my dad, but I hadn't seen the cruel part. You didn't deserve to be put on display like that, nobody does."

"All of those children were," I said softly, turning the glass in my hands. "Every photo in there was someone like me."

"Had I known ... I never would have invited you, Orla. I wouldn't have exposed you to that."

At that, I laughed. Turning, I shook my head at him. He still didn't really get it.

"Exposed me to what? I've already been exposed, Fin. You can't grow up in poverty and not be constantly exposed. If the government isn't involved and prying in your life, school workers are. If not there, then it's photos at the soup kitchens. Growing up like that literally is about exposure. You have no privacy. Nothing to call your own. This?" I gestured with my glass toward the building. "This is nothing. Not in the big scheme of things."

"It was mean-spirited. Even if in some twisted way she thought she was being helpful, it was wrong. And it wasn't fair to you."

"Oh, Fin." I gave him a small smile before making a tsking noise. "Don't you know the world isn't fair?"

"No, but it can still be kind."

At that I stilled, meeting his eyes.

"Orla. I think you're incredible. You've entranced me from the first moment I met you. You're terrifyingly competent, brilliant at what you do, and you constantly leave me in awe of your capabilities. And your stunning beauty only adds to the package. The world may have been unfair to you, but all I see is a goddamned warrior. And I've come to realize that I quite fancy you."

I blinked, stunned at his words, even as my heart swelled in my chest. Did he just say he fancied me? *Me?*

"Me?" I whispered. "But why?"

"Didn't I just list the reasons?" Finlay reached out and traced a finger along the neckline of my dress near my shoulder. "No goldfish badge?"

"It's in my handbag," I whispered, his touch at my neck doing weird things to my stomach.

"Show me."

I reached for my bag, having grabbed it when I ran, but now remembering my shawl.

"Damn it, I'm going to have to go back for my shawl."

"I'll get it for you, Orla."

"You don't have to—"

"Let me take care of you." Finlay's tone had an underlying note that I couldn't quite discern, and I shifted, unsure how to respond to someone wanting to take care of me. It made me uncomfortable the same way that it did when Hilda fussed over me by trying to feed me copious amounts of food. Not saying anything, I unsnapped the closure to the little silk bag that Willow had made and showed Fin the goldfish badge pinned to the green and white striped lining.

"See? How could I not fancy a woman who wields a handsaw with no problem but pins a goldfish badge in her handbag?"

"Oh, Fin." I bumped his shoulder lightly with mine, needing to take the tension from the air. We were so very different, me and him. It was pointless to even go down this path. "You're very sweet."

"*Sweet*," Fin all but growled. "Just what every man wants to hear."

"You are though." I grinned as Fin cursed low. The tension gripping me shifted, the mood lightening a bit.

"I am fierce. Strong. Some might even say a ninja." Fin sliced the air with his hand and I laughed.

"Wow, I didn't even see that coming." I nodded approvingly.

"Did you see this coming?" Fin turned my chin up with a finger, his face hovering close. He waited, his eyes on mine.

He could have claimed, taken my lips without my consent, stolen a kiss on a dark staircase on a misty night in Edinburgh. Instead, he seemed to understand that I needed to be the one who gave myself *to* him. And because of that, his waiting, his innate understanding of what I needed, I closed the space between us.

It was just a kiss.

Or it should have been.

The moment my lips touched his, my skin tingled, as though I'd brushed against a live wire, and energy zipped through me. A deep-seated craving rose, and I gasped against his lips, reaching up to twine my fingers through his thick hair as Fin angled his head and deepened the kiss.

Here. Here was heat, here was desire, here was everything.

Him.

This man, whom I'd been painfully aware of since the day he walked onto my job site, kissed like a demon, promising me my wildest desires, while cradling me close and protecting me from the world. A man who would lay down an expensive coat on a dirty street and pay thousands of pounds to save puppies, yet kissed like he could strip you bare and had the key to your most wanton needs. An ache bloomed, a lovely liquid need, heat coiling low in my core, and I squirmed, my body wanting more.

Fin's hands stroked my back, his kiss demanding, yet

oddly slow. The more agitated I grew, the more he slowed, his tongue dipping into my mouth, his teeth scraping gently over my lip. He savored. Teased.

Tormented.

And I was on fire. I wanted all of him, even if just to make the memory of how I felt inside the ballroom burn to the ground.

"Orla." Fin pulled back, bringing his forehead to mine. "Bloody hell, you're magnificent."

"Fin …" I almost mewled in distress, wanting to climb into his lap and have him touch me everywhere. Never in my life had a kiss ignited such desire before and it raged through me, a need I didn't know how to fulfill.

A door opened behind us, voices filling the night air, and I was sharply reminded of where we were. Fin put his arm around my shoulders, pulling me into his body, sheltering me as a group of people walked past us down the steps.

"Can I see you to your room?"

There was no way we could linger longer on these steps, as the rain was beginning to fall in earnest now, and the gala would be ending at some point. The idea of bringing Fin back to my lush hotel room excited me and I looked up at him, surprised by just how much I enjoyed being wrapped in his arms.

Shelter in the storm, and all that, I realized.

"Orla! There you are." At Lia's voice, I turned and found her and Munroe hovering at the base of the steps, Munroe's coat over Lia's shoulders. "I've been looking everywhere. Are you okay?"

"Yes, I'm fine." I shifted, hoping to pull myself away

from Fin's arms in front of Munroe, but Fin only held me tighter. *Damn the man.* It was just a kiss. He didn't need to imply to my client that I was messing around with his employee.

"Lia, can you help her to her room? I need to go back into the gala."

Of course he did. He couldn't just abandon his mum's charity gala because of me. I knew saving face was important, even as disappointment rose. Either way, he'd been kind when he hadn't needed to be, and even if the kiss had been fantastic, it was time to pull back from where my thoughts had been going about taking Fin to my hotel room. At the end of the day, no matter how satisfying a night with him might have been, it was still just a temporary distraction from a shitty night. I had learned long ago that distractions were just that—and the pain would still be there after. What I needed to do was dive back into work, my only refuge, and not into the arms of one very sexy client of mine.

"Thank you," I said, squeezing his arm as I eased myself to standing.

"There's nothing to thank me for." Fin's face once again returned to hard lines. "I'll check on you later. I need to speak with my mother."

"Please don't do anything ... like over the top or anything." I didn't want this to become a big deal. "I'm fine. Really."

"I know you are. But she doesn't get to behave like that and not have it go unchecked."

"It's not worth it." From my understanding, people like his mum rarely changed.

"Come on, Orla. Let's get out of this rain. I've been dying to see what's on the room service menu." Lia hooked my arm and tugged gently.

"Wait, you shouldn't have to leave ..." I trailed off as Lia shot me a fierce look.

"I absolutely should. Munroe and I both agreed that was unacceptable. We're all going to put our comfies on and watch silly TV while eating our heart's worth of food from the room service menu. Understood?"

I opened my mouth to protest, but the Green Lady drifted close behind Lia.

Let them help you. It's what family does.

Too tired and too cold to protest much more, I let Lia tug me back toward the hotel. Looking back, I caught Fin's eye as he brushed his coat off.

"Thank you."

He just pressed two fingers to his mouth, reminding me of the kiss, and I turned, a smile at my lips.

CHAPTER FIFTEEN

FINLAY

It hadn't been pretty, to say the least.

The confrontation with my mother had resulted in me leaving Edinburgh earlier than planned, along with a warning to my mother about her behavior. She'd grown increasingly bitter since my father had died, but deliberately cruel was a new low that I wouldn't be able to forget.

In time, I might forgive her, but for now, I had clearly and carefully outlined why she was in the wrong and what my expectations of her were moving forward. I set hard boundaries, limiting her access in my life, and most importantly? I cut her off from my bank account.

If anything, that had seemed the one thing that had upset her more than anything. Not that she'd hurt my friend's feelings or embarrassed a woman that I greatly admired, but the fact that her endless stream of income was coming to an end was enough to send her into a rage.

It had been a difficult lesson for me to learn. It was hard to watch someone you loved make choices that didn't align with your vision of them, like I had with my father. She'd always just been my mum, and I'd been protecting her since Dad had died. In fact, all I'd done was enable her laziness and lack of ingenuity. Mum was still of working age, well-educated, and capable of getting a job—or another rich husband, which was the route she'd likely take now that I'd cut her off. For years now I'd been working myself incessantly, squirreling away every last pound to keep her in the lifestyle she was accustomed to. Over and over she'd reminded me that the Thompson name meant something, and appearances were everything.

One act by her had burned that all to the ground for me.

I no longer cared about our reputation, nor about being at the upper echelon of society. At the end of the day, none of that mattered if you grew cold and callous, which my mother had. I feared I'd follow suit if I allowed her to dominate the trajectory of my life, and though this one moment for me had been the catalyst in dismantling our relationship, in reality this had been building for years now. Frankly, I felt freer than I had in ages, and I'd turned the music up and sang at the top of my lungs the whole way home from Edinburgh.

Home.

That was another interesting thought that had struck me on the drive back. Loren Brae was increasingly beginning to feel like a place that I wanted to grow roots in, and though it was an unusual feeling for me, it wasn't entirely unwanted. I had friends here, a business that I could look after, and there was Orla.

Beautiful, sweet, brilliant Orla.

That photo of her as a little girl had ... gutted me. Not necessarily in pity, although there was a lot of that too. But *knowing* that the little girl had been so destitute, so bereft of a home, of love, had broken something inside me. *How did she do it? How did she rise against that? How did she succeed?*

And then there was that kiss. Did she have any idea how her kiss had knocked my knees out from under me? Had I not had to deal with my mother, I likely would have scooped her up and taken her back to her room, simply just to hold her for one second longer. She'd closed up on me, I saw it happening in real time when I'd said I'd had to see my mother, and now I needed to find her so that I could explain.

It was early evening when I pulled in front of her wee cottage, having gotten directions from Lia, and light beamed in the window. I'd gambled that she'd be home, knowing she'd likely gone directly to the site when she'd returned from Edinburgh, and had worked through the day. Picking up Orla's neatly folded shawl, plus a small gift bag, I got out of the car and crossed to the front door. The soft evening light brushed against clean stone walls, likely recently power-washed, and a pot of red geraniums stood at the front door.

I knocked with the doorknocker—a wrought iron Scottie dog—and waited as I heard shuffling inside. The door cracked, just an inch, and Orla's eye peered out at me.

"Hi."

"What are you doing here?" Orla opened the door a few inches wider, but didn't step back and welcome me in.

"Delivering the shawl you left."

"Oh, thanks—"

Orla made to reach for it, but I held it back. No way was she getting this shawl and pushing me out. I'd only just made a chink in her defenses, and I wasn't going to lose the leverage I'd gained.

"I also brought a gift."

"Oh, you don't have to buy me gifts, Finlay." Orla worried her bottom lip.

"It's not for you. It's for Goldie."

Orla narrowed her eyes at me, clearly considering if it would be rude to send me packing, and then sighed. Opening the door wider, she ushered me inside.

"Sorry, it's a bit out of sorts in here. I'm just catching up on some paperwork."

"Ah, yes, the never-ending joys of running a business." I gave Orla space, since I could tell she was feeling self-conscious, and glanced around her place. Even though it was just one room, at least from what I could see, she'd made great use of the space. There was a cozy sitting area with a comfortable-looking love seat, a narrow table covered in ledgers and a laptop pulled close, and soft music pulsed in the background. A candle warmed the space, scented lightly of cinnamon or pumpkin, I couldn't quite tell, and a see-through bookshelf separated her bed from the living area. It was cozy and welcoming, and perfectly neat. Orla took care of her stuff. "Need some help?"

I wandered closer to the piles of notebooks on her table and glanced down. Looked like payroll. She should really have someone handling this for her, considering how many hours she spent on the job.

"Of course not," Orla said, her back up. "I've got it."

"I never said you didn't. I just asked if you wanted some help."

"Why would you help me with business stuff? Don't you do enough of that on your own?" Orla asked, a suspicious note in her voice.

"I do." I turned to her and grinned. "But I'm scary good at it, which is why Munroe puts me on most of the difficult projects. My brain just seems to love spreadsheets and organizational tasks."

"Sophie claims to love spreadsheets too." Orla's expression now mirrored her suspicious tone.

"Yes, I've heard. I'm guessing they're not your favorite?" I pointed at the sofa. "Mind if I sit?"

"Yes, go ahead. Um, I guess I should offer you tea or something? I don't really have beer, but—"

"A cup of tea is just grand, thanks." Tea would give her something to do and keep me here longer, which I hoped would ease her nerves enough to talk about what had happened in Edinburgh. I'd done some reading on needy children in Scotland that morning, and even if Orla's experience hadn't been half as bad as what I'd read about, I imagined it had to be a traumatic history to recount—let alone get highlighted in front of hundreds of rich people. The look on her face was still burned into my heart. I never, ever, wanted Orla to feel that way again.

Which was quite a thought about someone that I'd only shared one kiss with.

The thing was? I was a risk taker. Calculated risks, I

should say, but a risk taker, nonetheless. I liked to operate on the belief that hard work and dedication would see me through, and because of that, I was more willing to jump when others weren't. I'd lost some of that when my father had died, and we'd learned who he was as a person. So much of my life I'd been working hard to please someone that I found I couldn't respect when I'd learned just who he was. Then I'd worked hard to care for my mother, someone else who had just lost my respect.

But Orla?

I had nothing but admiration for her. Even more so when I got a glimpse at what she'd come from. It made me want to get to know her more deeply, to be vulnerable with her in a way that I wasn't with most, and I could only hope she would allow me to do so. One thing I think I could understand was that many people had let Orla down in this world. I didn't want to be one of them. If I could keep showing up for her, maybe, just maybe, she'd let me in more.

"Is it payroll that's stressing you out? I've got a good service that can help with that."

"Services cost money," Orla said, from where she filled a kettle with water.

"They do, but your time is valuable. At some point you need to delegate some things, or you'll fall behind."

Orla sighed, putting the kettle on, and turned to me. She looked adorably rumpled today, in baggy sweatpants and a loose gray jumper, her hair piled on her head in a messy knot. I wanted to cross the room, pull her into my arms, and bury my face in the crook of her neck.

"I am falling behind. I just don't have the time to hire

anyone because I don't have the time to see where I need to hire."

"Ahhh, you need a manager." I rubbed my hands together gleefully. "Right in my wheelhouse. Let's talk it out and I can offer some tips?"

"Finlay." Orla rolled her eyes as she put two mugs on a tray. "I can't afford your advice, or likely the services that Common Gin uses to streamline their business. I'm working on a far different budget here."

"Doesn't matter. There's always an answer. Your time is valuable. So first you need to look at where your time is best spent. What can you do that nobody else can do?" I wanted to keep her distracted with questions so she would keep talking to me.

"Manage the crew, oversee the work, build, payroll, work with the clients." Orla ticked the items off on her fingers.

"And which of those is most important to you?"

"Clients, crew, building."

"That's fine, so we'll list those as your top focused tasks. See the thing is that you have to assign a value to your time. For example, say your time is worth one hundred pounds an hour, well, then you need to start looking at tasks that you are doing that aren't worth that, and begin to find ways to delegate or streamline those tasks."

"Huh." Orla brought the tea over on a small tray and sat next to me. I was grateful it was a love seat because it forced her to be closer to me. "I never thought about it like that."

"You often don't have to think like that until your business grows to a tipping point where you're forced to hire more help or take fewer projects. Which would you like it to be?"

"I don't want to take less projects because I just hired more crew and I know they're depending on me."

"Then you need to hire more help. Let's talk it out. What do you absolutely despise doing?"

Orla nodded to the ledgers.

"Payroll."

"That's easy enough. I can give you some recommendations for affordable services that will make the process easier for you. What's the next biggest time suck?"

"Admin, likely. Answering emails. Speaking with clients. There's a lot of hand-holding and I want to make sure the clients feel heard and we're nailing their vision."

"Would a good customer service manager be able to answer some of those questions? It might not be everything, but at the very least they could run interference and maybe provide a tailored list of questions for you at the end of the day?"

"That ... that would be good. A lot of my time is spent responding to texts or emails that ping my phone."

"You're too available."

A hint of a smile came to Orla's lips. "That's the first time I've heard that."

"If you don't mind sharing some numbers, I might be able to create a budget for you based on recommended software programs and potential salaries for an admin person. Would that help?"

Orla leaned back, crossing her arms over her chest, and looked at me.

"Are you doing this because you feel bad for me?" Her

eyes were wary, her shoulders hunched. She reminded me a touch of a wounded animal.

"Why would I feel bad for you? Other than your taste in Caley Thistle."

"What?" Orla's eyes rounded and she whirled to see her jersey hanging on a hook by the door. "They're a great football team."

"If you like losing."

"We're Scottish, it's a rite of passage," Orla grumbled, and I threw back my head and laughed.

"True enough."

"Seriously though ... why are you trying to help? Is it because of what happened? I'm fine, you know. It isn't a big deal."

Exposing someone's past in a room with two hundred people was certainly not nothing, but I kept my tone light.

"Do you not like when people offer to help?"

"I can't say it's my favorite, no."

"But we're friends. And I love this stuff. Indulge me." I held my hand out to the table and waited until Orla sighed and leaned forward, plopping a book into my hand.

"I can't believe this is exciting for you."

"Never have I been more turned on. A beautiful woman and business ledgers? I'm in paradise here, Orla."

Orla's cheeks flushed, the curse of a redhead, I supposed, but I loved seeing it because I knew she was affected by my words. She smiled into her tea, not meeting my eyes, and I bit back a grin. I knew I had to take this slow with her, so I'd savor what moments I could that brought a smile to her face.

An hour later, I had a tidy list of to-dos for Orla to look

over. She'd largely kept quiet, working on her own tasks, but did answer any questions I had as I reviewed some of her larger pain points. It was cozy, working in this space, and I was deeply relaxed by the time I handed her my list.

"This is just a start. But I didn't want to overwhelm you." I leaned close to the notepad as she looked it over, her shoulder brushing mine. "See here? I've separated things by top recommendations as well as by potential budget as well as heavy lifting needed to execute the task. That way you can evaluate which one you want to tackle first based on budget or time restraints."

"This is smart." Orla nibbled her lower lip as she read the list, nodding in agreement. "And really useful. Thanks, Fin."

"Of course. Once you've gotten through this, I'll have a look and offer you the next level of recommendations."

"I'll pay you a consulting fee, of course." Orla looked up at me as I brushed a finger across her cheek, tucking a piece of hair back behind her ear.

"Nope."

"Why not?" Orla demanded.

"Because I don't want to introduce that type of element into our relationship."

"We don't have a relationship, Fin." Orla glared at me, leaning back and away from me. Luckily it wasn't far, being a love seat and all.

"Don't we?"

"We most definitely do not." Orla emphasized each word.

"We see each other most days. We enjoy each other's company. We're attracted to each other. And we've kissed.

185

The kind of kiss that will keep me up for many a night aching for more."

Orla's perfect pink mouth rounded into an O.

"Or maybe it wasn't as good a kiss for you? Should we try once again?"

"What? No, it was great. I mean, wait ..." Orla waved her hands in front of her face, fanning her skin. "My brain is short-circuiting."

"Is it because of my masculine presence? I do tend to overwhelm the ladies with my charisma." I flexed an arm muscle and Orla made a sound somewhere between a laugh and a choke.

"Should we try again? See if we both think it is just as good?"

"For what purpose?" Orla asked.

"For enjoyment? For fun?"

"Fun?" Orla arched a brow at me.

"Don't you find kissing to be fun?"

"I don't know that I've given it much thought, but yes, I guess kissing is fun."

"Well, you've finished work for the day, haven't you? That would mean time for fun."

"My after-work projects are crochet and listening to serial killer podcasts."

"Ah yes, I remember. You hold spikey instruments and learn about how people kill each other. A laugh a minute, I'm sure."

"Cheeky, aren't you?" Orla narrowed her eyes at me.

"Cute. Endearing. Sexy. Handsome ... I'll also accept those descriptors."

"Fine, just one. It's best to get it out of our systems and

then I can rid you of this notion that we're in a relationship."

"I wholeheartedly agree with this plan." I didn't want to point out the flaw in her logic that kissing someone again rarely disavowed a relationship, as then I'd talk myself out of a kiss, which would just be plain stupid after thinking about it constantly since I'd left her.

I moved slowly, inching slightly forward, and cradled her face in my hands.

"Impossibly beautiful. Your eyes look like mini universes. Incredible, up close, the depth they have."

"I don't need pretty words, Fin."

Oh yes, she most certainly did. Because I suspected that nobody had taken care with her before.

"Luminous skin. I love when it flushes pink after I've said something that excites you. Like now." I brushed a thumb across her bottom lip, and Orla's eyelashes feathered across her cheeks. "A perfectly pink mouth, with lips made for mine."

Her breath came out of her lips in a soft whoosh, warm and wet against my finger, and I couldn't hold back anymore. Leaning forward, I captured her lips with my own, sinking into the kiss as the world stilled around me.

I'd been right to think Loren Brae might become my home. All lingering doubt left my mind as Orla's kiss ignited me, a need to possess growing inside of me. Angling her head, I deepened the kiss, needing a taste of her. She surprised me, like she had the other night, by meeting me head on, her hands threading through my hair.

It drove me a little wild when a woman grabbed my hair like that.

When she crawled into my lap, straddling me, I let her, just happy to have her closer to me. I brought one arm around her back, supporting her, and traced my hand down her side. She was tiny, but so very strong, and her thighs gripped me as she rocked back and forth, lost in the kiss.

I wanted to spear upward, to drive myself into her, to take us both over the edge that we clearly so craved.

But I also knew that if we went that route, quick to bed, she'd also likely move me quickly out the door. If Orla hadn't had a lot of relationships in her life, then keeping things casual was likely the most emotionally safe route for her. I didn't want to be someone she dismissed quickly.

I wanted her, in every way, in my life.

And to do so, I had to make sure she didn't push me out.

As much as it killed me, I broke the kiss and pulled her to my body, simply holding her.

"What are you doing?" Orla's voice was breathy at my ear.

"It's called a hug, Orla."

"Why are you hugging me?"

"Because it feels nice."

"But other things were feeling nicer." To prove her point, Orla rubbed against where I'd grown hard in my trousers. I groaned, turning to press a kiss to her hair. "Keep doing that, darling, and I'll be embarrassed to walk out of here."

"We could—"

"Wheesht. Just try this for a moment." It wasn't surprising that a hug might seem more intimate to Orla than sex. Hugs were a vulnerable place to be with someone

188

you cared for and required a level of trust. Orla stayed tense in my arms, and I continued to lightly stroke her back, holding her in place, until I could feel her body begin to relax against mine. Only when the tension had eased from her, molding her into a loose pile over me, did I turn my head so I could brush a soft kiss over her lips.

"See? Not so bad, is it?"

"You told me you brought a present for Goldie."

Changing the subject, I noted, but allowed it. I considered my time here tonight a win. I'd become sharply clear on what I wanted for the future, and Orla didn't seem to hold resentment against me for my mother's behavior.

"So I did. You'll have to introduce me." I toyed with a lock of her hair that had tumbled out of her scrunchie. "I want you to know the only reason I left you on the steps was to confront my mother. She needed to know that her behavior was unacceptable. I've cut her off, just so you know."

"Fin!" Orla tried to rear back, but I held her tight until she grumbled and nestled into my arms again. "You don't have to cut your mother out because of me."

"I put up boundaries, for many reasons, one of which was for her cruelty. It was time for me to protect my own mental health, as well as that of the people that I care about. No longer will I cater blindly to someone who doesn't truly love me."

"Oh, Fin. I'm sorry. That must be such a hard line to draw."

"We'll see how it goes. She didn't take it well, but her own actions caused this."

"But is she your only family? Don't you want to hang on to that?"

I met Orla's eyes, bringing my hand up to hold her cheek.

"Wouldn't you say we get to make our own families? If we choose to?"

"Aye, I'd agree with that."

Orla surprised me by leaning forward and pressing a soft kiss to my lips, both a promise and a reassurance. She might not be thinking what I was thinking, about our future, but she clearly sensed something more was there. I would take what I could get for now.

"Now, are you ready to introduce me to Goldie?"

"It depends on the gift. If it's shite, she might not want to meet you."

"I would never bring a shite gift for Queen Goldie." I held a hand to my chest in mock distress.

"Well, in that case, let's see it."

"Bag is right there." I kept Orla on my lap as she leaned over and picked up the small gift bag. She took her time opening it, carefully unfolding the tissue, and I realized she was savoring the moment, as well as the paper. She'd use it all again, I realized, much unlike how my mother ripped open presents and tossed the wrapping away. This simple realization made me want to give Orla the world.

"A pirate ship?" Orla held it up to the light.

"Aye. It floats on top and she can bump it to get fish flakes out. It's meant to be a wee way to stimulate them, or so the shop owner assured me."

"She'll love this." Orla grinned at me like I'd just gifted

her with a diamond and sprung up off my lap. "Let's see what she thinks."

I crossed to the bookshelf with Orla and smiled at a wee goldfish doing circles in a large bowl with clean water, colorful gemstones on the bottom, and a few pieces of greenery to hide in.

"Look, Goldie. Your own ship." Orla tapped the glass and the fish did a wild spin around the bowl. I smiled as Orla took out a jar of fish flakes and added them to the boat. "Goldie, this is Fin."

"Pleased to meet you, Your Highness." I gave the fish a subtle bow and Orla chuckled as she plopped the ship on top of the water.

"Oh look." Orla grabbed my arm as Goldie instantly investigated the ship, bumping it with her head. When a few flakes drifted out, she ate them and raced a circle around the bowl before bumping it again. "Oh, Fin. She really likes it."

Orla gave me an adoring look and I all but preened under her happiness. Had I known a simple toy for her fish would make her so happy, I would have bought the whole damn store. Orla deserved joy, and I now knew two things.

The first was that I wanted her in my life.

And the second? That I was determined to keep showing up for her, because keeping a smile on her face was now my new favorite life goal.

CHAPTER SIXTEEN

Orla

Finlay was driving me crazy.

He popped up when I least expected it, stealing kisses left and right, disappeared, and then I wouldn't see him for ages. Which of course, made me look for him more, and then he'd surprise me with stopping by to steal a kiss or to tell me a funny story.

Every day he asked me for a date.

And every day I told him no.

It had been over two weeks since the gala in Edinburgh, and somehow Finlay had managed to unofficially have a date with me, in some capacity, almost every day since we had kissed. Usually it was bringing me a bite to eat at lunch or sharing an after-work soda and a snack while we talked about the updates to the site project. Well, *he* insisted they were dates. I ignored him because a proper date would be one where he asked me out, I accepted without taking any form of payment for doing so, and we did a proper activity or had a meal together. As such, I was convinced we weren't dating, but just having a wee flirt.

I was having fun.

Something I hadn't given much thought to in my life between work and trying to make ends meet. But flirting with Finlay was fun. And every night, while I watched Goldie play with her new ship, I tried to remind myself that I deserved to have fun. I was allowed to ease back here and there, wasn't I? Take a break. Leave work early. Have a holiday.

None of which I'd done yet, but I was working myself up to it.

Sweaty, and covered in sawdust, I finished cutting a beam for a door frame, and straightened, dusting my gloved hands on my overalls.

"Orla."

"Bloody hell." I whirled, shaking my head at Fin. The man had me so distracted on the job that I was daydreaming now. Usually I wasn't so jumpy when people approached me as the way of construction sites was constant interruption.

"Sorry. I waited until you were done with the big, violent scary tool thing."

My lips quirked. Fin liked to pretend that he didn't know any of the tools on-site and hated getting his posh clothes dirty, but I'd learned this was just an act. Even if he didn't know how to use a tool, it never stopped him from getting down and dirty or lending a hand when needed.

The crew respected him, as did I, and I could see why Munroe had brought him in to manage the buildout.

"Smart choice. I wouldn't want to slice an appendage off."

"Particularly a useful one." Fin wiggled his eyebrows at my look. "What? I find my hands to be quite useful."

"Mm-hmm." We both knew what appendage he was referring to.

"I've come to formally ask you on a date for tomorrow afternoon in Shona's garden. We'll be picking raspberries, eating homemade jam, and enjoying a proper picnic. The weather forecast promises no rain and it would be a shame to use the first proper sunny day for work. Plus, it's a Saturday, so you shouldn't be at work. You're allowed to have a life."

I opened my mouth to automatically tell him "no" but caught a glimpse of the Green Lady drifting over Fin's shoulder. She'd been more active of late, coming around to scold me on my choices, more vocal in her opinions of the decisions I was making. It appeared she was a big fan of Fin, and I couldn't help but wonder if she'd loved someone like Fin back in her time. She certainly fancied his looks.

It was hard not to. Today he wore dark denim trousers and a chambray shirt rolled at the sleeves, showcasing his muscular arms. I wanted to unbutton his shirt and lick my way down his chest. He was driving me crazy with all these wee kisses, leaving me breathless and wanting more, but refusing to have a casual hookup with me either. I was certain we just needed to scratch an itch, work it out of our systems, and both move on with our lives. He'd be going back to Edinburgh and I'd carry on with life here. I was a small-town girl. He was a big-city boy. Tale as old as time and all that.

You deserve a proper date. He's taking care with you. Let him.

I did my best not to glare at the Green Lady behind Fin's back because he didn't need to think that I was strange for seeing apparitions. That was another thing I worried about. What would Fin think if I ever told him that, apparently, I was a house witch that could see ghosts and help trapped spirits move to the next realm? It wasn't something one just brought up over a casual cup of tea.

"You're relentless, aren't you?"

"Come on, darling. Live a little. It's just a wee picnic on a bonnie day in Scotland. What say you?"

"Aye."

I grinned as Fin's mouth dropped open in surprise. He glanced quickly around, making sure none of my crew were near, before stalking toward me until I was backed against a wall. Surprising me, he pinned both of my hands against the wall and slid his leg between mine before dipping his head to take my mouth in a hungry kiss.

It shocked me, this need I had for him. It had come out of nowhere, blossoming on the night of the gala, and I'd been doing my best to ignore it over the past few weeks. Yet it was like the more I tried to pretend it wasn't happening, that I wasn't falling for Fin, the more my attraction seemed to grow. Which why I just wanted to get this whole thing out of my system. We could have some fun together as adults and move on. Whatever this dance he was doing with me was not what I had in my plans.

And still.

Still my heart swelled when he deepened the kiss. Still my blood thundered in my veins when he shifted his thigh, brushing against me. Still desire pooled low as I squirmed against him, delicious friction warming between my legs.

When he broke the kiss, we were both gasping for air, and he reached down to subtly adjust himself.

"Don't blame me for that." I pointed to his trousers. "You brought that on yourself."

"I was just so excited you finally said yes to a date. I couldn't help myself."

"Well, now you have to walk it off before one of the crew sees you." I slid my eyes down to the admirable bulge in his trousers. I couldn't help it, I licked my lips and he groaned.

"That's not helping the situation, Orla."

"Sorry. It's just that you're very well endowed."

"Gee, thanks. Only you would say it all prim and proper like that."

"Would you prefer I say something crass like I admire your thick schlong? Your bulging cock makes me want to—"

He had me pinned back against the wall before I could say more, his mouth on mine, wet and hot, and I moaned as he licked inside. My body trembled at his touch, and I wanted to wrap my legs around him and ride him until neither of us could think straight anymore. When he finally broke the kiss, I mewled in distress, and he hovered over me, his arms still caging me.

"You're doing my head in, Orla."

"Which one?" I asked cheekily, and he laughed.

"Both. And as much as I want to bend you over that

sawhorse and peel off those overalls to reveal every delicious inch of your body, I'm afraid the crew would be a touch distressed if I did so."

"Mmm, likely so," I agreed, though the image of him bending me over, anything, really, was making my legs shake.

"Tomorrow. Two at Shona's. Can you meet me there? I have to stop somewhere first."

"No problem." I liked driving to my dates anyway. That way if I needed an easy out, I didn't have to rely on anyone else. Typical for me, never wanting to rely on anyone. It wasn't even whether I wanted to or not. I'd just learned to fend for myself at a young age. That being said, it would give me time to get to know Shona a bit better and I might even get to meet one of those gnomes of hers.

Which, of course, I'd have to hide from Fin. Maybe I'd go a touch early then just to have a wee private chat with her.

"Boss?" A call from the other side of the work site came and I ducked under Finlay's arms, patting him on the shoulder.

"Gotta run. Best to take a moment here if needed."

"Or an ice bath," Fin said.

"A quick dip in the loch might sort you out."

"I'll keep that in mind. See you tomorrow for our first official date. Should I start calling you my girlfriend?"

I whirled in the doorway, my mouth dropping open. Finlay gave me a shit-eating grin.

"We are *not* in a relationship."

"Aren't we though?"

"I don't have time for this." I left before he could tie my

thoughts up again, or we'd get stuck in one of his ridiculous loops of banter.

By the time the next afternoon rolled around, my stomach was a bundle of nerves.

I changed my outfit three times before getting fed up with myself and leaving the house in a flurry of annoyed outbursts. It wasn't even like I owned that many clothes, let alone date-night type clothes, so I was a touch annoyed with myself for changing so many times. I'd finally settled on jeans and a dark blue scoop-neck long-sleeved top. I didn't really know how to use makeup, let alone owned any, so I just plaited my hair back as usual and left before I got in my head about having to try out different hairstyles for Fin.

He'd told me he liked me just as I was—in my overalls and covered in sawdust, hadn't he? The man had seen me at my most glamorous and had told me he preferred me just as I was. I was going to take his word on that, because I truly didn't have any fancy or flirty date outfits. Maybe I'd speak to Willow about gently introducing a few into my rotation, as my budget allowed, so long as they were serviceable and could be worn for other things.

Pulling up at Shona's gardens, I grinned. She stood outside, cradling a hedgehog in her arms and looking beautiful in jean overalls and a button-down shirt, with a sun hat clamped firmly on her head. She was all earthy goddess, and I could see why Owen had fallen for her. I'd met her partner recently, a filmmaker, before he'd jetted off to work on some project or another. He basically doted on Shona and it was sweet to see.

"Who is this cutie?" I asked, peering close at the wee hedgie. He poked his head out from where it was buried in the crook of Shona's arm and gave me a lopsided grin before burrowing his way back into the folds of her shirt.

"This is Eugene and he's very annoyed by that hot ball of light in the middle of the sky. I was just off to tuck him into his wee nest before you arrived. Come with?"

"This place is grand, Shona. I can't believe how big it is."

"Aye, we've expanded back quite a bit and have plans for more. We'll see how it goes along. I'm working on asking for more help, but that's a challenge in its own right. It used to be just me and a few part-time helpers, but I'm beginning to grow into a full-time operation. Thank God I cut back on the weddings."

"Did you supply for catering?"

"Nope, wedding flowers." Shona nodded toward one of two greenhouses set behind her pretty stone cottage. "That second one is all flowers. My gran loved flowers, and I couldn't help but follow suit. But I think I got in over my head with weddings. I'll still do some here and there, but I much prefer selling bunches of flowers and herbs at the market than the stress of wedding planning."

"I don't blame you. It sounds like it would be intense. I wouldn't even know where to start with all the color coordinating and matching dresses and so on."

"And I wouldn't know how to build a house, so I'm equally as impressed."

"You start at the foundation." I held the door to the greenhouse open so Shona could slip inside, cradling Eugene in her arms.

"Isn't that the way of it for most things in life?"

There wasn't much I could say to that, as I had to

agree, even if my own personal "life" foundation had been shaky at best. But that was the good thing about knowing how to build things. I could always shore up a foundation, fix it, make it stronger. Which was exactly what I was doing here, in Loren Brae, by joining the Order of Caledonia. I supposed I was building a house of sorts, built on friendships and trust, that would enable a stable future for me.

"She's good, Gnorman. One of us."

I whirled my head around from admiring Shona's expansive and healthy greenhouse, all bright light and humid air, greenery crawling every which way, to see a gnome statue on the table.

"For flower's sake, Shona. Warn us. I was about to have a picnic with Gnora."

My mouth dropped open as the statue shifted, morphing into a living, breathing thing. He wore a kilt, had tattoos lining his muscular arms, and a tiny leather biker vest buttoned to his beard.

"I did warn you. Earlier today when I said I had friends coming over. At which point Gnora reminded you that you never take *her* on picnics, and you got in a huff about it, and now, apparently, you're taking her on a picnic and you've forgotten that we have guests coming."

"How dare you suggest that I never take Gnora on picnics. I always—"

Gnorman trailed off as another gnome sauntered out of the bushes, this one dressed in a figure-hugging pencil skirt in leopard print, with a leather bustier that enhanced her curves. Spying me, she blew me a kiss before crossing her arms over her ample chest and giving Gnorman a look.

"You always what, Gnorman? When was the last time you took me on a picnic?"

"But ... but ... it's been raining for weeks now. It's spring. You said you didn't like the wet grass getting on your skirt."

"So you put down a blanket, don't you then?"

"Gnora, darling, you know I'd do anything for you." Based on his imploring tone and begging eyes, I suspected what the wee gnome was saying was true.

"Anything?" Gnora purred, a gleam in her eye.

"Anything," Gnorman promised, stepping closer to her. Gnora leaned over and whispered something in his ear, and the gnome's eyes widened, his cheeks pinkening. Turning, she sauntered off, a healthy swing in her step making every curve move, and then she disappeared back into the greenery.

"Right, well, I've just got to ..." Gnorman cleared his throat, glancing between me and where Gnora had disappeared into the plants. "Sorry to run, but ... erm, well. My name's Gnorman, with a silent G."

"Orla," I said, biting back a grin.

"Enjoy your picnic and all. Don't mess up my plants or I'll send my army after you." Gnorman raised a warning finger up at me before turning and running into the bushes after Gnora.

"And those are my gnomes," Shona said, with a laugh. Bending, she tucked the sleeping hedgehog into a nest of blankets in a box under the table, and he burrowed right in, nuzzling in next to another hedgie.

"Och, they're pretty incredible, no? I don't even rightly know what to think. Every time I think I'm growing comfortable with all this magick stuff, something new comes to basically show me that I know nothing about it at all. I mean, I would have bet money he was a statue when I came in. Not a live being. He looked just, completely fake."

"It's his resting gnome face. He does it well. They all do. There's quite a network of them, from what I can determine. They each have their own wee territories, based on our different gardens, and occasionally I drive them around to meet up with the others since they can't travel far on their wee legs."

"You facilitate clandestine gnome meetings?" I grinned at Shona's laugh.

"Something like that. Nothing much happens except they moan about how we're all ruining their gardens and that cats are the bane of their existence."

"Cats? Not dogs?"

"Dogs, yes, because they'll run up and pee on them sometimes, which I can imagine is pretty disgusting."

I gasped, covering my mouth with my hand. I would *so* not want to get peed on.

"I know, right? I don't blame the gnomes for being grumpy all the time." Shona laughed and leaned back against the table. "But the cats ... they are cunning. Even when the gnomes freeze, they seem to sense there's something more. So they mess with them, toy with them, you know?"

"Yeah, I could see that." A car door slammed outside.

"Sounds like Finlay is here. I've got a nice spot all set up for you two in the back." Shona's eyes gleamed. "How's that all going then?"

I opened my mouth to say this was just a nothing, a no

big deal thing, but I stopped. I shouldn't brush it off, not when Finlay was making a concerted effort, and when I knew in my heart of hearts that this was something more. Something was building between Finlay and me, a something that I couldn't ignore, and if I wanted to build friendships with these women who I now shared magick with, then I needed to open myself more even if it felt at odds with what I was used to doing.

"I don't know what to think of it all. He's a bit overwhelming, if I'm to be honest with you. He's ..." I bit my lip as I thought about Finlay. "Confident. Sure of himself in ways that I wish I could be. He navigates different worlds with ease where I would stumble, you know?"

"I get it. Owen's kind of like that. He just expects things to work out for him and they do."

"Yes! That's it."

"Annoying, isn't it?" Shona laughed.

"Totally. And now I feel like I'm kind of one of those things, you know? Just something he'll expect to work out. And I'm scared, I guess." I brought a hand to my heart, tapping my chest. "Like, scared it's going to leave a hole that I can't patch back up." *And I don't know if I can lose another person I care about.*

"Och, I so get that." Shona stepped forward and pulled me into a hug. I stiffened before relenting and hugging back. She pulled back, her hands on my arms, her blue eyes warm and friendly. "But from the little you've shared, it sounds like you've had a rough go of it growing up, right?"

"I have."

"So if you can get through all that, and still remain

standing, nae, flourishing ... I mean, you can get through this, right? Even if he ends up hurting your heart?"

"I guess I could. But why put myself through it if I'll just get hurt?"

"Because what if you don't?" Shona peered at me, and her words hit home. I was so used to anticipating disaster and shielding myself from it that I rarely considered what would happen if things worked out well. It was easier to prepare myself for the worst and be surprised at a happy outcome than the other way around, and I'd spent my life building nice thick walls to cushion my fall.

"Then ... we'd just be together?" Saying it out loud honestly shocked me. I'd never truly considered the possibility of Fin and me as an actual couple existing in the world. At best I'd thought we'd have a few weeks of fun while he was on the project, but now Shona had me thinking about having a real relationship with him. "He does keep asking me to be his girlfriend."

"See?" Shona pounced, her eyes lighting up. She poked my arm. "Listen to him. The man is telling you he's interested."

"Interested and being in a relationship are two different things, Shona. I just ..." I shook my head, trying to keep my voice clear as I said the next part. "Everyone leaves, Shona. It's the only thing that I know."

"Oh, Orla." Shona pulled me in for another hug and I was surprised I didn't jump out of my skin at all this affection. It was far past what I was used to receiving. "Nothing in life is permanent, you know? You gotta just grab on to the good and hold it close while you can. It's the best anyone can do, really."

Shona's words resonated with me as I left the green-house to meet Finlay at his truck. He was speaking to someone that I couldn't see, the passenger door open, and my heartbeat sped up at the sight of him.

Finlay was a good man. And Shona did say I needed to grab on to the good while I could. Turning, Fin saw me, and a grin split his face.

My stomach twisted as my heart cracked open a bit.

"There's a bonnie lass on a pretty spring day. I figured instead of flowers I'd bring you something better." Fin turned and spoke down to the truck again, and then I gasped as a furry beast jumped onto the ground and raced for me.

"Harris!"

"I sprung him from the shelter for an afternoon activity. He'd told me how much he'd miss you visiting him today, so I invited him along on our picnic."

"Oh buddy, it's *so* good to see you."

Yup, I was toast. This man knew what I'd needed even before I had. Having Harris there would ease my nerves on our first date, plus, it was damn sweet of him to bring my favorite shelter dog along for the picnic. I bent to accept Harris's delighted licks, scratching his ears and taking the lead that Fin handed me. He hurried around the truck and grabbed a cooler and a shopping bag. Hands full, he came up beside me, a grin on his face.

"I can't decide who is happier to see you—me or him."

I mean, what was I supposed to say when he said things like that? He just kept chipping away at my walls, ever determined. Sighing, I leaned up on my tippy-toes and planted a kiss on his lips. His surprised gasp made me smile, and I laughed a little against his lips.

"Damn it, Orla, I picked the wrong time to carry all the stuff from the car."

"Nope, this is just right." Desire threaded through me as I deepened the kiss, enjoying having the control, letting the moment linger between us as we stood in the gardens, a dog lead wrapped around my legs, his hands full of picnic stuff. As kisses went, it was perfect.

Now, I just needed to figure out if I was cut out for this whole falling in love thing. It seemed I was heading that way, even if I wasn't fully ready to admit it. And because I had no blueprint to follow, that alone made me nervous.

"Woman, you'd better stop now before I drop this on our feet and haul you into the back seat."

I laughed against his lips and pulled back, looking into his smiling eyes.

"Nope, I was promised a proper date. Let's see if you've nailed it."

"Challenge accepted."

CHAPTER SEVENTEEN

Finlay

It took everything in my power not to scoop Orla up and carry her home with me. There was something about her that made me want to protect her, even though I admired how confident and capable she was. It was just those glimpses of vulnerability she'd shared with me, a hesitancy to give more of herself, that made me want to show up for her.

Like many people hadn't in her past.

I'd spent some time over the past couple of weeks reading up on foster children, or those raised in poverty, and I was beginning to understand why Orla was distrustful of me. Or at the very least, not willing to jump into a relationship with me no matter how often I jokingly called her my girlfriend. Why should she trust me? I was new to her, and it sounded like many pivotal people in her life had failed her.

This knowledge had only strengthened the decision that I had finalized this morning. Now, I just had to settle in for the long game and see how it went. I had all the time in the world now, so long as Orla kept giving me a chance. As far as I could tell, she was worth it.

"Our first official date," I said, as I lugged the food toward the picnic table that Shona had set up under a tree, the branches lightly shading the spot from the sun that had decided to make an appearance for once. "And the sun shines upon us."

"You think it's giving us its blessing then?" Orla grinned at me from where she walked with Harris, who was taking his time to sniff and inspect each bush along the way. I couldn't blame the dog, it was likely far more interesting than the smells he was used to in the shelter.

"And why wouldn't it? A happy couple, enjoying a braw spring day."

Orla stiffened at my words, but I was getting used to her standoffishness and was learning to navigate her reactions. Once I understood where much of it was coming from, it made it easier for me to accept and adapt to her needs. I followed her gaze to where Harris had frozen, his head cocked at a gnome statue.

"Harris. No," Orla hissed, tugging at his lead. Harris twisted his body, moving to lift his leg. "No, Harris, *no.*"

She tugged, but the dog was stubborn, and the leg raised higher.

Seconds before the stream of pee would hit the statue, Orla managed to pull the dog back so it only splattered at the feet of the wee gnome. I could have sworn the statue's face grew angrier, but surely that was just my imagination, and I bit back a laugh.

"Harris! No peeing on the nice garden statues," I said to the dog, dropping the cooler on the table. "Here, I brought you a toy."

Orla was bent over the statue, whispering, and I squinted at her.

"All good there?"

"Och, just apologizing to the wee ... I mean, just seeing if any got on the statue." Orla gave me a guilty look. "Shona's been so kind to have us, I'd feel bad for Harris ruining one of her things."

"It looked like you caught him in time."

"Stubborn boy." Orla ruffled Harris's ears and took the tennis ball I handed her. "Up for some ball?"

Harris jumped, wriggling his body in delight, and it seemed he was indeed up for some ball. Orla tossed it across the grass and Harris took off running, chasing it down before racing back, his ears flopping in the wind.

"Oh just look at him go! He's so happy. Thank you, Fin. He needed this."

"Looks like you both did."

"I think you're right." Orla beamed as Harris dropped the already sloppy ball at her feet. "I love him so much."

I'd spoken with the shelter owner this morning. We all knew how much Harris loved Orla, but also that she refused to get a dog with her long work hours. I respected her for that, but we were going to try and come up with a solution. Maybe one that would benefit us all. I had to think on it some more, but for now this was today's solution—an afternoon in the sunshine with Harris's and my best girl.

"I wasn't sure what you'd like for a picnic, so I kind of went with everything." I unpacked the cool box, laying out cold cut meats, slices of deli cheese, several types of bread, sauces, two different salads, three kinds of crisps, and a jar of pickles. Orla's mouth dropped open as I pulled out two small cakes as well.

"Fin, we're never going to be able to eat all that."

"Nae bother." I laughed. "I'll pack it back in the cooler and we can have sandwiches for the week then."

"That's sensible." Orla bit her lower lip, worrying. "I hate wasting food."

"Nope, we'll get through it, one way or the other, I promise." I was about to ask her if she had a favorite meal growing up, maybe one for Christmas dinner or the like, but realized she might not have had much choice in what she ate. Instead, I shifted gears as I opened a can of juice and poured a glass for her. I hadn't brought wine, since we'd both be driving. "Tell me, how are things going down at the kilt shop? Such a shame, that fire."

"Right? Sad about it being Ramsay's brother too." Orla shook her head, her lips pursed. "Just goes to show that a lot of people have awful families."

"Unfortunately, that's the truth of it."

Orla glanced at me and winced, her cheeks pinkening.

"I wasn't implying your—"

"No, it's fine. Even if you were, I'm still raging about how she treated you at the gala. I hope you know that was truly the last straw for me."

"Fin." Orla turned to me, leaning over the table to grab

one of my hands. I liked when she touched me without thinking, since she so easily pulled back from me most times. "I don't want to be the thing that comes between you and your mum. You need to fix this."

"Do I?" I studied her, trailing my finger lightly across her knuckles, brushing my thumb over the palm of her hand. She sucked in a breath at my touch, and I continued, wanting her to get used to my hands on her. "Why?"

"Because she's family."

"So?"

"Family is everything." Orla's eyes were wide as she studied me. *Who was her family and why did she end up alone?* Those were the questions I wanted to ask, but I knew it wasn't the right time. That was given when she knew me better. Trusted me with her secrets. Her past.

JUST THEN, a bird chirped over us, having found a spot in the branches, and another answered merrily. Sunlight filtered through the leaves, and a light breeze carried the scent of wildflowers to us. I could see Orla's point about family, but I wondered where that conviction came from. Especially if she didn't have a family.

"Do you really believe that?"

I wanted to know her answer to this, because that particular phrase was often repeated, with little evidence to back it up.

"Och ..." Orla paused, considering her words. Lines appeared in her forehead as she gave my question more serious thought, and she threw the ball for a delighted Harris without even looking. "No, I don't suppose I do at that. For me? Family wasn't everything. But maybe because of that I have a glamorized version of how a family should operate so I hate to see when other family units break down. Maybe because mine was broken from the beginning. It's the idea of it all, this perfect vision of a happy home and family that I kind of hold on to, I guess?"

"Then you're advocating more for an ideal than a reality, right?"

Orla leaned back, looking a little hurt, and I rushed to explain. "No, I'm not slapping you back for that. I'm just seeking to understand. Because I had the perfect family life, or so I thought, until it crumbled under me. And I can keep wishing it would return to that, or that people were different from what they are, but how long do you keep chasing a reality that only lives in your head?"

"Then this thing with your mum has been going on a while then?"

"Aye, since even before my dad died. I kept giving her blind loyalty, bending over backward to keep her in the lifestyle she's accustomed to, and for what? She doesn't care about me, Orla. She cares about herself and what her peers will think. At what point do I step away and live my life for myself? I don't owe her anything. I'm the child, she's the parent. My duty is to myself and those that I love, not to a woman who's selfish beyond words."

"I'm sorry, Fin. I guess I was just seeing it from the night of the gala."

"The night of the gala revealed to me that my mother has moved past being difficult and into cruelty. The consequences for that will be losing her son."

"Fin." Orla's face twisted. "Do you really mean that? You're cutting her off completely?"

"I have to. For my own sake. And for her, as well. She's a healthy woman in her prime and certainly not stupid. It's time for her to figure things out on her own. I can't abide cruelty, even more so when it is against someone that I ..." I caught myself before I said love. "... someone that I care about."

"On the scale of things, it wasn't the worst that I've dealt with before, Fin. Kids can be quite mean." Orla had left her hands in mine, and I squeezed them, not wanting to break contact with her. "Particularly when you look different or are wearing the wrong sized shoes and all that."

"It was also likely because you're impossibly beautiful."

Orla's skin flushed, and I wanted to see her like that, her red hair spread out across my pillow, her skin pinkening as I brought her pleasure. Desire pooled low, my body responding, and I was glad a picnic table was over my lap, or I'd look like a creep getting turned on during a serious conversation. But, God, I wanted her. In all ways. In my life. In my house. In my bed.

"So you keep saying ..." Orla brought her hands to her face, a shy smile peeking out from behind them. "I don't know if I see what you see."

"How could you not?" I pulled her hands from her face, leaning forward, and brushed a soft kiss against her mouth. "I find you to be utterly bewitching."

At that, Orla stiffened, an odd look coming into her eyes, and her gaze darted away for a moment. What was she thinking about when I said these things? Did I make her nervous or did she just not believe me?

"I have a surprise for you after lunch," I said, switching gears to bring her to lighter topics.

"A surprise? After all this?" Orla swept a hand out to the food and to where Harris waited for his new ball toss.

"Aye, lassie. It's a good one too. But only if you finish your lunch."

"Tell me what it is," Orla demanded, picking up a piece of bread to start building her sandwich.

"It wouldn't be a surprise if I did."

"Give me a hint."

"No."

"Och, come on then. That's no fun." Orla pouted.

"Not good with surprises, are you?" I laughed.

"Hate them," Orla confirmed, adding some deli chicken to her sandwich.

"Too bad. You'll have to wait."

"Not even a tiny clue?"

"Nope."

"I don't like you very much right now, Fin."

"That's just the hunger talking. You'll be better after a sandwich." I laughed as she glared at me and Harris dropped the ball, coming to sit at the table, giving us the best puppy dog eyes to ever beg in the history of puppy dog eyes.

"Oh man, he's good, isn't he?" Orla gaped down at him, her resolve wavering.

"He is. I don't think I have the willpower to hold out." I reached for a piece of chicken and Harris, ever the gentleman, took it delicately from my fingers before wandering across the yard to eat it in a far corner. "Huh, look at that. I thought he'd scarf it down."

"Nope." Orla's expression was just a touch sad. "He's protecting it. And likely savoring every bite of it since he doesn't get chicken often. It's a prize for him, you ken?"

"Aye." But I wasn't looking at Harris, I was looking at Orla, my heart breaking for the young girl that nobody had been able to provide the most basic of things for. She glanced at me and shook her head, and then smiled. *That smile.* It was one of the many reasons I could see myself falling for this woman.

"Tell me how you started working for Munroe."

"Well, it started with a pool game ..." For the rest of the lunch, I kept things light, regaling her with tales of my university days with Munroe, all while making sure she had more than enough to eat. By the time she'd pronounced herself full, we'd made good headway through the food. I packed the rest away after giving one more slice of chicken to a delighted Harris.

"We'd best get on. Not only have you earned your prize, but we need to take this handsome fellow back to the shelter before they close for the day."

Orla's face fell, and I knew she was thinking about Harris having to return to the shelter. There was nothing that I could say to make it better, as I didn't have an answer for this problem.

Yet.

We packed up the picnic, and I helped Harris into Orla's truck since I knew he didn't want to be separated from her. Promising to follow me to the surprise, Orla waited while I backed my truck up with a wave goodbye to Shona. My stomach jittered with nerves, but at the same time, I was excited. This decision hadn't come lightly to me, but I hoped the choice I had made would show Orla that I was in this for the long haul. She needed to be shown that people didn't *only* let her down.

But in all honesty, I wasn't just doing this for Orla. I was hopeful for a future with her, but I also realized that this was something that I needed too. A fresh start, a new beginning, and putting down roots in a place that was beginning to feel like home to me.

I followed the road that hugged Loch Mirren, perfect cotton ball clouds reflected in her waters, sunlight bathing the rolling green hills in a warm glow. When I saw it like this, picture-perfect on a Saturday afternoon, it was hard to imagine the shrieks that split the night came from the loch's haunted depths. I'd heard them myself, hadn't I? We all had. The crew didn't speak of it, but after careful questioning, Munroe had opened up to me about the Kelpies. A known issue in Loren Brae, and one they were secretly trying to combat to help the village from dying off from people moving away out of fear. He hadn't exactly elaborated on how they planned to combat the Kelpies, but our conversation had been cut short by a meeting about delays in supplies. Still, this hadn't deterred me from my decision. If everyone else was staying to fight the Kelpies well, hell, so was I. Even if I had no clue what that meant. Maybe this was my own way of showing up for my *found* family— Munroe, Common Gin, the crew, and Orla—even if they didn't know I considered them such. The more I stuck around and ingratiated myself to everyone, the more I'd build a new future for myself here.

Humming, I put my indicator on and turned off the main road and down a small lane within walking distance of the little downtown stores. I drove a minute before pulling to a stop in front of a charming three-bedroom stone cottage with a walled back garden and cheerful flower boxes under the front windows. The door was painted bright red, and the flowers in the boxes matched the hue. I'd have to ask Shona what kind of flowers they were if I had any hope of keeping them alive. Getting out of the truck, I smiled at Orla as she pulled to a stop and hopped out, Harris at her heels.

"What's this? Are you taking me to bid on a new project? On my day off?" Orla shook her head sadly at me and I laughed.

"Not quite. I'm not so cruel as to force you to work on a date. Come on then, have a look."

"But what am I looking at?" Orla squinted up at me as I dug the keys out and unlocked the front door, a little hum of excitement going through me as we stepped over the threshold.

Would she be happy here?

It was my first thought when I'd seen the place, and one that I hadn't been able to shake every time I'd gone back. Even this morning, when I'd signed on the final papers, making this cottage my new home, I couldn't help but wonder if Orla would like it. Even if she never moved in here, I wanted her to feel safe in my home. Maybe one day our home.

I almost rolled my eyes at my thoughts. I'd only ever kissed the woman and here I was imagining living together? It made sense now, how Munroe had fallen so fast. I'd teased him about it at the time, before I'd met Lia, but now I was beginning to understand. When you knew, you knew.

And I knew it was Orla. Whether she was ready to see it or not was an entirely different matter.

"Welcome to my new home."

Orla's mouth dropped open and she pivoted, gaping at the space.

"Fin! You didn't. Did you really buy a house here?"

"I did."

"But why? I thought you were only here for the build-out. This seems extravagant. Even for you."

That rankled.

"What's that supposed to mean?"

"You know … being posh and whatnot." Orla waved a hand in the air, her eyes still taking in the house.

"I may be posh, but I'm not stupid with my money."

At my tone, Orla turned, and she must have caught something in my expression because her body tensed, and her shoulders went back. It was as though she was bracing herself for a fight, and I realized that in the past, she'd likely had to protect herself in more ways than one. Even though I was annoyed, I understood that I would need to reassure Orla in ways that maybe I didn't have to with other people that didn't come from a place of trauma. I'd read about this, and now I was witnessing her response in real time.

"I'm sorry," Orla said, taking a step back.

"I'm not mad at you." I didn't move, allowing Orla to take any space she needed. "And I understand why you think that I'm posh. I am. I come from money. But after my father spent it all, it made me re-evaluate things. While I do like to spend on nice things at times, I take care of them, and I usually keep them for a long time. Like this place. I plan to call it home. I've been ready for a change for a while and coming to Loren Brae has shown me what I've been missing in Edinburgh. A community. Friends. Nature. I'm happy here, and I want to put down roots. And ..." I trailed off as I searched her eyes.

"And what?" Orla's voice rasped.

"You're here," I answered simply. Honestly.

"Oh, Fin." It was just a whisper at her lips and I took a careful step forward, closing the distance between us. Her eyes searched mine as I leaned down and ever so slowly brushed the softest of kisses across her lips.

"It's a good home. But you'll tell me what needs fixing."

"Fin ..." Orla reached up and clutched my arm. "I hope you didn't buy this just for me."

"And if I did?"

Her eyes widened, her mouth working, and I saw panic flash.

"I didn't, Orla. It's also for me. As I said, I don't make these decisions lightly. But you should know that you deserve someone to show up for you. And I hope you'll see that I am."

"I don't know what to say to that." Orla tapped a hand at her chest, an unconscious movement that I'd seen her do before when she was stressed. It was as though she was tapping on her heart to give her the answers she needed.

"There's nothing to say in the moment. For now, just tell me if I've wasted my money on a pile of shite or not."

Orla laughed, and surprising me, she grabbed my hand.

"Show me around? I'll tell you if you've been taken for a ride."

"God, I hope not. I really like the place."

The ground floor held the main bedroom with an

ensuite bath and an open living area with a fireplace, dining area, and kitchen. Stairs led to two nice sized bedrooms that shared a bathroom between them. I'd make one room an office, and the other a guest room as needed. Orla wandered the space, tapping walls, muttering to herself, sizing up the thick wood beams that crossed the ceilings.

"Good bones." Orla glanced over her shoulder at me at the base of the stairs. "Can I go up?"

"Of course." Harris and I followed Orla. I did my best to not stare at her tight bum in the trousers she wore.

"Are you staring at my bum?" Orla demanded, catching me at the top of the stairs.

"It's a great bum. Hard not to when it's in my face, right?"

A grin flashed, and Orla turned, walking into the bedroom at the right. Harris followed and then skidded to a stop. A low growl emanated.

"What's wrong, boy?" I stopped next to him as he stared at an empty corner of the room. Sunlight filtered through the window but did little to bring warmth to this room. I'd have to check that the radiators worked up here.

"Shhh, it's okay, Harris." Orla stroked his head and the dog leaned into her leg, letting out a soft whimper. "That's a good lad. Yes, you are."

"I wonder what has him spooked," I said, turning in a circle. There was nothing that I could see that would have set him off. Two windows, one at the front of the house and one to the back, and deep green carpeting were the only things in the room. The entire place had been sold unfurnished, and I'd need some help with picking the right furniture for the space when the time came.

"Hard to say. Sometimes animals just get spooked. Let's go downstairs? Show me the back garden?" Orla turned and nudged me to move, and I did so, glancing once more over my shoulder at the bedroom.

For a second, I thought I caught a flash of something in the corner, and I shook my head slightly.

It must have just been the light filtering through the branches at the window. A simple enough explanation.

"Come on, Harris. You'll love the backyard. You can roam free as there's a wall all the way around."

"Oh, a new adventure for you, buddy. I'm so pleased you brought him today, Fin." Orla stopped me at the bottom of the stairs. "This is a great house, and I think you'll be happy here. I don't see many issues, but if you don't mind, can I pop back here when I have some of my tools? I just want to check a few things before you start moving in."

"Sure, no problem. I'd love to have your expert opinion." Didn't she have her tools in her truck? She could do it now. I didn't want to put her out, not when I knew how busy she already was. But before I could suggest it, she was leading Harris out back and I let it go. If she wanted to come back, I was more than happy with that decision.

It just gave me more time to spend with her and ease her into being comfortable with the idea of us here. Together.

As a couple.

Just the way I hoped it would be.

CHAPTER EIGHTEEN

ORLA

F inlay had a ghost in his new house.

And the man had no clue.

First of all, I couldn't even believe that he'd actually bought a house, here, in Loren Brae. And to say I had mixed feelings about it, well, that was true as well. The biggest feeling? The one that I was the most uncomfortable with? It was excitement. I was freaking excited that Fin was going to stay here. Long term. And that, och, well, that scared me straight down to the toes of my favorite work boots.

Not even having to clear a ghost from his house scared me as much as the meaning behind him putting down roots here. Nope, I wasn't going to examine that decision too closely. I wasn't ready to look at what I thought he might be offering.

All I could do was think one day at a time. It was what had served me well for years now, and it threw me off to try and think more deeply about an actual future with someone.

Why hope for something that could change on a whim? It was easier to focus on the things that I could control— like my business and helping the Order of Caledonia out. Which, apparently, meant I needed to sneak back to Fin's house and rid it of the little ghostly girl who had hovered sadly in the corner of the upstairs bedroom.

Harris had spotted her even before I had.

A damn good dog, he was. It had about broken my heart to take him back to the shelter, his eyes sad as I dropped him off. Maybe I could make it work to rescue him, I just had to figure it out. Surely there was some solution that would get him out of the shelter but not stuck at my house all day without me there to care for him. I hated that I didn't have an answer, but maybe I'd be able to find the perfect home for him soon.

"I can't believe he bought a house here." I said this out loud as I paced my room after work, trying to gauge when a good time would be to sneak back over to Fin's new place and do a ritual to remove the ghost. "It's too soon. He's only been here a matter of months. How could he know he wants to stay?"

With me, I silently added.

Why can't you trust him?

I whirled to see the Green Lady sitting on the edge of my bed.

"You make it sound so easy. When has trust gotten me anywhere?"

You trust yourself. You trust your crew. You trust your friends. I'd say it has gotten you a lot of places.

"That's different."

Is it?

"It is. That has nothing to do with my heart." I tapped my chest repeatedly, trying to soothe myself.

Doesn't it?

"Why are you even here?" I demanded, irrationally angry with this ghost who challenged me constantly. "Don't you have other people to haunt?"

Do you want me to leave?

"I want to know why me? Why do you always come back to me?" What kind of house witch was I if I couldn't get rid of my own ghost?

It's what I do.

The Green Lady shrugged one delicate shoulder, a compassionate look in her all-seeing eyes.

I help lost travelers. Or lead them astray. Depends on their intentions really.

"Their intentions? Why would you lead people astray?"

Depends if their path leads to harm or harming others.

"And me? You keep coming back to me. But I'm not lost. I'm doing good. I'm on the right path." I stomped my foot, my emotions twisting my gut.

Are you?

"You're almost as annoying as Fin, you know? Answering questions with a question." I glared at the Green Lady, frustrated because she wasn't giving me the answers that I needed.

Because it's not me that has the answers you seek.

"Great, just great. Talk in riddles." I stopped in front

of Goldie, watching as she bopped the ship with her head and went after the flakes that sifted out onto the surface of the water. "Do you know about the little girl in Fin's house?"

She needs your help.

"What happened to her?"

She was left behind.

My heart twisted at those words. I would forever have a soft spot for the forgotten ones, which is why I spent as much time helping at the shelter as I could.

"I need to do something about it, but I have to go when Fin isn't there."

Tell him.

"I can't tell him what I am. He'll never believe me."

You don't trust him.

"It's not that I don't trust him." I bit my lower lip as I thought about it. It was true. I did trust Finlay, as much as I trusted anyone, I supposed. He'd shown me kindness, repeatedly, and he was helping me with my business— something which I hadn't ever allowed other people to do. All things considered, these were big steps for me. It was just the whole hurting my heart thing that I wasn't so sure I was ready to sign on for. The grief of losing Jacob never really went away, and I could only imagine that same grief would arise if Finlay decided he tired of me. Losing someone I loved, again? Yeah, I wasn't sure I was ready to sign up for that particular ride.

You love him.

"Damn it. Can you read my thoughts?" I whirled on the Green Lady, annoyed that she had managed to pluck the word love right from my brain. "Isn't anything private?"

Love should be celebrated. It's the one thing in this world that universally links others. Why hide from it?

"Because it hurts?"

It only hurts because you aren't giving it a chance.

"No, not true. I loved Jacob. He was my best friend and I never held back from showing him my love. Same with Grandpa Lou. And they both left me. Everyone leaves."

The love doesn't. You'll always have that.

Her words slammed into me so hard that I gasped for breath, and I rubbed the spot where I'd tapped my chest so hard it was now sore. She wasn't wrong. Even though I no longer had Jacob or Grandpa Lou, my love for them never diminished. It just was. Maybe that was what she was trying to tell me—that once love was created it didn't just wink out of sight.

Unlike her. When I looked back up, she was gone, likely smug in the wee bomb she'd dropped on my head. Sighing, I tapped at Goldie's bowl.

"I need to go back out, sweetie. I've got a ghost to see about."

It was late, almost nine in the evening, but I figured my chance for sneaking in the house while Fin wasn't there was better at night. He'd given me the code for the lockbox, telling me to pop through whenever, as I'd told him I'd wanted to check a few things. Which wasn't entirely untrue, there were a few areas of concern in his new place I'd like to take a more careful eye to, but largely it had been an excuse to come back and see to the ghost girl haunting his upstairs bedroom.

I also still needed to go check that outbuilding at the distillery site. I'd banned my workers from going inside—

due to structural issues—and hadn't yet had a chance to have a look at what was really going on inside the derelict building. I'd make a go of it soon.

Happy to see no cars parked outside when I arrived, I made quick work of hauling my toolbox inside after I unlocked the door. Putting it down just inside the front door, I flicked on the light and dug in the box for my special hammer before striding upstairs. I needed to move quickly, just in case Fin was driving by and saw the light, and I didn't really know what I needed to do to help this little ghost girl.

Intent is everything, Miss Elva had told me, and I hung on to those words as I stepped inside the bedroom that I had seen the ghost girl in. Light spilled into the room from the hallway, illuminating the floor, and I immediately saw her cowering in the corner, her lip trembling.

Scared, I realized. *She's scared.* I couldn't blame her. Being left alone in an empty house had to be particularly sad for a child.

A glimmer of movement alerted me and I turned, surprise filling me as Clyde sauntered down the hallway. The ghost coo approached slowly, coming to a stop by my side.

"Hey, Clyde," I said, reaching out to scratch his ears as I watched the ghost girl. Her eyes widened at the sight of Clyde.

"Hello," I said, keeping my voice soft, not moving any closer. "I see you in the corner there. Are you all right?"

"You see me?" The girl jumped up, taking one step closer to me, and I tried to place her age. Maybe six or seven? Her dress looked old, as in old-fashioned, but I wasn't fashionable enough to be able to place the date of her death by her clothing.

"Aye," I said, nodding. "Can you see me?"

"Of course I can see you." The girl giggled and gave me a look like I wasn't very bright. "But nobody ever sees me."

"What's your name?"

"Elspeth."

"I'm Orla, and this is Clyde."

Her eyes grew huge as Clyde did a little dance and she brought her thumb to her mouth, sucking it. Self-soothing. Behavior I could certainly understand and recognize.

"Do you like coos?"

Elspeth nodded, her eyes huge.

"Do you want to pet him?"

"We used to have coos. Before."

"Before what?"

"My family ... they went away. They took my brothers."

"But not you?"

Elspeth's eyes filled and Clyde made a low keening noise.

"Go on, buddy. Go to her." I didn't trust she wouldn't disappear if I moved too fast and I needed to help her move forward, not have her hide from me and then still be stuck in this house. Clyde sauntered forward and to my surprise, he dropped and rolled onto his back, like a dog revealing his tummy for scratches, and beamed up at the girl.

"He's so fluffy," Elspeth said, reaching out to run a hand over him while Clyde mirrored a synchronized swimmer by kicking his legs in the air in delight. Elspeth giggled, and I blinked as tears threatened. Such an innocent thing, a child's laugh, even when it came from a ghostly apparition.

"I couldn't go with my family. I was told they couldn't take care of me. I was meant to stay with a family friend, but I ran away. Her husband was a bad man."

"Was this your home?" My heart twisted.

"No, it was a place I found to stay. Until ..." Her face grew sad and stony, and Clyde kicked up his legs some more, drawing her attention to him, so she continued to talk while she pet his shaggy fur. "There was a sickness of sorts. I don't really know. I was here and then I wasn't. But I still am."

Confusion threaded her words, and I pieced together what she was trying to tell me. The plague took her, and likely those who lived here, yet she didn't fully understand why she was still here. I wondered if she even really knew that she was dead. Maybe the concept was something that she wasn't ready to accept.

I couldn't say I blamed her.

"Are you ready to move on, Elspeth? It must be lonely here."

"Aye, it is. I haven't had anyone visit me in ages. I can't leave though."

"Why not?"

Elspeth looked up, longing on her face.

"I have nobody to show me the way."

God, if I didn't totally understand that feeling. To be endlessly lost, until finally, Jacob had thrown me a lifeline with his friendship. The Green Lady was right. Love did matter, in whatever form it came in, and that might just be what would help this wee lass out.

As if reading my thoughts, the Green Lady appeared in the corner of the room and I realized, in my own way, that I also loved her.

This weird ghost woman who had provided me protection and guidance for much of my life ... In some respects, she'd been a North Star to me when I was most lost. I don't think I'd ever examined my true thoughts or feelings for her, and now as I watched her slowly approach Elspeth, I realized how much I'd grown to care for her through the years.

"Will you help her? She's a lost traveler. And I think she needs our love."

The Green Lady stopped in front of Elspeth, and the two stared at each other. Clyde rolled over and pranced back to my side, as we watched the two ghosts regard each other.

I had a little girl once. One that I loved very much.

My heart twisted at the Green Lady's words.

"Will you help her home?"

Aye, I'll do so.

The Green Lady reached out a hand and Elspeth took it, the two winking out of sight before I could even let out a breath. Tears sprung to my eyes. I knew so little about the Green Lady, not even her name, as she'd spent so much of her time selflessly being a guiding force for me. Now as I realized just how much of a history she must have, my heart ached for her. *Would she let me in? Would she let me know her—*

"Orla? What are you doing here?"

CHAPTER NINETEEN

Finlay

I'd been driving home from a late meeting with a potential new supplier for botanicals when I'd felt the urge to swing past my new house. I was still living in my rental cottage, knowing my new house would need some shining up before I could fully move in, and I was looking forward to the challenge of making it my new home. Particularly because I knew I could wheedle Orla into giving design advice. I loved how cozy she'd made her cottage but had also kept it streamlined and functional without too much clutter. I hoped she'd be able to guide me in the same direction.

When I'd seen her lorry and the light spilling from the window, I immediately pulled over, annoyance lacing through me. Did this woman ever stop working? It was far too late for her to be at my house, making notes on projects that needed to get done, and I planned to tell her. *Even if I had to tuck her into bed myself.* The damn woman needed rest, not to be burning the candle at both ends.

What I hadn't expected was to find Orla crying, alone, in my upstairs bedroom. Instantly, I crossed the room and lifted her into my arms, carrying her downstairs and into the light-filled living room where the only piece of furniture —a faded couch draped in dust cloths—sat. Dropping onto the sofa, I cradled her on my lap, stroking my hands up and down her back.

"Shhh, darling. Shhh. I'm here. What's happened? Are you hurt?"

"No, no. I'm fine. I swear." Orla batted at my hands, trying to shift herself off my lap, but I was used to this by now. She always pulled back from my touch, but there was no way I'd let her close up on me, not when she was in a state like this.

"Tell me what's happened." I held her close, and she rested her head on my shoulder, finally stopping her attempts to push me away.

"Och, it's nothing, Fin. Just having a moment."

"Tell me."

"There's not much to tell." Orla shifted, a note of distress in her voice.

"Just spontaneous crying on job sites? Is this how you secure all your jobs then? You cry and they feel bad, so you get the work?"

Orla poked me in the ribs, and I laughed.

"Rude."

"Is it because you're in love with me and you're worried

I'll wallpaper the room mustard yellow when you really want it to be pink?"

Orla sighed and poked me again, gouging her finger in deeper this time.

"You can do whatever you like in your own home."

"Great, mustard it is."

"Such a soothing color," Orla said.

"If you don't like it, now's the time to speak up."

"Wouldn't you want like a soft blue or a sage green? Something relaxing?"

"I want whatever color doesn't make you cry."

"Fin, I'm sorry. I just had a moment is all. It happens."

"Why can't you tell me? I want to support you, Orla." At that, Orla pulled back, a world of emotions in her eyes. I waited as she considered, wanting nothing more than to lean forward and kiss her sadness away.

"I always wanted my own bedroom when I was a little girl. It just hit me wrong, I guess." Her eyes shifted away from mine and I understood that I wasn't getting the whole truth. And maybe I never would. Maybe that was something that I would need to accept about Orla and how she protected herself. It was likely easier for her to keep hurtful memories buried than it was to expose them to scrutiny. I couldn't say I blamed her for that either.

"That makes sense. Was it because you wanted space?"

"Aye. Just somewhere private to call my own. Nothing was my own. I didn't even have a journal or a box of toys or ... anything really. Not even a bag that my cousins wouldn't go through. It's hard to live with zero space or privacy."

"What happened to your family?"

Orla's eyes drifted away for a moment and then returned to mine.

"Not much to tell. Never knew my dad. Mum died of addiction when I was young. Her half-sister took me in, but just barely. There was nothing for her to give. Which is why I had no real space to call my own. When you finally get it, well, you treasure it, you ken?"

"Aye." I thought back to my own upbringing, where wealth had provided me with more space than I needed, to the point of loneliness at times. Different sides of the coin, but some of the same emotions, I supposed. "I wish I could take the hurt away for you, Orla. But all I can do is say that I'm always here to listen and I want you to know that I would give you the world if I could. Anything you want, and it's yours. Name it."

Orla lifted her chin, studying me.

"You're serious?"

"Of course, I am. You mean ... och ..." I stopped short. Now wasn't the time to tell this woman that I'd fallen head over heels for her. It had only taken one look, hadn't it? A part of me had known, even when I'd ignored it, that my life would never be the same after Orla. It was imperative that I move slowly with her because I knew she frightened easily at any semblance of closeness. Her walls were high, and I'd seen them from a mile away. But damn it, I wanted her. All of her. I wanted to be free to give her gifts and plan the future together. To wake up next to her and talk about our problems together. A partnership. In heart and home. I'd never craved this with someone before, not in the way I did with Orla, and it killed me to creep along as slowly as we did, each day nudging her closer to trusting me.

"I mean ... what?" Orla asked, her eyebrows winging up her forehead.

"You mean everything to me, Orla." My voice rasped and I brushed a thumb softly across her cheek, holding her gaze, wishing she could feel the emotions that threatened to strangle me. Never had I had this overwhelming need to protect and care for someone before, yet at the same time knowing she didn't need me at all. It was humbling, really, to know the things that Orla likely had gone through and still persevered. While every girlfriend before her had always wanted fancy gifts from me, Orla refused anything I tried to give her—aside from a gift for Goldie, that is. No, she didn't need me at all, but I hoped she'd want me at her side.

"You mean that, don't you?" Orla bit her lower lip, and my stomach clenched as need rose.

"I do. I promised myself I'd give you the time you need to grow comfortable with me. But I'm there, Orla. I'm already there. You have me."

Her eyes widened and her breath quickened.

"You're quite serious ..."

"Aye." I wanted to bury myself in her, both physically and metaphorically, and never come out. What had become absolutely certain over the last few weeks was that this woman was my sanctuary, my home, and I would do anything to keep her happy. It was scary, really, how months ago I thought I was fine, content in my life. And then Orla blew in and nothing had been the same since. Now I couldn't imagine a future without her in it.

Orla raised a hand, tapping it lightly against her chest.

"I have all these ... feelings. And I don't quite know where to put them."

My breath caught. It was the closest she'd come to admitting she cared for me, and I didn't want to scare her away. No sudden movements.

"Do you want to tell me about these emotions?"

"I'm not sure how to," Orla admitted, still tapping on her chest.

"Would you like to show me instead?"

Orla tilted her head, considering my words.

"Can I? Would you let me?" Her gaze sharpened, her pupils dilating slightly as she looked at me, and I realized she was talking about her desire for me. Instantly, I hardened at the mere thought of her touch.

"You can show me whatever you want, Orla." I chose my words carefully, not wanting to presume anything.

"And I can be in control?" Orla stressed the words, clearly needing confirmation from me.

"If you're suggesting what I'm thinking, then yes, one thousand percent you can be in control." I raised my hands and then made a great show of sitting on them. "There. See? All yours. Please. Show me anything you'd like."

"Nobody has ever just let me ... explore before." Excitement flashed and I bit back a groan as Orla shifted, reaching out to trace a hand across my chest. She sent me a flirtatious look, still biting that gorgeous lower lip, and a shiver of anticipation ran through me. I hadn't expected this side of her, and it was another aspect to Orla that I found myself falling for.

She had a mischievous side, it seemed.

"I told you that I would give you anything you liked. Explore away. I'm yours."

My heart is yours. My body is yours. My future is yours.

I left that part unsaid, my pulse picking up as she unbuttoned my shirt, trailing a finger across my chest and down to my pants, where I was *very clearly* affected by her touch.

"You're so strong. Stronger than you look," Orla said, bringing both hands to my chest to stroke my muscles, and I grinned at her.

"Us posh lads do love a personal trainer."

At that she paused, her mouth gaping open.

"You do not have a personal trainer."

"I don't, no. But I'll get one if it keeps you touching me this way."

Her lips curled up in a sultry smile and she shifted to straddle me, and I groaned as she settled over my hard length, still imprisoned in my trousers. Rocking slightly, she made a soft cooing sound of delight that would forever be imprinted on my brain.

"This feels nice."

"It does at that." I gritted my teeth, calling on my power to keep my hands under my legs, even though I wanted nothing more than to touch her until she cried out in ecstasy. Instead, I waited, allowing her to discover my body at her whim, and prayed that I wouldn't embarrass myself in my pants as her fingers stroked my skin gently.

"Is it hard for you? When I do this?" Orla rocked over me, a teasing light in her eyes, before lowering her lips an inch from mine.

"I'm hard for you, if that's what you're asking." I grinned as she chuckled, and then her lips were on mine, and I groaned into her mouth. She deepened the kiss, her tongue slipping inside, and desire shot through me as her slick tongue toyed with mine. I sucked gently, her soft mewl of surprise delighting me, and I wanted to thrust upward, to rub myself against her core. Instead, I stayed still, though it was becoming difficult to breathe, as our kiss intensified.

Orla broke away, burying her face in my neck, gasping as she continued to roll her hips over me, her body showing her what she wanted even if her heart wasn't ready for it. She was all strength and beauty, a powerhouse of a woman, and I wanted to sink myself inside her until the only words on her lips were my name.

She pulled back, removing herself from my body as she stood, and I almost whimpered I was so desperate for her hands on me. But still I sat on my hands, not touching, keeping my promise to her.

"You'll really let me do what I want, won't you? And I'll be in full control?"

"I'll give you anything you want, Orla." I'd meant the words when I said them, and I'd repeat them a thousand times over if she needed to hear it.

"I want to taste you." Orla licked her lips and the blood drained from my face as a rush of desire washed over me so hard that I swear I had wee dots dance across my vision from need. "I want my mouth on you."

"By all means," I said, gritting my teeth. "Be my guest."

Orla dropped to her knees in front of me, and I lifted my hips as she unbuckled my trousers, pulling them and my pants down my legs. I sprung free and I swear I almost lost it when she smiled, kneeling between my legs, my hard length at her lips.

When she took me inside, her soft lips encasing me, a

slippery slide of wet heat on my hard length, I almost shouted. I wanted to close my eyes, to loll my head back and stare at the ceiling, anything to make this experience go on longer. But I couldn't. I couldn't look away from where this entrancing woman took her power by pleasuring me. Unable to touch, only able to watch, caught on the slippery slope into love, it was the most erotic experience I'd had in my life.

Her small hand cupped me, fingers surrounding my length, and stroked, making soft sounds of pleasure that vibrated against me, her tongue wet against my skin. She sucked, the motion pulling deep, and I groaned, wanting to bury my hands in her hair. Over and over she licked and explored, leisurely taking her pleasure, while I did everything in my power to pull myself back from orgasm. I never wanted this moment to end.

Was there ever anything as beautiful as watching a woman take power in the bedroom? Granted, we weren't in the bedroom, but even so, I'd never expected this of Orla. The more she explored, the more excited she became, her body writhing on the floor as her kisses intensified, until she suddenly pulled back, her mouth making a soft popping sound when she stopped.

Her lips were slick, and I held my breath, wanting to kiss her so badly it made my stomach clench with pain.

"I want more," Orla whispered.

"Whatever you want," I promised her, wincing at the need that filled me. "But bloody hell, Orla, will you let me touch you? I'm dying over here."

Sweat had broken out on my brow, and I was physically shaking with my need to touch her.

"Really?" Orla's eyes lit as she realized just how on edge I was. "You want me that much?"

"You just drove me crazy with your mouth. You're a goddess among women, the only person I go to sleep thinking about, and I wake up with your name on my lips. I'm begging you, Orla. Have mercy. You're killing me."

"I had no idea I had this kind of power." Orla idly stroked her hand against my length, and I hissed, knowing how close I was.

"You have all the power. You always will. But just please, please, please ... let me touch you too."

Orla raised her eyes from where she kneeled and grinned at me.

"Och, go on then. Show me what you've got."

CHAPTER TWENTY

ORLA

Honestly, I'm not sure what had come over me. It had been a whirlwind of emotions tonight, and maybe Fin catching me at a vulnerable moment had made me open to him more. Or maybe we'd just been leading this way all along and I was finally ready to take this moment with him. Either way, I'd been emboldened enough to ask for what I'd wanted.

And he'd let me.

He'd kept his promise, sitting on his hands while I had my way with him. And the way his moans had echoed off the ceiling had made me feel like I was some sexual courtesan, well experienced in the nature of men and their needs. I mean, I had experience, but not a lot of it, and it had been sheer enthusiasm and excitement that had allowed me to explore with such abandon.

The man was seriously packing.

Between a rock-hard and chiseled chest—which by the way, I had *not* been expecting—and the fact that I could barely take him inside my mouth, well, my body was basically a puddle of lust. I wanted him, and I would think about the repercussions of that tomorrow. In this moment? All I could see was the adoration in his eyes as he begged me to let him touch me.

Begged me.

I mean, who was I to say no to a man's pleas? Particularly when I could see his body trembling with barely restrained need.

I was doing that.

I had made sweat break out on his forehead.

I had made his body tremble at my touch.

I had made his hips buck as I'd taken him inside my mouth.

Me. The man was besotted with me, dying for my touch, and never had I felt more womanly or powerful. Here I was, in my threadbare jumper and sweatpants, having been in my comfies when I'd left my house, and I felt like I could have been dressed in a lacy bodysuit and icepick heels for the way Fin was responding to me.

It was because of that, the way he looked at me, the way he'd told me he thought I was prettier in my overalls than in a ballgown, that had me peeling my jumper over my head.

"Let's see what you've got." I reiterated my challenge, loving that he hesitated before he pulled his hands from beneath his legs.

"You're certain?" Fin asked, checking in with me, and my heart cracked open even more so for this man.

This impossibly kind man.

Who seemed to understand what I needed before even I did.

Who was both silly and serious, equal parts commanding and friendly, who had ridden to my rescue when I'd needed him.

I nodded, biting my lip.

"Bloody hell." Fin pulled me to standing, stripping my pants down my legs, and buried his face between my legs before I could draw another breath. I jerked against him, shocked as his tongue slid across me, molten heat making my legs shake.

"Oh, God." I threw my head back, arching my hips forward as one of his hands came up to grip my bum, holding me tight against his face, as he used the other to slip a finger inside me.

I gasped, rocking against him, as he licked, his mouth wet against me, sucking gently as he stroked me, over and over, hitting the perfect spot inside of me. Desire shot through me, the wave of an orgasm riding across my body, as Fin scraped his teeth over me.

"Oh, Fin, oh, I'm close," I cried, grabbing his hair and holding his face close, not even caring that I was now rocking against his face, riding his hand, needing him to bring me to completion. When he pulled back, I whimpered.

"Not yet, darling."

"Noooooo," I moaned, my body shaking with need, unable to believe how quickly I'd been close to orgasming. Fin had the gall to wink at me and I glared at him.

"Get back to work," I ordered, surprising even myself, but damn it, I craved that orgasm I could feel hanging close.

He laughed and I wanted to punch him.

"Oh I plan to. But darling, the first time you come for me is going to be when I'm buried so deep inside you that all you can think about or feel is me."

Oh, when he presented it like that, I could see the merits.

"I can promise that the only one I was thinking about was you," I insisted, my legs shaky as I rolled my hips forward, hopeful for more. Fin bent, kissing his way down my inner thighs, and I sighed, thinking I was getting my way. When I heard rustling, I peered down to see him pulling a condom from his wallet.

"Come here," Fin said, after he'd protected us, and gripped my hips. Moving forward, I straddled him and moaned as I felt him at my entrance. Shifting, I tried to take him inside me, but he held me still, his eyes on mine. Leaning forward, Fin captured my lips in a searing kiss.

"Mine," Fin said against my mouth, and my breath left me as he slid deep inside of me.

Holy hell, but I needed him. All of him. I hadn't known it, not until this, that he would consume me so. My body stretched around his hard length, and I moaned into his mouth, gasping as he rocked his hips up into me, the pleasure excruciating. Desire built once more, and I mewled into his mouth, sucking his tongue as I rocked on him, my orgasm looming close. Just as I was about to shatter around him, he pulled me off.

"No," I cried out, knocking my forehead against his. "No, no, no."

"Not yet, darling."

Fin shocked me by lifting me, shifting down on the couch so his face was between my legs, and then his mouth was on me, his tongue slick with my need. I jolted forward, whimpering as I rode his face, needing the release he promised me. Never had I been so enthralled with a man before and when I almost broke, he pulled back.

"I think I hate you," I declared, furious that he was withholding my pleasure.

"No, you don't." Fin grinned as he gripped my hips, expertly bringing me back to his length, teasing me.

"Yes, I do." I might, if he kept this up, and Fin threw his head back and laughed before kissing me until I couldn't think straight.

"Gorgeous Orla, my stunningly tough warrior. Look at me."

I didn't want to. Caught between fury and desire, I wanted to ride him until all I could feel was pleasure rocketing through my body. Instead he held still, his gaze on mine, forcing me to connect.

"Say you're mine," Fin said, still not allowing me to slide onto him.

"Fin," I gasped, my body shaking with need.

"Say it," Fin demanded, refusing to let me take him inside, his arms like steel around my hips.

"You're ..." I gasped as he nudged me, little bolts of pleasure shooting through me.

"I'm what, Orla?" Fin rocked gently, teasing me with his tip, waiting until he got what he wanted.

I'd be lying if I said I didn't want it too.

"I'm yours," I said, giving up, giving in, knowing I was falling over that edge anyway.

"That's right, Orla. You're mine. You're my every fantasy and I finally found you." With that, he drove into me, and our eyes caught as pleasure took us both at the same time, our bodies convulsing together as the promise we made to each other blossomed.

Somehow, even when I'd thought I'd been in control, I never really had been. Or maybe we both were or not at all. Was that what love was? Giving over of control? Or was that simply just good partnership? I buried my face in his neck, not sure what to do next. I'd just bared myself for him and now I wasn't quite sure how to proceed now that we'd finished.

"Do you like pizza?"

"Pizza?" I looked up at him, confused.

"Aye, pizza."

"Of course. Who doesn't like pizza?"

"Perfect, I'm famished. Let's go."

"Wait, what? Where?" I gasped as Fin picked me up, still naked, and carried me toward the front door. "Fin! I'm naked."

"Oh, right. Clothes would be good here. I've got a frozen pizza at home. I'll meet you at yours in fifteen?"

I gaped at him, entirely unsure how to proceed.

"You want to come over and eat pizza? It's eleven at night."

"We'll be asleep by midnight. Promise."

He was sleeping over? Nerves shot through me.

"See you soon." Fin pressed a kiss to my nose before I

could say anything else and disappeared out the front door, his shirt still in his hands.

What the hell? He'd just rocked my world and now we were going to eat pizza?

What was a woman supposed to do with a man like that?

CHAPTER TWENTY-ONE

ORLA

Apparently, I was in a relationship now.

Or so Finlay kept reminding me.

Every time he snuck a kiss at work.

Every time he woke me, nuzzling into the back of my neck, his hard length pressing against me as he spooned me.

Every time he asked me a seemingly unrelated question, it pried a little bit more out of me about my past.

The man was unraveling me, a piece at a time, and if I wasn't so besotted with him, I'd be rebuilding the walls he kept tearing down. The man was nothing if not persistent.

It had been three weeks since the night at his house when I'd fallen for him, though I hadn't told him the depths of my emotions for him. Yet. The Green Lady kept reprimanding me to do so, but I couldn't quite bring myself to tell Finlay that I loved him.

Which wasn't fair.

He'd told me that he loved me, hadn't he?

It had been in the simplest of moments—a sunny morning enjoying a quick cup of coffee at my small bistro table in my back garden. And he'd just said it.

Out loud.

And waited patiently, an understanding look in his eyes, when I'd fumbled my response, spilling coffee on myself instead of responding the same way. Since then, he repeated it to me often, and still I hadn't worked the courage up to tell him how I truly felt. Finlay didn't seem to mind, though I had to think it must bother him a bit. What man wouldn't want his love reciprocated? Instead, I clammed up every time he said it, even though the words made my heart sing every time I heard them.

I'd never told anyone that I'd loved them before.

Ever.

Even sweet Jacob, my best pal in the world, and Grandpa Lou, had never heard those words from me. We'd all seemed to understand our shared mutual feelings. Knowing that Finlay would be the first to hear them from me terrified me, because what would happen when he left?

Because everyone always did.

Even if he didn't plan to.

Even if he promised me over and over that he saw a future in Loren Brae.

Even when he consulted me on decorating choices for his house, which he had casually started referring to as our place. Like I had anything to do with the purchase of such a grand cottage.

People leaving me was the only truth that I'd ever

known, and I was scared that the minute I told Finlay how I felt about him, he'd do just that. If I didn't give him that last piece of myself, well, when he did finally leave, I'd be able to lie and tell myself that it hadn't really been love. It would make the inevitable a touch easier, or so I was trying to delude myself into thinking. The reality was that when he left, he'd leave a huge gaping Finlay-sized hole in my heart, and I was certain it would be almost impossible to recover from that loss.

"Orla?"

"Yes?" I turned to find a statuesque woman with muscular arms, a curvy body, and a riot of dark curls standing before me in jeans and a tank top, a leather cross-body satchel at her waist. I was on-site at the distillery, working through my to-do list for the day, and my thoughts scattered as I tried to place the woman.

"I'm Kaia Bisset, the metalsmith? Your assistant pointed me in your direction."

"Och, right. Of course. Sorry, I'm a touch behind today so I'd forgotten about our meeting."

With Finlay's help, I'd finally hired an assistant, Stacey, and I had to admit, it had made a world of difference in my business. Not only was she scarily efficient, but I was no longer bogged down with handling admin when I was exhausted at the end of a long day. In turn, it had left me more time to be on-site with clients, as well as more time with Fin. An ulterior motive he likely had in mind all along when he'd insisted I hire someone, but I couldn't complain. I really enjoyed our time after work. At first I thought I'd be annoyed at having someone in my space, but Fin enjoyed quiet time as much as I did, both of us putting on headphones as we listened to our various podcasts, and he'd often work at his computer late while I worked on my next crochet project.

It was scary how easily we'd fallen into a routine.

Me, someone who'd never had a person to go home to before, now had a partner.

Honestly? It kind of blew my mind.

"No biggie. I'm pretty flexible with my schedule." Kaia looked around, interest in her eyes, and I paused as the Green Lady drifted behind her shoulders, giving the newcomer a nod. When Kaia turned sharply, looking directly at the Green Lady, my eyebrows winged up.

My my, what do we have here?

"Everything all right then?" I asked, wondering if she would tell me that she'd seen the Green Lady.

"Yup, just thought I heard something." Kaia rubbed one arm over the back of her neck, likely against the chill that the presence of a ghost would bring, and I studied her a bit more closely. Her accent was American, and she stood confidently, her blue eyes seeming to miss nothing as they surveyed the room behind me. "Pretty site."

"It is at that. I've had great fun working on it."

"I can't say I run into many women on the job, so I am beyond delighted to learn you're the master builder."

"No, I suspect you probably run into the same problem I do." We sized each other up, mutual grins of under-standing on our faces, and both nodded.

"Everyone assumes we should be men."

"Exactly," I agreed. Turning, I motioned for her to follow me. We were hoping to build some custom wrought iron gates for the entrance to the distillery, and Kaia's name had come recommended from someone that Hilda and Archie knew. Apparently, she was new to town, but not to the industry. At the very least, I was willing to give her a chance. "Particularly because my company is named Clarke Construction after my last name. It reads more manly than feminine, but I wasn't feeling particularly creative when I came up with the name."

"It's a good name. And why shouldn't you have your last name on the business? It's yours, isn't it?"

It was, even though I never gave much weight to my name. It was attached to a family line that I'd long disregarded, so what did it really matter? Lia had even searched for a Clarke in her spells book but had found no mention of an ancestor of mine. Which was fine, I was told, since not all women were written into her book.

But still. I'd been hopeful for a wee moment. Nevertheless, circumstances liked to remind me that I was on my own in this world.

"I agree. Plus, I enjoy putting men in their place when they make assumptions."

"You and me both, girl." Kaia laughed, a booming sound that had more than one man on my crew turning to check her out. I couldn't blame them. This was a woman who took up space and demanded attention. "So, it's gates you're thinking of, right?"

"Yup, out here."

We stepped outside the building to where the entrance was, and my heart did a little spin in my chest as Finlay waved at me from where he walked with two of my electricians.

"Whooo boy. Hottie alert."

"Taken," I said mildly, even though her words made me more annoyed than I wanted to admit.

"Noted." Kaia smiled. "Well done on that."

I couldn't hide my smile.

"I've brought a portfolio specific to gates that I've worked on in the past, but I also work with other elements, should you need something more specific." Kaia switched into work mode, digging a folder out of her satchel, and I opened it, flipping through glossy pages of gorgeous gates.

"Och, Kaia. This one. It's stunning." I tapped my finger on a gate made to look like thorns and leaves, with gold etching on the petals of the roses.

"Yeah, that was a fun one to do. I love when a client is willing to think outside the box."

"I was hoping to do something with the name or the logo, but maybe we could incorporate a thistle design too?" I stepped back, framing the entrance with my hands, noting how the creamy stone walls worked nicely against the backdrop of green forest and rolling hills behind the distillery. Adding an element of nature into the gates would make it go more seamlessly with the gardens and forest surrounding it.

"Could do that. What about swords?" Kaia turned and nodded to the castle. "Or something armor like?"

"Also interesting. Would it be a big deal to mock-up a few designs?"

"No problem at all. I love this kind of stuff. Particularly with a building like this." Kaia pursed her lips and shook her head. "It's why I came over here. You just don't get to work on spaces like this in the States."

"No, I don't imagine you have quite the history we do."

"Orla, hi!" I turned as Willow came out of the castle, her cat sauntering after her, and I waved.

"Willow, this is Kaia, a fellow American. She's just moved to town and is a metalworker. We're discussing designs for a custom gate."

Willow's eyes narrowed as she looked Kaia up and down before she brightened.

"What kind of metalwork? Is it industrial only? Have you considered chain mail? Or jewelry?"

"I do both, actually. Depends on my mood really." Kaia and Willow beamed at each other, fast friends, and I had to admire the woman. Where it took me ages to warm up to people, Kaia seemed to do so effortlessly.

"Even better. I'm a designer and I've been playing with some ideas for kind of a chain mail crop top of sorts? That you could wear alone or throw on over a band T-shirt, you know?"

"Totally. I can work on it, though chain mail takes time. It's an exacting work, hooking all those links together, and then soldering them closed as well."

"I can imagine. That's why we charge the premium price, don't we?" Willow grinned.

Calvin, her cat, brushed against her legs and Willow shot him a look before angling her head at Kaia. I wondered if the cat was communicating with her like she'd told me he was capable of doing. He was cute, I'd give him that, and I crouched to give his ears a wee scratch.

"You're a handsome wee lad, aren't you?"

"Brrap." Calvin bumped his head against my hand, and I gave him a good pet while the two women chattered about chain mail and fashion. Finally, I stood, knowing I needed to get back to work.

"Kaia, send me those designs when you can. I have to run."

"So great to meet you, Orla. I'll follow up soon with a few ideas." Kaia shook my hand, her grip authoritative, and I nodded my thanks.

"Say, Kaia. Got a moment? I'd like to introduce you to Sophie, the woman who owns this castle." Over Kaia's shoulder, Willow shot me a look.

One of those looks that seemed to say she wanted me to pay attention to something.

Or someone that was.

With a jerk of her chin toward Kaia, I understood what she was trying to tell me.

This woman might be the next in the Order.

Pursing my lips, I gave Willow a quick nod of understanding. If so, I was quite pleased. Having another woman who worked in the trades like I did, and with a personality like Kaia's, would be a benefit to the group. I still wasn't entirely sure what I brought to the table, but Sophie continued to assure me that I was doing just fine.

I'd passed my second challenge.

The night when I'd helped the little girl cross over, leaving Fin's house behind and reuniting her with her family. Or so the Green Lady had promised me that Elspeth was just fine. The next day, a new vine of gold leaves had appeared in the handle of my hammer, and I'd blown out a breath of acceptance.

Whatever was happening, well, I was doing something right. And if an ancient stone of truth deemed me worthy of my magick, then I just had to carry on and keep helping where I could, right?

The Kelpies had awoken us last night.

It was the first time in a long time that I'd heard the screams and I'd rushed outside, half-naked with my hammer in hand. Finlay had drawn me back, arms wrapped around my waist, and we watched from the window as the shadow of something had raced across the surface of Loch Mirren. It had humbled me, their sheer power, and Fin had cursed long and low at my ear, his muscular arms banding me to his body. He'd refused to let me budge an inch, furious with me for running outside, and I'd been powerless to tell him why I'd done so.

It was my job to help.

Except Fin didn't know that and I hadn't been able to bring myself to tell him, not when he'd whispered words of fear in my ear before the Kelpies had finally dissolved in a wicked splash of water.

Neither of us had spoken of it this morning. It still niggled at me, unsettled thoughts bouncing around my brain, and I knew I'd have to tell Fin what I was soon. He'd been pretty upset by the Kelpies, though, so I wasn't sure just how much to spring on him. Couldn't say I blamed the guy either. The shriek of the Kelpies was enough to make anyone cower in fright.

"Boss. Got a sec?" Derrick motioned to me from the entryway, and I nodded, striding forward.

Movement had me glancing toward the outbuilding—the one where Fin had first gotten himself into trouble—and I saw something flicker behind the windows. Damn it. I'd kept meaning to sort that out, as construction would begin on that space soon, but one thing after another had pulled me away. Remembering that Fin had an after-work meeting with Munroe later, I decided I'd deal with whatever ghost was haunting the wee cottage. The Green Lady had warned me it was tough magick there, but after my two recent successes I was feeling emboldened.

Surely I could help. It was what we did in the Order of Caledonia, and I needed to continue to prove my worth as a team player. Resigning myself to a difficult evening ahead, I bent myself to work, hoping I was making the right decision to tackle this on my own.

CHAPTER TWENTY-TWO

Orla

I'd waited until I was certain Fin was in the castle, meeting with Munroe, and my crew had dispersed for the day. Sneaking around the side of the distillery, I made a beeline for the abandoned cottage, sticking to the tree line so I'd stay out of sight of the castle.

It wasn't that I was trying to hide this from Finlay necessarily. It was more that I knew how scared he'd been due to his encounter in the building. I didn't want to subject him to those memories again, and I knew he'd come storming into the outbuilding if he found out I was in there. He was a protective sort, Fin was, and most of the time I liked it, even if I didn't fully know what to do with the feelings that arose in me because of his actions. I'd never had someone fuss over me before, and I had to admit, it was kind of nice. Unusual, but nice.

The cottage stood, silent and waiting, the canopy of trees hanging over it thicker here than in other parts of the expansive grounds. We'd need to clear some branches back and open up some space to walk around the building, if this was going to be a tasting room of sorts, as an outdoor garden with a few cozy tables would certainly be charming. Who would resist sipping a gin and tonic with the pretty view of the castle and gardens in the background? Stopping at the door, I closed my eyes and reached for that gentle ball of energy I'd found inside of myself when Miss Elva had taught me a spell for the Auld Mill. I didn't quite know what I was doing, but I'd done a little research, and it seemed like so long as I carried magick and my intention was pure, I'd likely be able to clear the cottage of whatever, or whomever, haunted it. Taking a deep breath, I put my hand on the ornate handle.

The door swung open, not even a squeak to the rusted hinges, and I narrowed my eyes. *Suspicious.*

I stepped inside and into another world.

Barely registering the door slamming behind me, I gaped at the cheerful fire burning in the grate, and the woman who stirred a cast-iron pot. Turning, she smiled at me.

My heart dropped.

What. The. Hell?

She had my eyes.

It was impossible to miss. The soft burnt ginger hair, the way her nose turned up slightly at the end.

"My child. You've finally come home."

Pressing my lips together, I stood, my back to the door, making no further movement into the room. I had come in, fully prepared to rid the cottage of a potentially scary ghost. What I hadn't expected was to encounter my own ancestor.

"I'm not your child." I needed to clarify this with the woman, in case insanity was making her see something different from what I was.

"No, I don't suppose you are." Something shifted in her eyes, lines deepening in her face, and her mouth turned down in anger. "You're one of mine, though, aren't you? The bastard kept you."

"I'm not certain what you mean." Still I stood, my hand at my hammer, and waited, as the woman picked up a small vial and added something to her cauldron, muttering beneath her breath.

"You're of his blood. And mine. Whether you know it or not."

"Who?"

"Your great-great-great-grandfather. A fancy Lord he was. Posh as could be. Couldn't be seen trifling with the likes of me." Her lips pressed together, harsh lines forming at the corners.

"What is your name?" I asked, my pulse picking up. I knew nothing of my history, and if this was true, at the very least she might be able to piece some bits together for me.

"Marie. A common name to be sure of it. Or a witchy one, if that's your way of thinking. It was theirs, you ken?"

"Aye," I said, shifting slightly on my feet. Marie tapped the wooden spoon on the side of the pot, and then laid it on the table. Turning, she dried her hands on a rag and then looked me up and down.

"You'll never find a man dressed like that."

I still wore my overalls from work, and my tool belt at my waist.

"Is that a bad thing?"

"No, I don't suppose it is." Marie pursed her lips, considering my words. "Maybe you're smarter than I was. Caught up in what I thought was love. Above my place, of course. He used to come visit me. In the afternoons. One warm summer day we snuck off to the meadow together. Never have I loved more."

"You fell pregnant."

"Aye." Marie shook her head, her eyes clouded. "It was, well, it was magickal. Though I shouldn't much be using that term, should I? If you speak of magick, they find you. They burn you. Hang you. Drown you. Fair trial or not, you're a dead woman walking as soon as they put the mark on you."

"Who did that to you?" I asked, sadness seeping through me. Scotland had a dark history with witch trials, and I was beginning to understand what might have happened to Marie.

"He did. Och, maybe not." Marie waved a hand in the air, her eyes flashing. "More likely the Lady did. She wasn't much for supporting other women. Particularly when I carried his bairn."

I wanted to point out that maybe the Lady had loved her Lord and his cheating had broken her heart, but it didn't seem prudent to do so. Arguing with a ghostly ancestor, one who had already been proven to be dangerous, wasn't a wise strategy.

"What happened?" I asked instead, since Marie appeared to be in a chatty mood. I reached cautiously into my pocket, fingering the bag of herbs for protection that Miss Elva had given me. Gris-gris, she'd told me, and I hoped it held strong.

"I birthed her, didn't I? My beautiful daughter. Worthless to him. He'd waited, you see? His Lady hadn't given him an heir yet. But once my daughter had arrived, well, it wasn't enough." Marie shrugged, but her face was anything but nonchalant. Anger warred with sadness, and I lifted a hand.

"I'm so sorry that happened to you."

"The world is an unkind place, blood of mine."

"Not always," I whispered, though I'd seen more unkindness than most. If I fully believed that there was no good, however, I'd never find happiness. An image of Goldie flashed in my mind, happily booping her pirate ship, and then Fin's face. Warmth flooded me. A reminder of some of the good I'd known.

"Och, that's a face in love." Marie barked out a laugh, stepping forward, and I visibly saw the shift in her. "Careful, child of my blood. They always lie. And when they find out who you are? The power that runs in your veins? They'll kill you for it."

"It's not the same now," I said, though her words sent a shiver down my spine. "They don't prosecute witches anymore."

"Och, aren't you the lucky one then?" Marie threw her head back and laughed, her hair spiraling out around her, and when she dropped her chin back down, madness careened in her eyes. "Because I was murdered for it. On this very spot, while my babe cried for me in the corner."

"I'm sorry," I said again, helpless to offer any other

support. What could I say? She'd been horribly wronged, but I couldn't make it right.

"He'll do the same. As soon as he sees what you are ... he'll never be able to love you."

Right, enough of this. I caught a flash of movement and the Green Lady appeared behind Marie.

You need to move her on. She'll hurt you out of sheer jealousy. If she can't have happiness, nobody can.

Marie whirled, spying the Green Lady, and raised her arms, a scream spiraling from her very core.

There's blood magick here, Orla. You'll need to use your own.

I gaped as the Green Lady winked out of sight and Marie whirled, fury radiating from every inch of her body. A smile pulled the corners of her mouth up, adding to her fierceness, and I froze as a layer of ice coated the cottage. It even encased the fire, though the flames still danced behind a thin layer of ice, and I realized that I was dealing with a deeply powerful ghost. This was nothing like I had seen in the past, and though Marie wasn't as physically intimidating as the nuckelavee had been, her immense power had me rooted to the spot as my brain scrambled to figure out how I was going to banish her.

"If I couldn't have joy, neither should you," Marie hissed, and I ducked as an icicle flew across the room and shattered over my shoulder.

I needed to crack on with some magick here because this was definitely not an apparition. The sting of ice shards against my face informed me that this was very much real, no matter how much I wished that it wasn't.

"That's not a very nurturing sentiment for your own

blood," I said, vying for time as I pulled the gris-gris bag out of my pocket. "Shouldn't you want the daughter of your daughters to find happiness?"

Marie gaped at me, incredulous.

"We witches aren't destined for a normal life, child. You'll only know pain. Why don't you come join me? On this side? At least we'll have each other then, won't we?"

Oh hell no.

I quickly sprinkled salt at my feet, praying that I made some semblance of a circle around me, and then rattled off the quickest circle protection spell that I could think of.

"I call on the East, South, West, and North to protect this circle I stand in."

"A spell? What is this? You call *this* a spell?" Marie threw her head back and laughed once more and I shouted when a small icicle dropped onto my head, splitting it open. A warm rivulet of blood seeped down my face, blurring one eye, and sweat broke out down my back. *So much for a protective circle.*

Reaching up, I wiped blood from my eye, and it dripped onto the protective bag that I had. I remembered the Green Lady's words. *There's blood magick here, Orla. You'll need to use your own.*

My own blood to banish those who came before me. Could this be more appropriate? Finally I meet kin of mine, and I have to send her packing. How many times would the universe bash me over the head with the understanding that family *wasn't* everything? Blood meant nothing if the heart cared only for itself.

Again, Goldie flashed in my head. Jacob. Grandpa Lou. Then Derrick, my head joiner. Fin. Sophie. Shona. And so on. Faces of people who I'd allowed myself to care for, even when I knew I'd lose them someday. Because even if everyone did eventually leave, love still mattered. And the hodgepodge family that I'd pieced together had somehow become the ones that I loved, deeply, and would always do so. For a woman who'd been given no roots, I finally understood that I had to grow my own.

Marie shrieked again. I needed to do something, quick, or I might not make it out of here alive. She was raging now, tossing icicles around the room, whirling with her hands outstretched to the ice-coated ceiling, her screams ricocheting around the ice cave she'd formed inside the cottage.

"Blood of my blood, mother of my own, the time has now come, to send you on home."

Marie froze as light flashed, the ice shattering around us, the cottage restored to its normal state.

As in normal in the now. No fire warmed the grate, no furniture filled the room. Marie's image flickered in front of me, like a television set with bad reception, and her eyes filled with sadness.

"My own blood … you, too, would banish me."

"You seemed to have no problem hurting me," I said, wiping the blood from my eye again.

"Foolish woman." Marie's grin stretched open, and I understood I needed to do more magick.

"It is with my blood—"

"He comes for you." Marie threw her head back and laughed.

"That I now shall send—"

"He'll never love you." Marie danced in a circle, madness consuming her.

"Those who came before—"

"Once he sees. He'll betray you. Just as I was betrayed." Her laughter shook the building, and I whirled as the door blew open, showing Fin standing there, his hand raised as though to knock. His eyes widened as Marie shrieked with laughter, and I turned back, needing to finish the spell before all hell broke loose.

"On their way out the door."

Listen, it wasn't the prettiest spell, but Miss Elva told me intent was everything. And my intent to move Marie on seemed to work, because once more, light flashed, and Marie disappeared from sight, her laughter lingering in the air, like dust particles caught in a beam of sunlight. I struggled to catch my breath. I didn't want to turn and look at Fin. I couldn't handle what was about to come.

Because I knew, as much as I knew that I could love my found family of hodgepodge friends, that he would leave me now that he saw who I was. I'd lied to him, all these weeks, hiding this power from him. And now he knew who I truly was. Trembling, I turned, wiping my face once more. I had to imagine I looked a fright, sweating and bloody, the soft burnt smell of magick used shifting in the air around us.

"What the hell?" Fin asked, crossing to me, and I stopped him, raising a hand.

"Don't. I have to close the circle." When his face shuttered, hiding his emotions from me, I wanted to weep. Quickly, I recited a short closing spell, muttering the words under my breath before I stepped from the circle of salt at my feet. Fin's eyes trailed down to the salt and then back up to my face.

He looked amazing. As he always did. Polished and posh, and the most handsome man I'd ever seen. Both familiar friend and stranger, and I had no idea what to say to him. My mouth worked as the silence grew between us, as we both struggled to understand what had just happened. What I'd inadvertently revealed to him.

And how I'd lied to him by withholding this part of myself from him.

"Are you all right?" Fin gestured lamely in the air, nodding at my head, and I pressed my lips together. This distance from a man who would rush to care for me when I got a sliver. Now, he stood back, the distance both noticeable and as sharp as a knife slicing through my heart.

"Yes," I said softly, though I wasn't. Not even close. I forced myself to box off my emotions, a tool I'd long used through the years, and lifted my chin, refusing to cry.

"What are you?" Fin asked, his voice a rasp in the stillness of the cottage.

"I'm a House Witch. A member of the Order of Caledonia, tasked with protecting Loren Brae."

"I don't even know what that means."

"No, I don't suppose you do."

"You have magick. Actual magick?" Fin's eyes implored me to tell him anything but.

"Aye."

Fin stepped back, and my heart broke.

"You hid this from me."

"Aye." There was nothing else I could say. I was wrong, oh so wrong to have kept this part of myself from him.

"You're ... you're a witch? An actual witch? And you never said one bloody word to me. After I shared so much of myself with you. I can't ... I just can't." Fin wiped a hand over his face, his expression a mixture of sadness and agony.

"Fin ... I ..." I raised a hand, my emotions fighting with my thoughts and clogging the words in my throat.

"Don't, Orla. Just don't. I can't ... I just ..." Fin stepped backward, outside the cottage, and looked at me. "Get out here."

"Fin, please. You have to understand ..." I raised a hand, but he just shook his head.

"Please get out of the cottage so I know you're safe."

I did what I was told, my legs moving mechanically, until we both stood, shrouded by the canopy of branches over our heads.

"I'm sorry—"

"Don't. I'm not ready to hear it." Fin's voice vibrated with fury, and I flinched. Even though I knew this would be goodbye, I had hoped for some understanding from him. If only he'd let me explain. Instead, without another word, Fin turned on his heel and stomped away, leaving me, broken-hearted and bloody, on the steps of where my ancestor was murdered.

Marie's laughter carried to me on the wind.

"He'll do the same. As soon as he sees what you are ... he'll never be able to love you."

CHAPTER TWENTY-THREE

FINLAY

I had to walk away before I scared her.

My temper was a rare thing to behold, and I knew, particularly because of Orla's past, that showing it to her would potentially make her feel unsafe. So I left.

I walked away before I lost it.

I wasn't just mad at her for lying to me.

I was furious that something, some *thing* that I couldn't fight or do anything about, had hurt her. It had taken everything in my power not to rush to her, to check her head wound, to make sure she wasn't hurt more deeply. Only when I realized that she was practicing magick had the other shoe dropped.

Orla was a witch.

And she'd been hiding it from me all along.

It was such a blow to my heart, the one that had been

singing love songs and mapping out a careful future for Orla and me. I trusted her, or so I'd thought, and she'd hidden something monumental from me.

Just like my father had.

It all came crashing back. Once more the person that I'd put on a pedestal had shown me their true colors, and I was left with my heart broken in bits, trying to find a way to tape it back together. Maybe I'd been stupid to believe in love, if even my own father couldn't stay in a committed relationship, maybe the world didn't revolve around love.

"Finlay—what's wrong?"

Footsteps crunched on the gravel behind me, and I sighed, passing a hand across my face. I'd almost made it to my lorry without being seen.

"It's nothing."

"It doesn't look to be nothing. Mate, you look shattered." Munroe put a hand on my shoulder, and I kept my eyes on the ground, unable to look up at him.

"I need to go."

"Nope, not a chance. Come on."

"No, Munroe."

"It's an order."

"Bloody hell," I shouted, needing him away from me.

"Och, you're definitely not driving. Get inside. I have whisky." Munroe, for all of his easygoing manner, had a steely determination to him that I rarely butted heads with. One time, we'd almost come to blows at university, and from there on we'd acknowledged that we both had a side to us that we rarely showed the world.

But we respected it.

Now, I let him push me toward the castle, fury making

my blood heat. I wanted to punch something, anything, and I stomped down the dark corridor toward the games room where I'd enjoyed a game of pool a time or two with Lachlan and Munroe.

When the apparition of a coo—a ghost coo—jumped out in front of me, I didn't even pause.

"No!" I shouted, once, and sharply, and breezed right through the ghost, no longer caring if it would take me to my death. What did it matter anyway? The woman I loved, that I'd uprooted my whole life for, hadn't been truthful to me. She'd hidden such an important part of herself, so what else did I not know about her? *Is she like my dad too? Thinks I'm a pushover, someone who doesn't mean shite to her?* Did she think concealing her lies was acceptable?

"It's okay, Clyde. Just a bad time," I heard Munroe murmur from behind me, and my eyebrows winged up. Were ghosts just the usual thing for him? Was everyone else in on this whole magick thing other than me? If so, that made me even more furious, since I considered Munroe to be one of my very best friends. If he'd lied to me as well ... bloody hell.

The games room was a classic room with a fireplace, tartan lounge chairs, and a sidebar stocked with whisky. Striding over to it, I chose a bottle at random and poured myself a dram, swallowing it in one gulp so the liquid burned down my throat.

At least I wasn't entirely numb.

"So you're in on it too then?" I poured myself another dram, gesturing with it as Munroe walked slowly to me, like a man approaching someone with a gun.

"Please clarify."

"The ghost coo. Magick. All of this?" My mind flitted back to the day I'd seen the unicorn. Then even further back to being trapped in that cottage with the scary ghost who tried to kill me.

The same ghost that had bloodied Orla.

"Bloody hell," I hissed, taking a sip, and Munroe poured his own glass.

"Sit with me?" Munroe gestured to the armchairs and crossing the room, I dropped into one, running a hand through my hair. Finally, I faced him, my expression mulish.

"Well? It's a simple question. Aye or nae? You knew about the magick here or not?"

"Aye, I do, Finlay."

"Of course. Just fecking grand. All of you, just running around behind my back, laughing at me."

"Nobody was laughing, Fin."

"Easy for you to say when you're in on the game."

"It's also not a game." Munroe sighed, stretching his legs out, and pushed his glasses up his nose. "It's deadly serious."

"Oh, don't I know it. Kelpies shrieking in the night. Ghosts trying to kill me. Yeah, it's great fun for all." I shook my head, clenching my jaw, and looked out the window to the placid waters of Loch Mirren. "Would have been nice to be let in on the secret."

"Orla didn't tell you?"

"You fecking knew she was a witch?" My eyes widened and I gaped at Munroe. He'd known before me and hadn't said a damn word. My fury intensified. "That's real class, Munroe. Thanks for that."

"I can explain if you'll calm down enough to listen."

"Oh, I'm calm. Perfectly calm. See?" I waved my hand holding the glass in front of me and whisky slopped close to the rim but didn't spill.

"I know you're about two seconds away from burying your fist in my face."

"There's that too." I tipped the glass at him in acknowledgement and then took another long searing sip.

"Lia is also a witch."

I paused mid-sip, the liquid sloshing against my lips, and stared at him over the rim of my glass.

"Um ..." Pretty Lia who ran an extraordinary restaurant? "A witch?"

"Aye, mate. It's a lot to take in, but it's also really amazing and beautiful. She's a kitchen witch, a member of—"

"The Order of Caledonia," I said faintly, recalling Orla's words.

"That's it. There's more of them here, Fin. They're protecting the town and the people here. Orla just found out and she's learning."

"She didn't know she had magick?"

"No. Many don't until they join the Order. It's a whole thing."

I blew out a breath.

"When did this all happen?"

"Recently. Over the last couple of months. At least for Orla. For Lia, when she arrived here."

"I don't know what to say."

"Tell me what happened?"

I gave him a quick rundown of what I'd seen in the

cottage, and how I'd walked in on Orla, bloodied and working her magick, shock and fear igniting my anger.

"Is she still there?" Munroe's face creased with worry.

"I made her leave the cottage. She's safe."

"Still." Munroe pulled his phone from his pocket, tapping a message out.

"She lied to me. *You* lied to me."

"Aye. And no. For me? My choice was to protect Lia. It's her story to share, you ken? I trust you with my life, Fin, but it's her decision who she tells. It wasn't about lying to you, it was just about respecting my fiancée's story. I don't see why she wouldn't tell you, other than we've all been so busy lately you've barely seen her."

That was true enough and I nodded, accepting his words.

"Plus, when is a good time to drop that on someone? Guess what, Fin? My woman's a witch? We already had enough drama at the gala, which is one of the few times you've even had to hang with Lia lately."

"Point taken." I sighed, feeling my shoulders relax slightly.

"As for Orla, I can't say why she didn't tell you. She's still learning about it all, I'm told, so maybe she wanted to figure it out for herself first?"

"She lied to me. I love her and she lied to me. I put her on a damn pedestal, Munroe. Just like—" My voice broke. "Just like my father."

"And he knocked himself off that pedestal, didn't he? Aye, it was a shite thing he did, Fin. To you and your mum. But this is not the same."

"How is it not?"

"Because when are you going to realize that everyone has faults?"

I froze, staring into the dregs of amber liquid left in my glass.

"Of course they do," I said automatically.

"You say that, but I don't think you mean it. You were taught to idolize those you love by a hard and controlling father who insisted you live up to his standards. I know this, because I had much the same, remember? The problem is because your father never showed weakness, at least not until his death, you were gutted when the illusion fell to pieces. But he made it black and white, Fin. When in reality, we all exist in shades of gray. Orla is not your father, and she had every right to be careful with her story as she figured herself out. You can't go around putting people on pedestals and then freaking out when they fail you. Because they will. Every damn time. It's only human."

"I—"

I didn't really know what to say. He was right. Damn him, but he was fecking right.

"Don't. Just let that sit for a moment." Munroe stood and crossed the room, bringing the bottle back and topping up our glasses. I stretched my legs out, confusion whirling inside me.

"It's clear Orla came from a tough upbringing. Don't you think that would make it hard to trust?"

"Aye." Nerves kicked up as I began to see how I'd treated her.

"And maybe she was right not to trust you. Because, what did you do?"

"I yelled at her, and I left her."

"Just like everyone else before her," Munroe finished for me, and a wave of shame crashed over me. Here I was supposed to be the one to show up for her, and instead I just did the one thing she knew to be true of people in this world.

They left her.

"Bloody hell. Och, I've royally screwed this up. I need to go—"

"No, not now. Lia's with her. Just ... give this a moment to settle." Munroe checked his phone. "Lia said that Orla went home. She wants to be alone."

"I could go there."

"Not after three whiskies you're not. She needs more from you than a drunken apology."

"You're right." It went against my Scottish stubbornness to admit that, but I couldn't fault the man's logic. *Lia is a witch.* How did he process that when he found out? And more than that, was he right about how I love people?

"You were taught to idolize those you love by a hard and controlling father who insisted you live up to his standards. You can't go around putting people on pedestals and then freaking out when they fail you. Because they will. Every damn time. It's only human."

In other words, I love ... conditionally. Was that why it had taken years for me to see my mother for who she truly was? Had I been blinded by my father's deceit but not really considered that he'd never been perfect and worth idolizing in the first place?

Was that why I'd reacted to Orla as I had?

"Orla is not your father, and she had every right to be careful with her story as she figured herself out."

Fecking hell. Orla didn't need me to put her on a pedestal, not in an unhelpful way. But she still deserved to be loved and adored. *Believed in*, no matter what it was about her that needed to be championed.

I just had to figure out how to communicate to her ... after groveling and begging for forgiveness. Sighing, I sipped my whisky.

"So a ghost coo, huh?"

"Clyde's the best. Let me tell you ... he made Lia pee her pants one time."

"Is that right?" I smiled faintly, but my heart wasn't in it.

What I needed was a plan. A good one.

And it had to start with regaining Orla's trust.

CHAPTER TWENTY-FOUR

ORLA

Not even Brice cuddling Calvin the cat had been able to shake me from the depths of my despair.

When Lia had found me, still standing outside the cottage, I'd been stuck in shock. Bullying me into her kitchen, she had forced the story from me while mixing up some magickal blend of tea that she'd made me promise to drink once I went home. Because even though she'd done everything she could to get me to stay, I knew where I needed to be.

At home. By myself.

Or with Goldie at least. It was the only thing that I'd been able to use as leverage to get Lia to allow me to leave—that I needed to feed Goldie—and now I stared glumly at my wee fish as she swam in delighted circles around her bowl, attacking the pirate ship I'd refreshed with fish flakes.

Just when you thought you had it all figured out.

I sighed and went to the bathroom, giving myself a wee shock in the mirror. Goodness, maybe I was more hurt than I had realized? Dried blood stained my forehead and cheeks, a rusty sticky brown, and I carefully threaded my hands through my hair to look for the wound. Tilting my head, I found the small cut in my scalp and sighed gratefully. No need for stitches. Head wounds tended to bleed more than necessary, so all I needed was to clean myself up and put a wee plaster on the gouge in my head and I'd be fine. Lia had tried to do it already, but I'd been too on edge to let her touch me, and she'd respected that.

I showered, keeping care to be gentle with myself, and anytime my thoughts landed on Fin, I forced them away. I'd told Lia about Marie and she'd promised to spend some time looking in her spell book to see if there was any mention of her.

At the end of the day, I just felt bad.

I felt sorry for Marie, and a life cut short.

I felt sad for myself and how somehow, I couldn't manage to keep people in my life.

I felt bad for Fin, who had been so optimistic for a future with me.

I'd never even told him I loved him.

I'd held that part of myself back, maybe because I'd always thought I'd end up right here, alone, crying in the shower.

Pity party table of one.

Sighing, I dried off and wrapped myself in my fluffy robe, stopping at the table where I'd placed the packet of tea. Next to it sat my hammer.

A third gold vine had entwined itself around the handle.

I'd passed all the challenges and was officially a member of the Order of Caledonia. I'd thought I would be happy when I did, but instead I just felt empty inside. Crossing the room, I put the kettle on. I'd promised Lia I would drink her tea tonight, and I didn't have the heart to let her down. Waiting for the kettle to boil, I turned the packet over and looked at the words written on the wee envelope of tea.

For courage to see just how lovable you are.

The words punched me so hard in the gut that I took a physical step backward.

Such a simple sentiment, but one I'd never considered before. Here I'd always been focused on people leaving me, for whatever reason, and just how awful that felt. But I'd never truly looked deeper to think that I'd internalized that to think I wasn't lovable. But seeing it here, in front of me, made me realize how much I'd allowed this subliminal belief to drive me.

And was it really true?

Adding the tea to the water, I let it steep while my mind whirled, flipping through a photobook of memories of people I'd met in my life. Was I not lovable? Or had I been loved and people had to leave for their own reasons—none of which truly related to me?

Addiction, a deadly sickness, had claimed my mother.

My aunt, already at poverty level, had still given me a room.

My cousins, barely able to find enough food for themselves, hadn't had the capacity to care for me. They, too, were just children and younger than me.

Jacob had been taken from me, but he hadn't chosen to leave me.

Grandpa Lou had died of old age.

Ex-boyfriends had left, mainly because I'd kept them at arm's length, or had never given a relationship a serious go.

None of which said I was unlovable.

All of which pointed to the fact that some people were dealt shitty circumstances, and they dealt with it the best they could. I'd finally built a life I could be proud of, happy even, and still I held on to a core belief and kept people away from me, on the off chance they'd one day leave me.

Life certainly wasn't fair, sure enough, but I wasn't being fair to myself either. I'd kept my walls up for so long that I'd been missing out on any opportunity to truly move into a brighter future for myself. Here I was, in Loren Brae, having been offered a veritable magickal sisterhood, as well as an incredible boyfriend, and still I pushed them all back. I wouldn't let Lia help me much tonight. I refused to tell Fin how I truly felt about him. I couldn't even bring myself to adopt Harris because I was scared to lose him. And now, here I stood, feeling sorry for myself because once again, someone had left me.

It looked like it was time for me to fix my cracked foundation.

Drinking my tea, I settled on my bed, not bothering to turn a podcast on as I watched Goldie twirl about in her bowl. How did one go about changing their life?

You can start by apologizing.

The Green Lady sat at the end of my bed, and I smiled faintly at her. My oldest friend, I guessed she was. Odd, wasn't it, that the longest relationship I'd ever had was with a ghost.

"I tried to apologize to Fin, but he ran off."

Do you blame him?

"I don't know. I guess witchy stuff is scary to people. Particularly him. I mean, he did have the incident in the cottage a while back. He'd been full on panicking after."

He was protecting you when he walked away.

"Och, come on now. That's a leap."

Is it? He was angry, but he wants to keep you feeling safe.

I considered that. Fin had always been very protective of me.

"Safe from what? Hadn't I just banished the bad guy?"

Safe from his anger. He didn't want to scare you.

"Does it matter? He took one look at witchy stuff and ran. I don't really see how this will work." Yes, I know I'd just said that I was going to fix my foundation, but I was still bitter about the way that Fin had run from me before giving me much of a chance to explain. I took another sip of my tea.

The Green Lady just looked at me in silence.

"What? Maybe he *is* doing us a favor. Would we ever really have worked out? Remember. He's the type who holds galas for people and I'm the one people hold galas for."

Tears pricked my eyes, shocking me, and I tried to shore up the walls that held my emotions in a wee box inside me.

Oh, Orla.

I blinked through the sheen of tears, a shiver of disquiet working through me. The Green Lady rarely used my name.

"It's true enough, isn't it? I'm not wrong."

No, you're not.

"See? So maybe this is all for the best. Why even put all this work in just to end up in heartbreak anyway?" To end up alone?

He bought a home here. He's building a life. With you. For you.

"It's for him as well. He told me he was sick of Edinburgh. He likes it here. He has friends here. Plus, it doesn't really matter. He walked away. This is all too much for him. I'm just a mess, all right? I'm a messy difficult person and the magick is probably just one thing too much for him. You had to have seen him. Don't lie ... I know you were around. He was furious. Raging. He's done with me."

People are allowed to be mad. That doesn't mean they'll leave you.

"Well, he did."

Orla.

"What?" I looked up at her and stilled. The expression on her face. I knew it. My stomach twisted and I set my cup of tea down before I spilled it on myself.

This is goodbye.

"Why?" I whispered, my tears finally spilling over. "Why now?" How could she do this to me? After all these years of protecting me and guiding me? She was actually leaving me?

You don't need me anymore.

"That's ... what?" I barked out a laugh. I was literally at my lowest point. How could I not need her? "How can you even say that? Look at me."

I am. And I'll say it again. You don't need me anymore,

Orla. You have everything you need. Right here. She tapped her chest, mirroring my unconscious movement that I was doing on my own, and then disappeared from the end of my bed.

This time, I didn't try to stop the tears. Burying my face in my hands, I wept. The Green Lady believed I didn't need her, but my heart ached. *She* was choosing to leave me, after I'd just deduced that *leaving me* wasn't always a choice. And somehow, losing the Green Lady caused a deep, deep chasm inside my heart.

I was now part of the Order of Caledonia, I had women who loved and respected me, but I just felt so utterly ... *alone.*

CHAPTER TWENTY-FIVE

Orla

I wanted to call in sick the next day.

I never took a sick day, well, I needed to be on death's doorstep for me to call in. As much as I wanted to hide out, burying my face under my blankets, the reality was, I couldn't walk away from this job. Seeing Fin would be unavoidable, so I just needed to deal with it. At the end of the day, I had a job to do, and I was a professional.

A professional whose eyes were still puffy from crying most of the night.

Once the emotions had busted through, it was like someone had shaken up a bottle of champagne, and I couldn't seem to stop crying. I cried for it all. For those I'd lost, for the little girl I'd been who'd desperately wanted family, for hurting Fin.

Because I *had* hurt him. I understood that now. Keeping my abilities from him was likely similar to how his father had hidden his life from Finlay. Even I could see the parallels, even if I hadn't hidden magick because I thought I was doing something bad. I just hadn't been ready to share it with him. Or anyone, really.

But one thing about a long night of crying, is you learn some hard truths about yourself. And in the bright light of morning, because yes, the sun insisted on shining this morning much to my annoyance, you can either backpedal and go back to what you've known, or you can make a change.

It was time for change.

Or so I'd told myself, but when I pulled up and saw Fin's truck in the car park, my stomach twisted. I'd even come early today, hoping to get immersed in work so I could take some time to get my bearings before I approached him. Because I couldn't avoid him forever and even if he was done with me, at the very least I hoped he'd hear my explanation.

Slamming my door, I made my way toward the construction site, but then paused. Tilting my head, I looked at the site, and then back at the car park.

That was odd.

Even though I was early, Derrick was usually on-site long before me. He liked to cut off work earlier than most so he could have a leisurely dinner with his wife, and I didn't mind in the slightest. Instead, the distillery was empty.

Nerves kicked up and I turned again, hands on my hips,

and tried to sense if I was missing something. Was magick at play here? Much like yesterday when I'd walked into Marie's cottage and found another world, had I just done the same? Pressing my lips together, I wandered closer, uncertain of what to do.

A happy bark sounded, and I turned to the gardens.

"Harris!"

I dropped to my knees as Harris ran to me, barely containing his excitement, and the tears started again as he slathered my face with his big sloppy, wet, tongue. Apparently, I was a crier now, much to my chagrin.

"Buddy … what are you doing here? Who sprung you?"

Harris rolled over on his back, wiggling in the grass, and I scratched his tummy, loving how enthusiastic he was when he was outside the shelter. It was like he was a different dog entirely with an extra spring to his step. When he turned over and buried his head in my stomach, his collar caught my attention.

It was new, a dignified blue tartan, and had his name etched on the fabric.

"Buddy! A new collar. Aren't you fancy?" Running my hands along the collar, my breath caught as I found the tag. Twisting it, I flipped the metal tag to read the inscription.

"If lost, please contact Orla and Fin." I read the words out loud and then the tears really came on. Collapsing to the ground, I buried my face in Harris's fur and cried and cried.

When I lifted my head Fin was there, kneeling on the other side of Harris. He looked tired, dark smudges beneath his eyes, and still, impossibly perfect. Frankly, I couldn't believe he was kneeling in the grass, what with his trousers potentially getting dirty.

"Fin."

"Orla." Fin gave me a gentle smile.

"I'm—" My voice cracked, and I swallowed, forcing my eyes away from where I drank in the sight of him. "I'm confused. The tag here seems to indicate that Harris belongs to us."

"Aye, the lad has found his forever home."

Cue more tears.

"But ... but ... how?"

"We'll make it work. Together, Orla." Fin's voice was steady, and we both stroked Harris's back, the dog loving the attention.

"But work? We'll be away all day—"

"I've been assured that Harris is welcome at the castle any time, much to Sir Buster's annoyance. Lady Lola didn't seem to mind, which might be why Sir Buster is annoyed."

I coughed out a laugh, wiping the tears with the back of my hand.

"And after? When this job is over?"

"He's a work dog. He'll come with us. Sleep in our lorries. Or we can drop him by the castle. Or some days he'll stay at home and sleep in a patch of sun on the rug. Either way, we'll figure it out."

"We will?" Hope bloomed.

"Aye, we will." Fin studied me, seeming to wait while my world recalibrated around a future with both him and Harris in it.

"Fin, I'm sorry," I rushed out.

"No, *I'm* sorry—"

"No, please, let me." I needed to say what I had to say before he started talking. I'd rehearsed it enough that if I didn't get through it, I might go back on my resolve. And I'd drank my courage tea and cried all night and had a stern talking to about my future life choices, hadn't I? Now it was time for me to make good on my decision to shore up my life's foundation, so to speak.

"While I'm sorry for not telling you about my magick, so, so, so sorry ... there's something I'm even more sorry for." I looked up as Fin's face fell, and I realized he was worried I was going to reveal something worse. "I should have been honest with you about my feelings."

"Oh." Fin stiffened.

"I love you," I hurried out before he could think the worst of me. "I've loved you for a while. You've been so good to me, saying it over and over, and still I held back. I was so scared that you would leave me, and if I didn't say it to you, well, then I'd be okay, you see? When you eventually left, I'd be able to tell myself that I never really loved you anyway. And that you didn't own my heart and weren't taking it with you when you left. But that would have been a lie, a lie I told myself, because it isn't true. Not even a little bit."

Fin's eyes were on mine, steady, gentle. Patient.

"See, I can feel it. Here." I was tapping my chest, as I usually did, understanding now that this was how I self-soothed. "I see now, that is what love is. I don't really own my heart anymore, so it doesn't matter how much I hide my love from you, it's yours anyway. You could leave or stay, and I'd have no say in it. My heart has decided. It knew, long before my head did, that you were it for me. And I'm trusting you with it, knowing that one day, yes, you could still go. But it's worth it to me, Fin. I want to take this chance. I don't want to be scared anymore. I don't want to worry that I'll be left alone and sad. You know what? I already have. And I survived that. And I could survive losing you in the future, but oh, God, please don't make me feel that pain."

"Orla." Fin reached for my hand, entwining my fingers with his in Harris's thick fur. "I understand. I'm not going anywhere. I bought a house here hoping you'd see that you're it for me. I'm not going anywhere, and you can't make me leave, no matter how many spells you do to try and get me to go."

I barked out a laugh. Was he really joking about this already?

"I don't know, I might be able to make you go."

"Maybe, but you wouldn't."

"No," I said softly, my eyes searching his. "I wouldn't."

"I wasn't leaving you yesterday, Orla. Not really. But I *was* angry. I am a surprisingly patient person, but some-times I'm pushed to the edge. That was one of those times. I don't like to take my temper out on people, particularly with someone like you who has had a difficult past. I walked away so I could deal with my emotions. But being angry with you doesn't mean I'm going to leave you, Orla. You need to know that because it's going to happen. We're going to both make each other mad. I can be mad and also still love you. One doesn't cancel out the other."

My heart filled, the hope that bloomed spilling over, and all of a sudden the sun didn't seem so annoying anymore on this beautiful morning.

"I understand why you were upset. It wasn't fair of me to hide that part of myself from you. I know how much it hurt you when your father did the same. Even though I wasn't hiding it because I thought I was doing something wrong."

"So why did you then?" Fin asked, but again, his tone was gentle, unaccusatory.

"I was coming to terms with it myself. I ... I don't know. I guess I was so used to not sharing about myself with people. And something as big and weird as this? Yeah, well, it wasn't like I was ready to shout it from the rooftops. I'm a witch, Fin. Historically, that hasn't always gone down well for people. It made me nervous, and I guess I wanted to be surer of myself before I shared it with you."

"That makes sense. Particularly since I had such a difficult time in the cottage when we first met."

"Something that you still didn't share with me," I pointed out to him, and Fin's face dropped.

"Well, shite. I didn't, did I? Now who was keeping secrets from whom? Och, I'm a real arsehole, aren't I?"

"Nope, not in the slightest. You didn't know me then. And trust me, after I met Marie, the ghost inside the cottage, I can understand why you didn't say anything."

"She was terrifying."

"She was my family."

Fin's fingers gripped mine.

"Is that the truth of it?"

"Aye. My own bloodline. She was put to death for witchcraft."

"Bloody hell." Fin looked away, shaking his head.

"Maybe it was instinctual not to say anything."

"I don't doubt it. I'm sorry I took off. Truly. And in hopes you'll know that I'm with you—no matter what—I have a proposal for you."

"Sure, what's that?" I tilted my head, waiting for his proposition.

A mile-wide grin split Fin's face.

"Still not getting it, eh?"

"Getting what?" I looked around and when I looked back, Fin had a gold ring in his hand. My mouth dropped open and my heart hammered in my chest.

"Fin! Like an *actual* proposal?"

"I believe I was clear."

"Oh, oh my God. What am I supposed to say to that?" I tapped at my chest until Fin pulled my hand away and slipped the ring on my finger. I looked down to see a wide gold band with a Celtic chain design wrapped around the ring, a small diamond deeply inset in the middle, so it didn't raise off my hand. It was a perfect ring for a builder.

"When did you have time to make a ring?" I glared at him, suspicious, and he laughed.

"I made this weeks ago, Orla. I told you that I knew you were the one."

"Oh." Damn it, but he'd been showing me all along that he wasn't going anywhere, hadn't he? I held the ring to the light.

"A chain, as a symbol that I'm, quite literally, chaining my heart to yours. For life, Orla. If you'll have me?"

Harris turned his head and licked the ring, nudging my hand and making me laugh.

"Of course, I'll have you. Oh, this feels impossibly fast but also so right. Damn it, Fin. I love you so much."

"I love you too and I'm not going anywhere. You're stuck with me for life."

And then his lips were on mine and I sunk into the kiss, my heart thundering in my chest, as giddiness swept me away. When loud cheers broke out behind me, I pulled back, gasping to see my entire crew, along with Sophie, Shona, Agnes, Lia, Willow, Hilda, Archie, and their respective partners all lined up with balloons and flowers.

"Did she say yes?" Sophie shouted and I laughed.

"I wasn't kissing the lass goodbye, was I now?"

"I hope not."

Harris jumped up, tearing across the lawn, delighted to meet everyone and be free from the shelter. Never had I seen a happier dog, free from the burdens of his past.

Just as I was, now that I was starting my new life with Fin by my side. Turning, I grinned at him.

"You're cleaning up his poop," I said.

"Absolutely not."

"We'll take turns."

"Nope, that wasn't in the deal."

"That's all part of it."

"Surely dogs only poop once a week."

I burst out laughing, feeling a lightness that I hadn't ever felt before, and for a brief moment my eyes caught on movement by the forest.

The Green Lady and Marie, walking side by side, smiles on their faces. Understanding dawned. The Green Lady had left me for someone who had needed her more. Tilting my head, I waved discreetly, and the Green Lady blew me a kiss before winking from sight.

I'd always wanted a dog.

I'd always wanted a partner.

And now I had both, because Fin got it.

He understood me. Which was incredible timing as I was just beginning to understand myself as well.

Most importantly, it seemed I'd finally found my way.

EPILOGUE

ORLA

I was going to a party.

Somewhat in my honor, it seemed.

Ramsay Kilts was finished, my second crew putting in long hours to have it up and running ahead of schedule, and today they were hosting a grand opening party for the whole town. They told me I was the guest of honor, and Willow had even sent over an outfit, much to my chagrin.

"I'm scared to open it."

I eyed the wardrobe bag that hung on the bathroom door.

We were at my place, as Finlay was still taking his time with getting his new house together, and we'd made a cozy space of it together. And I do mean cozy. Our bed barely fit us, let alone Harris, who once he'd spied my soft comforter had instantly decided that was his new favorite spot. It didn't matter that I'd bought him a nice fluffy dog bed. Nope, he only slept in it when we hung out on the couch. But if we went to sleep? Well, he was coming with us. It had been an adjustment, to say the least, and some days I woke up spooning Harris, and others, I woke to find Fin's arms wrapped around both me and the dog.

I loved every second of it.

"You'll break her heart if you don't wear it."

"You don't even know what's in there." I pointed at the bag, suspicion in my voice. "It could have ruffles. Thousands of ruffles. I could look like a feather duster or something."

"The sexiest feather duster I've ever seen." Fin dropped a kiss on the back of my neck, and I shivered, desire rippling through my body. Even though we were both exceedingly busy, our sex life hadn't diminished. Not in the slightest. In fact, I was certain the man made more excuses to find new and exciting ways to corner me for a quick shag whenever he could.

This week's had been particularly entertaining, though I didn't think Fin saw it the same way I did. Thinking back, a snort escaped me.

"What was that for?" Fin demanded.

"Och, just thinking about the storage rooms at the castle."

Fin grumbled something, likely cursing at me, before ducking into the bathroom to hide his embarrassment. We'd just, uh, *finished*—having snuck away to a deep dark hallway of the castle—when Clyde had jumped from the wall. I'd sensed it seconds before he'd arrived but had been unable to warn Fin in time.

In time to pull his trousers up, that is.

Instead, Clyde had sent Fin running down the hall, pants-less, with everything hanging out for the world to see.

I'm not sure when I'd ever laughed harder. To the point where I had to cross my legs or soon there would be a story going around about *me* peeing my pants. I wanted Lia to hold on to that particular honor. Luckily, it had only been Munroe who had appeared at Fin's shrieks, and apparently the two had seen each other naked a time or two in passing during their university days. All in all, no harm had been done, except to Fin's ego that is, and I still laughed about it at least twice a day. Not that I'd admit that to Finlay, of course.

Smiling, I unzipped the garment bag and gasped.

"Is it bad?" Fin ducked his head back out of the bathroom and whistled. "Damn, baby. You're going to look fabulous."

"I'm in awe. Won't I look like a big disco ball?"

"Even so, you'll look amazing. This is perfect for you. Willow nailed it."

She'd designed sparkle overalls for me to wear, mirroring my work overalls exactly, except she'd coated the material with sequins. Shiny rose gold sequins.

"Pink," I grumbled.

"Which goes fabulously with your ginger hair." Fin kissed the top of my head. "Go on, try it on."

I reached for the zipper and then paused, bursting out laughing as I leaned close.

"Look!"

At the collar she'd embroidered both a goldfish and a smiling puppy dog face. Harris and Goldie, by my side.

Right, okay, this whole found family thing was pretty damn cool after all.

"I love it." Fin pulled his kilt on as I stripped and slipped into the overalls. They weren't much heavier than my work pair and I blinked down at myself, amazed by how much I loved these. "There's a note that says to wear them with your sparkle trainers."

"Of course." I laughed. She knew me so well. I still only had about four pairs of shoes.

By the time we'd arrived at Ramsay Kilts, I had only attempted doing the robot once, feeling like some sort of sparkly dance machine, and Willow's cry of approval told me all that I needed to know.

"You look fabulous."

"I agree." I beamed at Willow, hugging her, and then pulled back. She looked radiant in a leather bustier top with a huge tulle maxi skirt that floated around her and was dotted with sparkles. "Love this look. It's all like, badass and fairy princess in one."

"Exactly what I was going for. Come, get a drink. Everyone is coming today. I can't wait for people to see your hard work."

The shop had turned out beautifully. Even though the fire had destroyed much of the shop, the bones of the building had been fine. We'd leaned into making this place a custom boutique experience, and Ramsay had spared no expense on the extension that turned the wee shop with a small flat over it into a comfortable two-bedroom house with extra space for Willow's business to grow as well. Wood beams, which we'd had engraved with Celtic insignia, crossed the ceiling, the fireplace mantel mirroring the same Celtic artwork, and we'd painted one wall a lush deep evergreen. Cream-colored stone, gorgeous new hardwood floors, and floor-to-ceiling windows allowed light into the shop space, making it earthy, rich, and welcoming.

Apparently, Ramsay was going to have to get over his zero-customer policy.

"It's a beautiful space," Ramsay said, coming forward to shake our hands. "Now everyone's going to want to come here."

"Much to his annoyance," Willow said cheerfully, grinning up at the towering grump. His eyes softened as he looked at her, and I'd learned since working with them that he was all bark and no bite. At least not for whatever Willow wanted, that was.

"Damn it, Willow. How many people did you invite?" Ramsay glared past us, and I turned to see a crowd making their way down the lane toward the shop. Biting back a grin, I turned to watch the show.

"Just a few of our friends."

"I thought I had discouraged this whole friend-making propensity of yours."

"I can't help that people love me, Ramsay. It's a curse, I swear it." Willow hung her head, pretending to be repentant, and Ramsay grabbed her waist, whispering something in her ear that sounded suspiciously like "punishment" and I grinned as her cheeks pinkened. The door swung open and in moments, the party was in full swing.

An hour later, I was exhausted with the number of people who had come up to either congratulate me on a job well done or to ask me about potential future jobs. Grateful that Fin had prepared me for this, I'd dutifully tucked cards in the pocket of my overalls.

Yes, it came with pockets.

"Oh my, this is going to be interesting." Agnes, looking sexy in the way of people who just are without having to think about it, wore a simple midnight-blue silk dress that slithered over her body and a necklace with a small book charm at her neck. It made me think of being wrapped in sheets, sexy ones at that, and I'd caught Graham eyeing her more than once while she remained oblivious, chatting to everyone in the room. Turning, I glanced out the window.

"She's back!"

Miss Elva sauntered down the lane in a sequined caftan, with a tartan turban on her head. A single crystal sparkled at the center of her turban, and big doorknocker earrings sparkled at her ears. Nothing about this outfit should work together, and yet it all worked, seamlessly so. Her three hotties followed, all in tartan caftans and black sequined waistcoats, and there was not a shirt to be seen among them. Muscles rippled as they walked, almost in unison, guarding Miss Elva as she strolled to the shop.

Listen, if you had told me that I'd find a man in a sequined waistcoat sexy one day, I would have called you a liar. And yet, here we were.

"Well now, I heard there was a party so I had to swing on through on my way back to Tequila Key," Miss Elva announced to the entire party, who naturally had gone quiet as she'd swung in the door. Out of deference or out of surprise, I wasn't quite sure, but either way, Miss Elva commanded the room.

"Miss Elva!" I waved to her, and she came over, her smile wide and shining in her face.

"Child. Just look at you. I swear, I never would have thought about a sequin jumpsuit in that style. But it works. It really works."

"That's all Willow. She's one of my friends. And part of the Order."

"Well, now, child. It seems you found your place after all, doesn't it? I told you friends were everything, didn't I?"

"You did. You were right. I need them as much as they need me."

"It's a good thing to remember. Now, introduce me to this Willow. I want a jumpsuit."

I introduced her to Willow. The two women looked each other up and down, sizing each other's outfits up, and instantly became best friends.

"We need to talk. Where did you get this skirt?" Miss Elva demanded.

"I made it. I'll make one for you if you'll get me one of these caftans."

"I make these," Miss Elva crowed, and Willow clapped her hands in delight.

"My new best friend."

"Looks like she has a new sister from another mister." I started but didn't turn at the voice over my shoulder. Rafe was here, and it seemed the pirate ghost was in a mood. I'd only met him for a short time, but I'd quickly understood volatile was his standard operating procedure.

"That's okay. I'm happy to share Miss Elva. I'm sure you're used to it, aren't you?" I hissed over my shoulder, unable to resist poking at the ghost. I mean, he'd saved my life and all, and then insulted me the rest of the time. Maybe insults were just his love language.

"Rude." Rafe winked from sight, and I stifled a grin as Agnes beamed up at the trio of beefcakes.

"Lads. Good to see you again. How were your travels?" Agnes asked, twirling a curl around her finger. She choked as Graham appeared at her arm, neatly hooking her elbow, before dragging her to the corner behind me.

Naturally, I eased a bit closer.

I mean, we were at a party after all, it wasn't like I was eavesdropping on a super private conversation.

"You're fairly obvious," Fin whispered at my ear.

"What? I'm just admiring the view." I kept my eyes on Miss Elva's boy toys and grinned when Fin pinched my side.

"If I was a lesser man, I'd be jealous."

"Thank God, your ego is intact. Now wheesht."

I sipped my drink, pretending to nod at something one of the sparkle kilt-boys said, but instead I was hanging on Graham and Agnes's whispered conversation.

"It's getting old, Agnes."

"Och, I certainly can agree to that, Graham. But it's not me that's dating every lass that blows through town, is it?"

"In fairness, I might not mind if you did."

I bit down on a laugh at that.

"You wish."

"I wouldn't mind the view, that's all I'm saying."

"Graham. You can't control who I date or even whom I lust after."

My eyebrows rose at that.

"Lust after? You're lusting after these lads?"

Och, now she was really winding him up.

"I mean, they're not hard on the eyes. Will give me something to think about later. When I'm alone."

With that, Agnes sauntered back into the party, Graham's muffled groan following her. She'd played that one perfectly, in my opinion, because now Graham was going to think about her in that sexy silk dress, alone, and being all lusty and whatnot.

In fact, I was getting my own self worked up. Fanning my face, I looked up at Fin.

He grinned, a knowing look in his eyes.

"I know that look."

"It's warm in here. Shall we get some air?"

"I'd love nothing more." Fin looked around, his eyes narrowed. "So long as there's no ghost coo about."

My laughter boomed across the room, and hooking my arm in his, we ducked through the back and into the garden, strolling home toward the cottage. *Home.*

It looked like I finally put down roots, finding friends, family, and my love all in one spot. I'd only needed to accept that the wee girl who was given nothing still deserved everything. Because she did.

I did.

"I love you," I said, smiling up at Fin.

"I love you too, my wee disco ball."

"We'll be finding sequins for days."

"Who cares? It's about time you shared your sparkle with the world."

Indeed, it was.

Love Orla & Fin? Take a quick peek at their future plans in this sweet bonus scene: A Home of their Own.

. . .

JOIN my mailing list and download the free bonus scene here - triciaomalley.com/free

FANCY A WEE DRINK and some grub in your favorite Loren Brae pub? The Tipsy Thistle has its own line of merchandise! Shop here - triciaomalley.myshopify.com

WILD SCOTTISH GOLD

The tension is ramping up in Loren Brae. Will the newest
member of the Order of Caledonia be ready to join?
Order Wild Scottish Gold today!

KAIA

"What is this place? I thought we were going to Cartier."

I bit back my suggestion that they, indeed, should go to
Cartier and instead angled the tray of gold rings to better
catch the light.

"No, baby. This is *better* than Cartier. An original artist.
Don't you want something unique that nobody else has?"

The woman, who wore every brand name under the
sun, so many logos on her outfit that I gave up trying to
read them all, glared at the man beside her. She towered
over him, likely from the spikey heels she wore, and he
grinned up at her. Tanned, reeking of wealth, and likely
dating more than one such arm candy, the man slid me a
quick glance.

I pasted a polite smile on my face.

I didn't feel like being polite. I wanted to take my tray of rings and boot the people out of the shop that I was showcasing my jewelry in this weekend. It was a trial run, to see if there were clientele for my pieces, and I was hating every moment of it.

I'd even dressed up for this, but apparently not well enough, based on the look of derision in Arm Candy's eyes. Even so, I kind of wanted to ask her what she used to get her hair so shiny. When she stuck out her lower lip and pouted, I knew I wasn't getting a sale. But at least I could get some intel.

"Sorry to ask, but your hair is just so pretty. What product do you use that gets it so shiny?"

Instantly the woman transformed from annoyed and petulant to engaged. Swinging her glossy mane over her shoulder, she leaned forward, nudging the tray of rings aside.

"Listen, I'll tell you this because you probably can't afford the product that I tell people I'm using …" She tapped one manicured nail on my arm, her eyes earnest. "But the secret is a touch of castor oil—not too much— while your hair is still wet."

"Is that so?" Hmm, maybe I'd give it a try.

"Good for the dark circles under your eyes too." The woman gave me a pointed look and I internally winced. Right, so I hadn't been sleeping well these days.

Who could blame me when my life was falling apart?

If this woman looked close enough, she'd see where I'd hastily filled the scuff marks on my only pair of black heels with a permanent marker this morning. She didn't need to, though, having sized me up and dismissed as not one of her ilk the instant she walked in the door and scanned my outfit. That being said, she'd warmed up marginally, and at least conversation would make the time pass. Any conversation.

To say business was slow was an understatement. Why the jewelry store owners had insisted on a Fourth of July sale *on* the actual holiday, I did not know. My luck had only worsened when they'd also picked that same day to allow me to showcase some of my new work. *Finally.*

Now I couldn't help but wonder if they'd just been looking for someone to run the store while they got sunburned on the lake with a cooler full of cold Corona beers. I couldn't say I blamed them. If someone was stupid enough, in other words, *me*, to say they'd work on a national holiday, well, I'd probably be at the beach too.

Sighing, I waited while the brunette nudged the tray of rings, finally giving them a quick glance. Only then did her eyes widen a bit.

"Hey, these aren't so bad."

Gee, thanks.

"See, baby? I'm telling you, sometimes it pays to be the person who starts the trends." Sweat glistened on the man's brow and I suspected he might be struggling with money issues. My prices were considerably cheaper than Cartier's, so if he could convince his special lady friend to buy a piece from me, he might be off the hook. For whatever it was he was atoning for.

I just needed to sell one more ring. Two would be ideal.

It would be enough to cover my plane ticket to Scotland and out of hell.

Dramatic, much?

Why yes, yes, I was. That being said, my current life situation had degraded to the point of barely tolerable and was lackluster on a good day. My bags were packed. My tools were ready to ship. The rest I'd sold or was in storage.

I just needed a few more sales and one extremely awkward conversation before I'd be on my way to Scotland, where I'd been promised a new beginning.

In the form of one meager inheritance of a tiny cottage, a barely running car, or so I was told, and a bed to lay my head on. Furnished was the key word I'd heard from the solicitor who had called me when a distant auntie had died. With no kin of her own, somehow the cottage had worked its way down to me, and frankly, I was happy for it. The pictures made it look charming, if 1970s pea-green carpeting and faded cabbage rose wallpaper was your thing.

It could be my thing if it got me away from Stan. Boring, dull, ever so patient Stan. Somehow, he'd worked himself into my life, rescuing me when my apartment building had flooded, and the relief I'd felt at not having to worry about rent for a few weeks had turned into a much longer room-mate situation. One where Stan was convinced I was meant for him. I slept fully clothed on the couch, waking before he rose so I could shower and disappear to avoid the awkward conversation that, no, I wouldn't put on a Princess Leia bikini and role-play while he laughed like Jabba the Hutt.

"You know ... this one is quite pretty actually."

I snapped back from daydreams of sleeping in a real bed again and beamed as the woman picked up one of my rings. I'd had a lot of fun with that one, hammering the gold and melding it so it twisted and coiled around the finger like a snake, and had dotted it with pave diamonds down the back.

"Even better? You can stack it with this band, like so."

I showed her how she could interlock it with another band, making it seem like two sparkly snakes twirled around her finger, and she gasped.

"Oh, I love the mixed metals. White and rose gold. This is like Bvlgari, but cooler."

"See, baby? I told you this stuff was neat."

"We'll take it." The woman nodded to me, and I beamed at my new best friend. Unbeknownst to her, she'd just secured my ticket to a new life. I just prayed the man's credit card wouldn't be declined. The woman stepped away to wander around the room, looking at the other cases, while the man turned to me.

"How much?"

"Four thousand for the pair."

He blanched and pulled out his wallet. I saw a wad of cash and worry kicked up.

"Discount for cash."

The man opened his money clip and counted his bills.

"Can you do three hundred off?"

"Yup, no problem."

No problem at all, *sir*. Cash was king and I would be more than happy to take his money. He handed it over, and I quickly tucked it away. Out of sight, out of mind. Wrapping up the packages in pretty navy-blue boxes with gold etching on the outside, I handed the woman a bag with a bow knotted at the top.

"I hope you enjoy it as much as I enjoyed making them."

"Thanks." The woman breezed to the door, the man following one step behind her. Just before they left, she bent her head to his, and I caught her words.

"But we're still going to Cartier, right, baby?"

I shook my head, walking over to lock the doors after them, seeing the guy pleading with the woman in the parking lot.

I didn't care that the day was only half done.

I had what I'd come here for.

Picking up the phone, I dialed the owners.

"Hey, Debra? So sorry to do this to you, but I'm sick. Yes, horrible stomach cramps. I have to go."

I didn't like to lie, but Debra didn't seem to mind. Seeing as they'd only had one customer in four hours, I couldn't blame her. Instructing me to lock up for the day, I followed her orders and then hightailed it out of the store, already looking up flights on my phone. The good thing about last-minute Fourth of July sales?

I scored myself a killer deal on a ticket to Scotland.

Now to discover this so-called family of mine and just what kind of inheritance I'd really been granted.

Will Kaia's brash approach clash with her new-found rival? Or will sparks fly as they battle it out for best metalsmith in Loren Brae?
Don't miss the fun and magick in Wild Scottish Gold!

HIGHLAND HEARTS HOLIDAY BOOKSHOP

Delicious banter, bookstore magic, adorable puffins, and a heartwarmingly happily ever after makes this an enchanting Christmas treat.
Order this magical stand-alone today!

AFTERWORD

Orla and Finlay might be some of my favorite characters I've written. There's something so vulnerable about people looking for family, even when they're determined to go their own way. I've often felt like that in my life, and I know when you do find the kind of love that feels like a soft landing after a long struggle, it's a gift not to be taken for granted.

I also really enjoyed writing this book in Scotland! We are now living part of the year at our flat in Edinburgh, and I am just falling in love with the city. Everywhere you turn looks like a photo out of a magazine. I'm looking forward to exploring more of Scotland and bringing you more stories enriched with myths and legends from Scotland's long history.

Speaking of, I'm also very excited to spend my first proper Christmas and Hogmanay in Scotland this year! And I have just the perfect Christmas book to give you all those magical cozy vibes: Highland Hearts Holiday Bookshop. Set in Kingsbarns (you met some of the characters in

Starting Over Scottish) you'll get to visit with your favorite book club again and fall in love with new friends. Even better? There will be puffins. Which means - puffin merch. I'm already making up my *Merry Puffin Christmas* jumpers now!

Thank you, as always, for joining me on my journey. Sparkle on, friends!

-Tricia O'Malley

ALSO BY TRICIA O'MALLEY

THE ISLE OF DESTINY SERIES

Stone Song

Sword Song

Spear Song

Sphere Song

A completed series in Kindle Unlimited.

Available in audio, e-book & paperback!

"Love this series. I will read this multiple times. Keeps you on the edge of your seat. It has action, excitement and romance all in one series."

- Amazon Review

THE ENCHANTED HIGHLANDS

Wild Scottish Knight

Wild Scottish Love

A Kilt for Christmas

Wild Scottish Rose

Wild Scottish Beauty

Wild Scottish Fortune

Wild Scottish Gold

"I love everything Tricia O'Malley has ever written and Wild Scottish Knight is no exception. The new setting for this magical journey is Scotland, the home of her new husband and soulmate. Tricia's love for her husband's country shows in every word she writes. I have always wanted to visit Scotland but have never had the time and money. Having read Wild Scottish Knight I feel I have begun to to experience Scotland in a way few see it."

-Amazon Review

Available in audio, e-book, hardback, paperback and Kindle Unlimited.

THE WILDSONG SERIES

Song of the Fae

Melody of Flame

Chorus of Ashes

Lyric of Wind

"The magic of Fae is so believable. I read these books in one sitting and can't wait for the next one. These are books you will reread many times."

- Amazon Review

A completed series in Kindle Unlimited.

Available in audio, e-book & paperback!

A completed series in Kindle Unlimited.

Available in audio, e-book & paperback!

"Love her books and was excited for a totally new and different one! Once again, she did NOT disappoint! Magical in multiple ways and on multiple levels. Her writing style, while similar to that of Nora Roberts, kicks it up a notch!! I want to visit that island, stay in the B&B and meet the gals who run it! The characters are THAT real!!!" - Amazon Review

THE ALTHEA ROSE SERIES

One Tequila

Tequila for Two

Tequila Will Kill Ya (Novella)

Three Tequilas

Tequila Shots & Valentine Knots (Novella)

Tequila Four

A Fifth of Tequila

A Sixer of Tequila

Seven Deadly Tequilas

Eight Ways to Tequila

Tequila for Christmas (Novella)

"Not my usual genre but couldn't resist the Florida Keys setting. I was hooked from the first page. A fun read with just the right amount of crazy! Will definitely follow this series."- Amazon Review

A completed series in Kindle Unlimited.

Available in audio, e-book & paperback!

"I have read thousands of books and a fair percentage have been romances. Until I read Wild Irish Heart, I never had a book actually make me believe in love."- Amazon Review

A completed series in Kindle Unlimited.

Available in audio, e-book & paperback!

STAND ALONE NOVELS

Highland Hearts Holiday Bookshop

As Christmas looms, and lonely hearts beg for love, I'm tossed into the world of magic and romance, aided by a meddling book club who seems more interested in romance than reading.

Ms. Bitch

"Ms. Bitch is sunshine in a book! An uplifting story of fighting your way through heartbreak and making your own version of happily-ever-after."

~Ann Charles, USA Today Bestselling Author

Starting Over Scottish

Grumpy. Meet Sunshine.

She's American. He's Scottish. She's looking for a fresh start. He's returning to rediscover his roots.

One Way Ticket

A funny and captivating beach read where booking a one-way ticket to paradise means starting over, letting go, and taking a chance on love...one more time

10 out of 10 - The BookLife Prize

ACKNOWLEDGMENTS

Thank you to everyone who helped me finish this book. To my lovely editor, Marion, whose comments always make me laugh, but inevitably helps make my stories shine - I thank you! I'd also like to thank Dave, Julie, and my beta readers for catching all those pesky typos that fight so darn hard to slip through.

Thank you to my readers, for your endless support and boundless enthusiasm for my stories. I hope each book I bring you is better than the last and that we can keep shining our lights for everyone.

To Alan, despite my protests, your silly dances really do cheer me up. Love you always.

Sparkle on, friends!

CONTACT ME

I hope my books have added a little magick into your life. If you have a moment to add some to my day, you can help by telling your friends and leaving a review. Word-of-mouth is the most powerful way to share my stories. Thank you.

LOVE BOOKS? What about fun giveaways? Nope? Okay, can I entice you with underwater photos and cute dogs? Let's stay friends! Sign up for my newsletter and contact me at my website.

www.triciaomalley.com

Or find me on Facebook and Instagram.
@triciaomalleyauthor

Made in the USA
Middletown, DE
16 August 2024

59173227R00198